The Man of My Schemes

ALSO BY LESLIE J. SHERROD

Like Sheep Gone Astray
Secret Place
Losing Hope
Without Faith
Sacrifices of Joy
Sweet Violet and a Time for Love

The Man of My Schemes

A Novel By

Leslie J. Sherrod

Write On Time Publishing

Baltimore, MD

Write On Time Publishing, LLC

ISBN: 978-0-692-98016-3

First Write On Time Publishing, LLC trade printing
Manufactured and Printed in the United States of America

The Man of My Schemes

DEDICATION

For NiNi, Ney, and J.H.
Chase after Him and Love will always find you...

ACKNOWLEDGEMENTS

Book number seven! Who would have imagined? I am excited to introduce a new character to you. A little zany, and a lot of fun, the star of this novel took me on a crazy ride complete with loops, spins, twists, and turns. Brace yourself and enjoy.

As always, there are some key people I need to thank who helped make this project possible. First, I need to thank my family who gives me time to write, encouragement to continue, and feedback that is honest and helpful. Without my husband, kids, parents, in-laws, cousins, aunts, uncles, and the rest of my extended family, not sure how any of this would have been completed. I also want to thank important people who have continually provided prayers, writing support, and words of encouragement: Angela, Charese, MaRita, Yolonda, Joylynn, Carla, Angelique, Ms. Sheila, Ms. Machell, Cheri, and Burnett. Your prayers and encouraging words help keep me going. Also, I have had amazing co-workers through the years who have blessed me more than anyone (including them) will ever know. Thank you. There are other friends and loved ones who have been supportive as well and I sincerely thank you. If I didn't mention you by name, know that you are still close to my heart.

There are two more people I want to especially thank. The first is you. Yes, you, the one reading this book right now. Your love of books and your willingness to keep flipping through the pages of my novels are why I keep pressing forward with these dream-filled books of mine. I write because you read, and I thank you for going to the bookstore, or the library, or pulling out your e-reader. For telling your cousin or your co-worker about what you've read and getting him or her to read it too. For posting your reviews, coming out to events, sending me emails, reaching out on Facebook and Twitter. I appreciate it and I wholeheartedly appreciate you.

Last, but certainly not least, thank you, Jesus! I am grateful for the chance to share a story about love, mistakes, and grace. Be glorified and help us all draw closer to You.

"Search me, O God, and know my heart: try me, and know my thoughts: And see if there be any wicked way in me, and lead me in the way everlasting."

–King David *(Psalms 139: 23-24)*

"So, this is me. No disguises, no pretending, just me. You can rightfully hate me. You can have grace, and forgive and love me."

–Berry Jenkins

Part 1:
"You've Been Struck by Love…"

Chapter 1

My first boyfriend was also the bully of my fifth-grade class. Our relationship began over a pack of butter crunch cookies he'd stolen from the teacher's desk. The cookies had belonged to my best friend at the time, a girl we called Kiwi. Our teacher had confiscated them after Kiwi started rustling the plastic package during a spelling test.

Anyway, the boy, Dontay, had the cookies in his pocket by recess. He approached me under the sliding board and told me he would give me the whole pack if I let him kiss me.

Now, don't get me wrong. I wasn't a fast girl or anything like that – my mother wasn't having that. However, I was a loyal friend and Kiwi had been my bestie since second grade when we both showed up with *Jem and the Holograms* lunch boxes the first day of school. So, I did what any good friend would do. I puckered up and let that turd put his little cold, wet lips on mine for all of a half second. He immediately stepped back and frowned.

"Ew, your breath stink," he snarled. "I don't want you to be my girl no more. Get some mouthwash." He turned and walked away, the cookies still in his pocket.

Somewhere in there might be a lesson about not giving away your cookies; but in that one moment, my first kiss was forever ruined, I didn't get those butter crunch delights, *and* I lost my best friend.

How was I supposed to know that Kiwi had a secret crush on Dontay? The boy used to flush people's lunches down the toilet and go running and screaming down the hallway kicking lockers.

Really, Kiwi?

Anyway, she never forgave me for that kiss and never let me tell her why I let my lips be desecrated.

That was my introduction to love.

Hidden agendas. Loss. Betrayal.

Now that I think about it, sounds a whole lot like my parents' marriage, too.

I wish I could say that my lessons in love got better as I grew older, but by the time I hit young adulthood, I'd fended off enough cheaters, leeches, and beggars to be more than a little disillusioned by the whole relationship thing. A date here and there was okay with me, but something more permanent? Naw. I didn't feel the need to have that kind of drama in my life.

That's why I still don't understand what the heck happened and how I fell so fast and so hard.

No, I'm not talking about falling in love. I'm just talking about falling period. There were no strong arms or sweet embraces to cushion or comfort my fall. What I've experienced is a hard splatter on the cold concrete of reality – the reality of who I am and what I'm capable of. I've learned a lot about myself lately, and I can't say that I'm proud.

I'd like to say that my massive downfall began because of everyone else; that the push was from a text I received from a coworker, or a conversation I overheard in church. But who am I kidding? If I had to start at the beginning, I'd be covering the chaos of my childhood, the dark ages of my teens, and the confidence-shattering episodes of my twenties.

But that's just too much to get into right now.

Let's just start with the day I climbed up the steps to the biggest downward slide of my life. Before I'd realized it – and after it was too late – I'd sat down and let go.

***

"That ring is ridiculous. How many carats did you say it was?" Gina, the girl from the cubicle next to mine, pushed her shoulder into my back as we all gathered around our assistant manager for a better view.

"One point nine seven." Celeste waved her manicured, rock-heavy ring finger in front of us. "And no, he did not just mistakenly fall short of two carats," she continued. "Remember, Greg and I first met at the 1.97-mile marker of the marathon I ran in Scotland last year. I tripped right into his arms and the moment our bodies touched, it was fire and sparks, just like this diamond." She held the ring up to the office light. The jewel sparkled and flashed more brilliantly than the salon-quality highlights in her gleaming, blond hair.

"That is just too sweet." Naomi rubbed her bulging, baby-filled belly as she spoke, the multi-carat diamond on her own ring finger flashing. Naomi was the site manager at our office.

"Jeffrey already told me that he was going to get me at least a two-carat, princess-cut solitaire when he proposes." Gina's shoulder still poked into my back and the pretzels she'd eaten for lunch weighed heavy on her breath. "I think it's going to happen on my birthday next month. He's booked a trip to Virginia and keeps saying it'll be a vacation I'll never forget. Even his mother's excited. Can you imagine? A proposal with the scenic backdrop of the Shenandoah Valley?"

Nope. I could not imagine it. Not at all; but I wasn't going to say that out loud.

"Well, when it happens, Gina, call me," Carolyn, the district director and the fifth and final member of our small office suite, finally chimed in. The diamond glittering on her finger had been there for over three years. "I'll give you my wedding planner's contact information. She's absolutely the best. Are you sure you don't want her number, too, Celeste? She would totally ace the Victorian theme you said you wanted for your special day. You should see what she's planning for me and Ricky's *Gone with the Wind* ceremony."

My head swung back and forth while the four of them talked. It was 8:23 and I could think of a few other things I wanted to do before the phone lines opened instead of listening to the continual talk of wedding plans. We'd have all lunch break to hear about it, and a few moments after work, too. Because only the five of us worked at this location, the work day was filled with incessant conversation about every detail of everybody's lives.

Well, not mine.

"Thanks for the offer, Carolyn, but we're thinking now that we're going to go with more of an American colonial theme." Celeste's whitened teeth glowed. She'd gotten fully prepared for this proposal. She must have known it was coming and planned accordingly.

I stared at the bright whites of her teeth as she continued. "Greg's sister has offered to be our wedding planner since she just came back from her sabbatical in London. Did you know she's a professor at Harvard? And did I tell you Scott is a descendant of one of the signers of the Declaration of Independence? One of the partners in his law firm has offered to host our engagement party at his estate in Philly. Apparently, the estate used to be the summer mansion for Greg's great-great-great-uncle."

"Awww, that is so perfect." Naomi clasped her hands around her stomach. She looked ready to pop any day now. Her husband had taken off from his banking job to finish carving a rocking chair and a matching toy chest just for that reason.

"It's going to be a great year for our office," Naomi continued to gush. "Weddings, baby showers. Everyone has something to celebrate." The four of them giggled and sighed.

And then they all looked at me and sobered.

Was something wrong?

Had one of my hair twists come undone? I'd tried a new gel that morning and I usually didn't experiment with new hair products mid-week, but this one strand of hair that didn't cooperate with the rest of my two-day old twist-out had needed an intervention and nothing else in my hair closet had worked.

Darn carrot oil and mayonnaise concoction. I wondered if it smelled.

Or maybe I had food stuck in my teeth from the breakfast sandwich I'd gobbled down on the bus. I looked back at the blue, green, hazel, and gray pairs of eyes staring sympathetically at my dark brown ones and tried to use Gina's glasses as a mirror to check my pearly whites. No luck.

"Don't worry." Celeste looked at me and gave some kind of version of a half-smile. Naomi reached out her hand to stroke my arm as Celeste continued. "On the night I turned twenty-nine last year, I was so worried that I would have to go through my thirties alone, no husband, no family, no kids. Now…now… This." She held up her ring finger and the four of them squealed again. "I'm right on the edge of all my dreams coming true. You just don't know what can happen for you. All it takes is one single moment for your life to change."

Look, I turned twenty-nine not last year, but five years ago, and I don't remember having any sort of night like the one Celeste had just described. I was having too much fun to get down and depressed about who or what wasn't in my life back then. My girls from college, Keisha, Leilani, and Meeka had made sure that I did nothing but celebrate the first day of my last year in my twenties. We'd all been fashion majors in school and we partied together all through our twenties until one by one we parted and went our separate ways. But that night of my twenty-ninth birthday? We ate, drank, laughed, danced, and ate some more.

Oh, we celebrated, *and* it wasn't just because I was turning twenty-nine. I was twenty-nine and I had been promoted to manager of my department at work. That was back when I had my old job. Yup, I was the head woman in charge, manager of logistics and operations for the small electronics delivery company where I worked at the time. I'd had the corner office complete with a lighted waterfall fountain on my desk, and a view of the trees that bordered the company parking lot. No, it wasn't the dream job I'd had in mind when I graduated with my degree in fashion marketing in my early twenties, but I'd spent that decade of my life, my twenties, working hard to be the queen of the hill, even if that hill was a mound of outdated electronic equipment and unheard-of technology.

By the time I turned thirty-one, however, the company had begun its crumble. Electro Management no longer had a logistics department, and I no longer had a job. I was forced to start all over again, and sitting in the ruins of smoking circuit boards and broken monitors, I didn't have time to mope around and cry over the absence of a man's love in my life.

I needed money to pay my bills.

I looked over at the bronze name plate that hung outside my current cubicle and thought back to the platinum one that used to hang on my former office door.

Customer Service Assistant, the current name plate read. I didn't even have a name anymore. Not even a mid-level title like everyone else in my current office. Even Gina was *Lead Customer Service Assistant.*

At least I had a job.

"When you have your big day, what do you want your theme to be?" Gina's voice brought me back to the conversation. I realized they were still looking at me. An uncomfortable silence had taken over as nearly all of them seemed to be shielding their blinging rings from my view.

Um, really?

"When I get married, if I even get married," I kept myself from rolling my eyes, "I'm going to have a *Soul Train*-themed wedding."

The girls – all of them at least three years younger than me – looked at each other and paled.

"You're kidding, right?" Celeste tried to chuckle.

I let a smile ease onto my face. "I want the preacher in orange polyester, the bridal party to have humongous afros, and I want to go down the aisle doing The Bump."

Honestly, I'd never given serious thought to a wedding theme. I had more important matters to figure out, like paying bills and getting my car out of the shop again. Honestly, I wanted to be left alone about my lack of a love life.

"Well, if that's what you want." Carolyn shook her head, clearly unimpressed. "I guess a *Soul Train*-themed wedding can be...graceful." They all had the same look of pity on their faces as they walked to their cubicles. I turned toward my own, wanting to shake my own head.

Truth was, of course I'd thought about marriage and men, babies and diamonds and my lack of any of those things. But to hear those words and dreams come out of my co-workers' mouths with their Victorian-Colonial-Scotland-law firm realities, I didn't feel like I could relate to what they were describing and desiring. Whatever dreams or desires I had of my own felt distant, removed. Undisturbed.

At least at that moment.

"You're so funny, Berry." Celeste smiled just before

disappearing into the cubicle across from mine. "With your sense of humor, I know the right man will come along one day and sweep you right off of your... broom? No, jump over your feet...sweep the broom, whatever that wedding tradition in the Afro-American community is called. Have a good day!"

"It's 'jump the broom'," I murmured more to myself than to her as I settled back into my desk chair and adjusted my headset. She meant well. They all – Gina, Carolyn, Naomi, Celeste – meant well. I wasn't mad at them.

8:30 exactly.

I shook my head one last time before pressing the button that put my phone in the call center's queue.

"Good morning, you've reached Cole Financial Services. My name is Berry. How may I help you today?"

Okay, let's just get this out on the table. Yes, my name is Berry. Berry Martini Jenkins, to be exact. I never tell people my middle name. My first name is usually enough of a shock.

Were my parents drunk when they filled out my birth certificate? Yeah, probably. They only giggle when I ask, refusing to give me the details about the day or circumstances of my birth. What they do tell me, however, is something about a trip to the Bahamas nine months before my birth, a Barry White record, and some chocolate-covered blackberries. I've stopped them from giving me any more details. I don't want to know more.

Anyway, I digress. I need to get back to my story, because there is a lesson in it somewhere. At least that's what I'm hoping for. Things have gotten pretty bad for me since that day Celeste showed us her new engagement ring at the office, so the idea of a redemptive moral, feel-good ending appeals to me right now. For all that's happened between that morning at the office and today, I need a glimmer of hope to know that I didn't completely ruin my life over the past few months.

I know what you're thinking. Berry has a story to tell and it's going to be all about her finding Mr. Right and living happily ever after and wedding bells and fairy tales and ribbon and flower-decorated bouquets and, well, brooms…No, this is not the cute and cuddly romance story you're expecting.

Oh, and before you get political on me and start thinking this is the woe-is-me tale about the only black girl in the office who alternates between feeling inferior and feeling all "black is beautiful," let's get it straight. That's not the road my story takes, either. That being said, I can only write from my experience, and if *my* experience as a woman of color in a world where white is the standard offends *you*, then imagine for one second how *I* feel.

I digress again.

The day that Celeste showed us her brand new, 1.97 carat diamond ring and regaled us with the story of how he proposed, I wasn't bothered one bit that I was thirty-four, single, and completely out of the dating scene. Nope, I wasn't bothered at all that day.

But that night?

Now, that's really when my downfall began…

Chapter 2

"Girl, if you don't put a relaxer back in your hair, I might just have to disown you. How in the world am I supposed to go into Bible Study with you looking like a field hand next to me? Look like a darn pickaninny with those little twists coming up out of your hair. I didn't raise you like this."

My mother, Frederica Jenkins, was one of those women who kept her hair short and sassy, chemically-straightened with razor-sharp curls that flicked in whatever direction her stylist's flat-iron felt moved that week. Yes, she had a weekly appointment with her beautician, Sharlazena, and another weekly stop to see Soo Yung, her favorite nail tech and eyebrow artist, at a place on Greenmount Avenue. My mother made good money at her job as an administrative assistant at Johns Hopkins Hospital – and even better money from the divorce settlement with my father after he left us and his banking management position to live on a sailboat somewhere in the Caribbean with a blond, twenty-three year-old named Dynasty.

Yeah, that was her stage name.

Anyhoo, with her two children out of her house and somewhat out of her hair, my mother had earned the right to spend as much as she wanted on her tresses, nails, and whatever other body parts she wanted altered, fixed, dyed, or straightened.

"I will never understand what made you mess yourself up like this." My mother frowned at me as she pulled into a parking space in front of Rock of Life Church. "I hate naps. Hate them. That's all your head is full of now. Naps and pickaninny twists."

I'd ended up working late that day. For once, I just didn't

feel like joining the afternoon discussion of wedding plans that I knew would only be at a rabid frenzy now that Celeste's ring finger had joined the club. I kept my phone on in the queue two minutes longer than everyone else – and ended up on a forty-minute call with an irate customer. Since my car was still in the shop waiting for a new transmission, well, really the money for me to pay for a new transmission, I'd called my mother for a ride. She didn't mind. Her masseuse was not far from my office building and she never turned down an opportunity to look me over.

Getting a ride from my mother meant only two things: a head-to-toe critical analysis and Wednesday night Bible Study. I knew these facts of life when I dialed her, which shows how much I hadn't felt like dealing with the bus that evening.

"Mom, this is just how my hair grows naturally out of my head. Not trying to make a political or spiritual statement. I've just accepted this part of me. Not to say I won't ever go back to the straight look. I'm fine with who I am right now." How many times had I said this to her over the past few months since I'd chopped off all my relaxed, bone-straight hair ends?

My mother groaned as she shut down the engine. "Ain't never going to get a man looking like that."

I could tell she had more to say, but Sister Evangeline Willow was coming across the parking lot. Sister Evangeline was one of the last women at the church who still wore hats, and yes, she even wore them to Wednesday night Bible Study. Tonight, she had a wide-brimmed, white, straw one.

I could wear jeans at my job since I worked in a call center, well out of the view of customers. Since my mother had picked me up, I had not been home to change. Not that I would have anyway. I lived in jeans and tennis shoes. That was my fall/winter ensemble. In spring/summer, I traded them out for yoga pants and flip-flops.

Today was a hybrid day. Though it was early spring, the weather in Baltimore had not fully warmed. I had on jeans and flip-flops, two blasphemous articles of clothing in Evangeline's eyes.

"You could have at least gotten a new pedicure if you were going to wear those cheap things. Your pinky toenail polish is chipped," my mother hissed as we both got out and Sister Evangeline neared us. My mother knew what was coming, too. "Oh, God, help us," she mumbled as she reached for a thick, hard-covered Bible she kept on the back seat of her white Cadillac and then looked down at her own feet. My mother had on flip-flops, too.

"Sister Jenkins and Daughter Berry." Evangeline Willow enunciated each syllable of her every word with great fanfare and formality. "How are you two doing this marvelous day that the Lord has made?"

"God is good." My mother's smile was the complete opposite of the scowl that had been on her face just seconds earlier. "I woke up this morning with a song in my soul and the melody hasn't left me all day."

"Very well. Beautiful." Sister Evangeline turned to face me. "Berry, it is so good to see you come out to the house of the Lord. We've been missing you. It's been some months, now, but you're here, praise God, and on a Wednesday, no less. You must have some kind of big prayer request, a huge petition for the Most High to have you come out and grace us with your presence tonight."

I stood silent for a few seconds looking back and forth between her and my mother before realizing she was asking me a question, not just making an assumption. "Oh," I spoke up, "there's not any special prayer request that's bringing me here tonight. Just spending time with my mother, that's all."

"Oh, I see." Sister Evangeline looked at me with the same

pitiful glance my co-workers had given me earlier in the day. "We all stand in the need of prayer, even, especially more so, when we don't realize it. I'll be praying for you, Daughter Berry." She gave both me and my mother a final and obvious head-to-toe look-over, and after turning down the corners of her lips even further, she turned and walked toward the main entrance. "I'll see you two ladies inside. Amen?"

My mother exhaled right alongside of me as we followed behind her and entered the glass doors of the church. As I listened to the music piping from the organ at the front of the sanctuary and stared at the scene around me and at the people there, I wondered why I hadn't just caught the bus home. Sister Evangeline had been correct in stating that I hadn't been there for a while. And, as far as I was concerned, for good reason.

I hated fakery, and this church – the people in it, the things they did – was the epitome of fake-titude.

"Oooooooh! Bless God!"

A sudden shout sounded in the foyer and several folding chairs that had been leaning against the wall clattered down in a loud, metallic collapse. Brother Fitzgerald, the choir director, had begun his weekly spin-around. Hopping on one foot, stomping sporadically with the other, he twirled and whirled as his body shook with what looked like convulsions.

"Praise Him! Praise Him!" Some out-of-uniform ushers grabbed some fans and went to encircle him as his stomping and whirling intensified.

Don't get me wrong. I have no problem with anyone praising God, but this man did this exact same move every single time he entered the foyer of the church, whether it was Sunday service, mid-week Bible Study, or church picnic committee meeting.

He spun, and swayed, and shouted, usually until Daphne Brooks, the lead soloist, came to him with a cup of water and a handkerchief to wipe his sweating brow. She was already on her way up from the basement steps, I noted. A paper cup filled to the brim was in one hand. She clutched a lace hankie tightly in the other. Her pink dress had a lot of lace on it, too. Tight, short, cleavage. Need I say more?

Like I said.

Fakery.

"He would be such a good man for you," my mother smiled and mumbled in my ear. "He's God-fearing and has a great voice."

I had no idea those were the sole qualifications for a future husband, but I guess my mother thought so.

"I bet if you would do something with your hair, he'd have his eyes on you and not that skinny Daphne. She's not that good of a singer anyway. Good evening, Mother Langley," my mother's voice boomed again as she walked toward the pews with one of the elder women who'd just disembarked from the church shuttle.

My brother, Davis, was the driver, so I knew that next up in the foyer would be all the single women of the small congregation. My brother was one of only three unmarried males between the ages of eighteen and fifty-three who attended Rock of Life on a regular basis. One of the other three was currently getting wiped down by Daphne in the corner of the foyer and the last of the trio, Brother Will Gaynes, usually sat in the back row of the church, rocking back and forth, mumbling to himself. He came and left with his mother, Wilma Gaynes, the church secretary.

"Where is everybody?" I wondered out loud a few moments later as the testimony portion of the Bible Study began. My brother had already come through the foyer, but the usual crowd of sisters that followed had not yet appeared. The doors to the sanctuary were being closed by the out-of-uniform ushers, meaning the service was truly underway. One of the ushers gave me a glance to see if I would be entering. I shook my head no. I'd had enough of the fakeness. I started to sit down in the foyer with a hymnal to browse through to wait things out, but my curiosity had the better of me. "Where is everybody?" I wondered aloud again, peering out the foyer window to the parking lot.

Tressa, Vickie, Shaneka, Raina, Pat. I saw all of their cars parked in the lot. They made up the bulk of the thirty and over crowd of young women I usually sat with the Sundays I did come, if it wasn't their choir day. I looked again at their cars on the lot. They were here, but where were they?

A little kid burst out of the basement to get into the sanctuary before his mother came looking for him. Just before he shut the door to the lower level behind him, I heard the unmistakable sound of squeals and laughter.

Tressa and them.

I headed down to the bowels of the church.

"Girl, you sure he didn't get that from *Avon?* You know they can make some real diamond-looking cubic zirconium rings now."

"No, Shaneka, this is the real deal." Vickie stood in the center of the basement as the other four women pressed around her. Her left hand was raised and a rock that rivaled Celeste's sat on top of her ring finger. I joined the circle and Raina's shoulder jabbed me in the back as everyone pushed in closer to see the double halo engagement ring.

"Wow, Vickie, I didn't realize Micah rolled like that. That diamond is the truth." Tressa's eyes were wide, drinking in the fire and light and the brilliance of the stand-out gem.

"Yeah, Micah owns a barbershop. Owns it. He has seven employees and is doing quite well for himself, but his business is just a minor detail about him. He's really a great guy overall, the perfect gentleman. You know he even bought my mother a present for her birthday last month? A *Michael Kors* bag."

"Girl, we do know how to get them, don't we?" Raina weighed in. "Ain't nothing finer than a brother in a business suit. Drew's real estate investment firm is doing well and he's talking about us taking a trip down to Miami in a couple of weeks to celebrate our tenth wedding anniversary." The two had met in college when he was a power forward for a Big Ten basketball team. They'd married young.

"Uh, well y'all need to be making some babies while you're down there," Pat playfully scolded. "I don't know what you two are waiting for. Ten years is a long time not to have some little ones."

I didn't miss the quick flash of bitterness in Raina's eyes. "Well, Pat, ten years is also a long time for Reverend Cook not to be asking you out," Raina retorted and everyone laughed.

It was no secret that the young, assistant pastor of Rock of Life's sister church, Stone of Peace, had had his eye on Pat Green for years. "Keep us posted on when he finally does."

"What do you mean 'finally'?" Pat gave a playful grin. "We went on our second date last night."

"Two nights at a revival hardly count for dates in my book." Raina rolled her eyes.

"Maybe," Pat countered, "but the dinners afterward were definitely divinely directed dating appointments. I know it's early, but my spirit is telling me that Reverend Cook may be The One, and he's not disagreeing."

"And let me just say," Shaneka spoke up, "that a brother doesn't only have to be in a suit to be fine. That cop that stops for lunch in the deli where I work, y'all he just gave me them digits. We are going to *Phillips* to eat some crab cakes on Friday night."

"Business suit, uniform, greasy overalls, girl, you're right. It doesn't matter." Raina nodded. "A brother with a good job, a nice smile, and the knowledge of how to treat you with respect is a fine specimen indeed. We are some lucky women."

"Yes, and I can't wait to get started with the wedding plans," Vickie rejoined the conversation. "I'm thinking I want to have the reception right here in the church basement. Mother Wallace already said she'll fix her chicken and green beans. I'm going to ask Deacon Lloyd about his potato salad."

"Girl, why are you going so cheap?" Tressa frowned up her face. "Why don't you rent out a hall and hire a real caterer?"

"I thought about it, but to tell you the truth, I'd rather use the money for our honeymoon. We want to spend two weeks in Paris. Plus, Micah's getting us a house built in Woodstock. Five bedrooms, three baths, and a fire pit out in the backyard."

"Um, um, um, look at how God is moving. All of us are finally getting settled. Go on, ladies," Tressa clapped her hands. Her engagement ring had been a fixture on her finger for over seven years. Despite the two children she had with her live-in, Darius, they still didn't have a date set. Nobody asked and she didn't answer.

And then… For the second time that day, all eyes turned to me and the room grew quiet.

"Don't worry, Berry. God has a man for you, too," Raina's lips went into a pout.

"In His time. He's going to reward you with a really good one for all this waiting you're doing," Vickie chimed in.

Silence. Were they waiting for me to say something?

"If that's what God wants for me." My words came out slowly as I looked from eyeball to eyeball. "I can't say that I've been too worried about it."

Should I be? The thought started nudging some part of me I hadn't noticed before.

Here I was, having the same conversation I'd had earlier that day, but with a different group of women. This time, unlike the last, something bothered me, but I couldn't quite put my finger on it. I knew about *Avon,* chicken and green bean church dinners, cops, greasy overalls, and fine brothers in business suits. Was it the familiarity that felt different? That this time, the exclusion I felt was more personal...more relatable?

"Well, it's good that you're not worried about it," Vickie eyed me. "I certainly had been worried. We're not getting any younger, and I still want to have children. If marriage and family isn't really your goal, then I guess you have no reason to start sweating."

"What are your colors going to be, Vickie?" Shaneka blurted and the conversation turned back toward the ring.

As discussions swirled about shades of lavender, midnight blue, black and white, and something about cherry blossoms, I found myself feeling lost in their midst. I stared at Vickie, her perfect weave, the smooth, almond foundation on her cheeks and forehead, the slightly imperfect alignment of her teeth. She weighed about thirty pounds more than me, but that weight had been put to good use in her hips, her chest, her shapely legs.

She was going to be a beautiful bride. I felt happy for her and her plans for a Parisian honeymoon.

I smiled, swallowed, wondered what this feeling was that had suddenly grabbed me by the neck and wasn't letting go.

"I have to get up early for work tomorrow and it sounds like Bible Study is going to run late tonight," I mumbled at some point in the conversation. I headed toward the steps, headed back up to the foyer.

"Bye, Berry," Tressa called after me. I turned to say bye

to all of them, but all I saw were their backs. They wouldn't have heard me anyway, I realized, as they all talked over each other. Something about bridal gowns, and wedding cakes, and unique favors from *Etsy*...

"Davis, can you take me home?" I was glad to see my brother stepping out the church door, shuttle keys in his hand. I stepped out with him and immediately rubbed my hands over my arms. The night air had a chill in it that I hadn't noticed before.

"I thought Mom was taking you home, little sis." Davis shifted from one foot to another, his eyes darting from the van to me.

"She was... I just... Can you just take me home real quick before you have to come back to drop off everyone else?"

He let out a loud sigh, then nodded. "I got you, Berry. Come on."

I stepped onto the shuttle and saw the reason for his hesitation. Sister Ertha Bellvue, the pastor's niece, sat in the front seat. From the disappointment that immediately flashed on her face, I knew I had interrupted something.

"I'm dropping my sister off, and then we'll go grab something to eat, okay?" My brother's words made her smile.

In the way.

Alone.

Disturbed.

I tried to figure out what words could best describe how I felt at the moment.

"Thanks, Davis," I nodded back at him ten minutes later as he let me off in front of my apartment building. The doors shut right behind me, but not before I heard Ertha giggle.

Chapter 3

"Huxley, I'm home!" My voice echoed in the foyer as I clicked on the lights. My cat, a brown and white tabby I found by the trash bin in my complex last year, frowned from his perch under a side table.

"Aren't you glad to see me? Did you miss me today?" I moved toward him, dropping my purse and phone onto the blanket that covered my sofa. He turned away, faced the wall, resettled. I shrugged, headed to the kitchen to grab a water bottle. As I studied the empty shelves of my fridge, my cell phone chimed from the living room, so I headed back. A text message from my assistant manager, Celeste.

Hi Berry. I know it's late but I've been thinking about you all day. There's an Afro-American man at my fiancé's law firm who would be a great match for you. He is a little older (48 maybe?) but if you see him dance at the firm's holiday party, you'll know he's in good shape. He led the limbo line last year. He's a little of a heavy drinker, but aren't we all, lol? His name is Wesley and his divorce was finalized a couple of months ago. I'll see if Greg can introduce you to him. I'm excited. C u 2morrow. Have a good nite! XOXO, Celeste

'Delete.' I pressed that button fast and then threw my phone back on the couch. Did she think I was that desperate that I'd be willing to take someone's leftover, alcoholic ex-husband? *Should* I be that desperate?

The thought scared me.

Everyone, from my coworkers to my church friends, heck, even my own mother, seemed worried about my lack of a love life. Sure, I was aware that I didn't have one, but…but what? Should I be worried?

Skipping dinner, I poured my favorite bubble bath into the tub and then sank into the warm water until the apple-scented foam touched my chin. My neighbor's kids were arguing next door again. I could hear their doors slamming and the parents of the two boys scolding them, threatening to take away their toys if they didn't get along better. One more door slam, and then quiet.

Too quiet.

No household noises for me. No laughter, or arguing, or small talk, or sloppy kisses. My cat barely meowed and, well, he wasn't quite the sociable type.

Maybe I could get a dog. I pictured a hyper Chihuahua barking and racing around my place and then jumping into my bath water, its little wagging tail splashing water all over my face.

Naw, not my thing.

"God?" My voice echoed on the bathroom walls. "Am I supposed to be alone? Is this the plan you have for me? Or am I supposed to be getting a husband? Starting a family?"

I waited. Of course, there was no answer. Truth was, I had no sudden feelings or revelations about it either. But maybe, just maybe, I didn't like being alone all the time. Maybe, just maybe, I was supposed to be doing something about this.

I sloshed out the tub, dried off. I slipped on my night shirt and wrapped my hair up in a silk scarf. I thought about my friends who'd taken me out for my twenty-ninth birthday five years ago. Keisha had married and moved to Norfolk, Virginia where her military husband was based. Leilani and I had lost touch after she took a job at a fashion house in New York, and

Meeka had a different man, a different party, a different group of friends nearly every week, it seemed.

Yeah, I was alone. The realization settled in me, got up in my bones, messed with my psyche, disturbed my comfort zone.

I didn't like it.

But what was I supposed to do about it?

Ready for bed, but nowhere near ready to sleep, I pulled out my tablet, pulled up the website for Celeste's fiancé's law firm.

"I can't believe I'm doing this." I felt ashamed of myself as I scrolled through the pictorial profiles of the partners at the firm. I got to Wesley Grimes and my stomach turned, dropped, and turned some more. A little older? A little? If that man was actually even forty-eight, the years had been horrid to him. He looked more like he was seventy-two. Despite the high quality suit he wore in the unsmiling picture, his face could have been one of those faces I saw hanging out on the stoop of the liquor store around the corner from my apartment complex. Gray stubble covered his cheeks and neck and one of his eyes bulged out a little larger than the other. He reminded me of someone's Uncle Grady.

Specialized in contract law. Interests included chess, bottle cap collections, and Sudoku. Favorite quote: "Toothpaste is external. Democracy is eternal."

"Huh? I don't get it." I minimized the profile, closed out of the website. "How on earth are we a perfect match, Celeste?" I argued as if she sat in front of me. "What do we even have in common other than we're both black?" Then again, I guess the bigger question was, why had I even looked?

Then, a thought occurred to me. If I had been willing to look at the profile of an old lush, why not look at profiles of actual potential soul mates.

Soul mates? Where had that notion even come from?

I did an internet search for online dating sites. "I'm not really doing this. Just looking for fun."

The results that came up overwhelmed me. *Looking for men? Old men? Young men? Black men? White men? Asian men? Just friends? Sugar Daddies? Travel buddies? Married men?*

What on earth?

Is this the dating scene now? A wide expanse of confusing opportunities?

I scrolled through the results and then clicked on a random link. *Make a free profile.* This particular site was part dating connection, part social media.

Why not?

First things first: a profile name.

Looked like all the 'Berry' combinations were taken. Berrylicious, Berry Good, Berry Bad Girl, Berry Kisses. I shook my head, as the pictures that accompanied those profile names looked even more desperate than the names. Lots of skin, too many boobs, and daunting facial expressions.

Can't someone just be normal on these sites?

I typed in B.M. Jenk and then stared at the B.M. No.... I didn't want anyone calling me B.M., or, even worse, asking me about my middle name.

BerryLady34.

There.

Skipped the picture upload for the moment and then I got to the description box.

About Me.

I was doing this for fun, so no need to put too much thought into it.

I'm a 34 yr old non-diva. I like plants, swimming, the color orange, and one day I want to learn how to ski.

"Is this dumb?" I frowned at what I had written. What was I doing? What else could I say about me that could attract a potential soul mate? *Listen to yourself, Berry. Soul mate?* Is that what I thought I was doing? Throwing out a hook and line to catch The One?

I read the next box. Describe your fantasy romantic weekend.

Hmmm..

What was I supposed to write? *Lost* marathon on Friday night? Dinner by candlelight on Saturday? Church and Sunday brunch to cap it all off? My mind drew a blank.

How would Celeste and Gina and the other ladies at work answer this? With all of their trips and traveling, they seemed to always know exactly how a romantic weekend should look. For that matter, the women at church seemed to know as well; but then again, the idea of clubbing the night away in Miami or sweating down the church aisles at revivals, like they had planned, didn't quite sound like the ultimate fantasy romance dream date to me.

Although I had been joking about the *Soul Train*-themed wedding, the look of disgust on my coworkers' faces bothered me, I realized. I needed a dream date weekend that would impress, no, *exceed* their highest expectations of the best date ever.

"I know exactly what to write, Huxley." I grinned as my fingers whizzed over the touch screen keyboard. My cat glanced up at me before burrowing his head back into his bowl.

My romantic fantasy would be a cozy weekend in a log cabin in the mountains. Snow. Hot chocolate. Fireplace.

Yes, that sounds like something they would say.

Why was I even taking this so seriously? Nobody was even going to see this profile, especially my coworkers or church friends. Especially since I was probably going to delete it as soon as I was finished.

Hot chocolate. Fireplace.

Switzerland, I went back and added. *A log cabin in the mountains of Switzerland.*

If that was not an ultimate romantic fantasy, I didn't know what was.

"Why am I doing this?" I looked at the screen. I moved the cursor over the delete button about to eliminate my entire free profile when a sudden animated arrow shot across the monitor and landed in a bright red heart. Robins, roses and butterflies burst from the arrow-shot heart and danced around the screen. A sound like harp strings and wind chimes boomed out of my tablet's tinny speakers. *This site gives notifications?* I frowned at the frilly commotion. Notifications of what?

"You've been struck by love." A sultry voice whispered as the harps and wind chime sounds continued and the arrow-pierced heart pulsated on the screen.

"What is this?" I clicked on a box that began swirling out from the center of the heart. It was a profile picture of someone else. *I'm aiming for you*, the words captioned underneath.

Someone was checking out my profile. I didn't know whether to be alarmed or flattered. I didn't even know my profile was live. I clicked on the small box to enlarge it and see my "admirer."

Hmmm... Not bad, I conceded. The man in the photo wore a suit, tie, and leaned against a silver BMW. Charming smile, engaging eyes, gorgeous chestnut skin, curly, precision cut fade. *Electrical Engineer, Lover of book clubs, black and white photography, anything and all things jazz.*

"Okay, I see you." I smiled back at the beckoning grin in his snapshot. I scrolled down for more. *Looking for a woman who appreciates the finer things in life and who will cherish the gifts I will give her.*

"What's the catch?" I looked back at his picture, re-read his description. "You seem a little too perfect, a little too good to be true, Mr..." I scrolled back up, realizing I had missed his profile name. "Mr...*MakeUPant*...um..." An instant message from him popped up on the screen as I tried to make sense of his profile name.

Are you breathing hard yet?

Am I really supposed to answer that? Another message popped up on the screen.

If you ain't moaning yet, I've got a picture to send you that will really get you going - but you gotta send me a pic first. Where's your profile pic at, gurl? I wanna see you. ALL OF U!!!!

"DELETE." I used my finger to shut his profile down with such strength, I nearly shattered my generic tablet's sensitive screen. His profile box spun away into a sudden garbage heap of broken harps and shattered hearts that appeared on the screen. Dissonant chords played and a flock of creepy looking vultures landed on the pile and picked and tore at what remained of his profile box.

It was all a game. The thought that my sudden intense desire for love and meaningful companionship could be cheapened into a sleazy experience with really great graphics both sickened and angered me.

"Huxley, the world is crazy. How am I supposed to make sense of anything as complex as love? How do I even begin to find it, I mean the real thing?" My cat sashayed over to me, jumped into my lap. He purred as I stroked his head and patted his chin. "See, I knew there was a part of you that understands where I'm coming from." I smiled as his purrs continued. And then he jumped down, trotted back over to his now empty bowl and gave me a severe look. His rare act of affection had nothing to do with me and everything to do with his bottomless pit of a stomach.

I shook my head as I got up and grabbed his bag of kibbles. "I ain't mad at you, Huxley. You do what you have to do to get what you need."

You do what you have to do to get what you need. My words echoed back to me as I went to shut off my tablet. I might not be sure how people the world over were getting their love grooves on, but I knew this online option was not for me. Now to get rid of my free profile before some other nasty, panting stranger aimed his arrow at me.

"Nice. They warn you." I noted another window had popped up on the screen. *Profiles similar to MakeUPant.* A list of other names, with, well, let's just say disturbing pictures and *About Me* links with way too much TMI filled the window. I could not delete my account fast enough. I wanted nothing of this foolishness.

But then a thought...

"Huxley," I looked over at my cat, "if this site can tell me about men who are similar to that one guy's profile who I don't want, what if... What if I created a profile of the perfect man - the man of my dreams - and then see who comes up as similar to that one? What do you think, Hux?" The cat's bowl scraped along the kitchen floor as he finished up the dry pellets without giving me another thought or glance.

Maybe I should have asked Jesus and not a cat about what to do about my non-existent love life, but at the moment I didn't realize what I stood to lose from this single, simple, seemingly harmless idea.

I just didn't know yet.

"I'm going to do it; make a perfect profile and see who comes up as similar so I can aim my arrow at him." I sat back down with my tablet and a bowl of peanut butter fudge ice cream.

Name. I studied the blank fields that needed to be filled in to create a new profile.

"What should it be, Huxley?" I didn't want to end up with any creepy or disturbing or otherwise inappropriate monikers when the "similar" profiles came up. "How about a man who isn't afraid to share his real name. No games, no hiding behind the screen. That would be different, right?"

My cat stepped into his covered litter box, his tail the last thing visible before the door on it swung shut. I shrugged, feeling silly for consulting a feline. "Think, Berry. What would be the perfect name, the right combination of sophistication and sexy, maybe a little exotic too?" I thought about it a few seconds before deciding.

"Sebastian Brooks." I typed onto the screen. Sebastian. Made me think of *The Little Mermaid.* Delete.

"Gage West." No, not that, either. I backspaced.

"Jasper Pearce?" Not quite right.

"Dexter Schneider." I didn't even finish typing that one out.

"Okay, maybe I do need some divine intervention. God, can you help me out?" Hey, commit all things to prayer, right? I was being proactive and I thought my plan to find the perfect man was genius. I reached for a Bible for some name inspiration. Guess I figured if I found a way to get my Bible involved, then my whole approach could be deemed biblical and God would have to make this work.

I opened the Bible, letting the pages fall somewhere near the middle. The Old Testament. The book of Malachi.

"Malachi." Had a nice ring to it. Sounded strong, daring, maybe even a little sexy. A hint of spicy cologne, a half smile, five o'clock shadow, and a business suit with a slightly crooked shirt, partially unbuttoned. Child, I could see it. Malachi.

Classic name, but… I frowned. It needed a modern zing to it, some kind of twist to make it unique. A different spelling to juice up this classic.

I wasn't looking for the business-as-usual type of man. I wanted a stand-out. I grinned and imagined who I would end up hooking up with. I imagined the girls at work and at church salivating over my perfect catch.

"Malikai." I typed, "Malikai Carter." I liked it, but did it sound too... too different? Would the similar feature just return men with names like D'jontae, or Acquwon, or La'Veetrius? Nothing wrong with those names, but I was open to expanding my horizons beyond the names of the guys I grew up with. I thought about my *Soul Train*-themed wedding joke and the subsequent horror on my coworkers' faces.

Why do I care so much? This isn't even real. I shook my head at my own self, but knew that I could make this profile perfect to nearly anyone's taste by just adding one thing.

An awesome job title.

Chief legal counsel at an international corporation. Not quite a signer of the Declaration of Independence, but this was a pretty darn good seven-figure position, if I said so myself. And I was saying so. This was my perfect profile to create. I couldn't wait to see what profiles would come up as similar to this one. I kept typing.

I love to travel for work, but I'm looking for a special lady who will travel with me for fun. Let's see the world together. I want a woman who is as comfortable relaxing in my beachfront San Francisco condo as she is in my Swiss Chalet. I want a woman who can dine with me in Paris, and dance with me in New Orleans. My dream woman can appreciate Carnival in Brazil, accompany me to landmarks in Rome, and enjoy soul food in Harlem.

"Yum." Ooh, this was going to be good.

My love for travel began during my days playing professional ball overseas and continued when I started a charity for orphans in Africa. Maybe my dream woman doesn't exist, but if she does, I hope she'll be ambitious and graceful enough to complement my life's mission of service; and free enough in body, soul, and spirit to contain my admittedly untamed passions. Let's connect. Soon.

Fully yours, Malikai...

"Huxley, where is the fan? It's feeling kind of hot in here." Little did I realize then just how much heat I was going to be feeling because of these two, innocently written paragraphs.

There were still other fields to fill out, plus I needed a picture, but I didn't bother with either. All I wanted was to see what would be offered as similar profiles. I pressed submit and immediately the inbox of "Malikai's" profile started filling up.

Really? Had I created such a perfect profile that some women (and a couple of men, I noticed) were willing to aim arrows at him without even a picture? Didn't matter if Malikai was pretty or pretty ugly (of course he was gorgeous in my mind); the description alone was enough to serve as bait.

But I didn't care about his admirers. I only wanted to see who would come up as similar. That was my sole aim.

"Where is the list of similar profiles?" I sat waiting for a few moments, but nothing. Maybe I had set the bar too high and there were no similar men folk who could measure up to my fantasy. After about fifteen minutes of nothing but a threatening message that my inbox was near filling without paying for the premium services, I felt the yawns coming. "It's bedtime, Huxley. Enough of this foolishness."

I shut off my tablet, finished my ice cream, and settled

into my bed dreaming of blue water beaches and Mardi Gras parades, not realizing that this would be one of my last peaceful nights of rest before the nightmare took over.

Chapter 4

"Snow White!" Celeste squealed the moment she entered the office. Her engagement ring looked even bigger than what I remembered as all my coworkers gathered around. "That's going to be the theme for my wedding. I know it sounds a little crazy and different, but it's going to be beautiful. Imagine apple and flower bouquets, and twigs for centerpieces to make it feel like woodlands. We'll have mirrors everywhere to make it feel magical. We've set a date for the fall and we're going to go to *Disney World* for our honeymoon."

As everyone discussed this new change of events in Celeste's wedding plans, I headed to my cubicle and sat down all of my belongings. I had a few moments before the phones lines went live. One day my prince will come, I guess. This time yesterday, I hadn't really cared. Now it seemed like I needed my fairytale to begin immediately.

I couldn't help but wonder if any new developments had happened overnight with my perfect man profile. Checking to make sure no one was behind me, I quickly pulled up my fake account. Malikai Carter. There were over fifty messages waiting in my inbox, but no similar profiles.

I clicked on one of the messages. A woman's voluptuous and bare rear end filled my screen. *O Lord, my workstation is going to get flagged for inappropriate images.*

I quickly deleted it, but the next message had an even worse picture. Is this all people wanted to do online to find love? Or maybe nobody was really looking for love. Maybe this was all just about getting a one night or two nights or one month stand. I wanted more. All these darn nasty responses and not one single similar profile to my Malikai Carter.

Then a thought… A revelation, really. I only got the list of similar profiles after *MakeUPant* aimed his arrow at me and sent me an instant message. Perhaps if I recreated my *BerryLady34* profile and had Malikai respond, then that magical list of men on his level would make it to my screen. The account I had created for myself was still in my history. I restored it with one click. Then, I opened up Mr. Carter's profile and found the button that would allow "him" to respond to me. *But what would he say?* I was taking this a little bit too seriously, I knew.

Hi BerryLady34, I saw your profile last night and then it appeared you had taken it down. So glad to see you renewed it! When you'd written something about wanting to drink hot chocolate in front of the fireplace in a log cabin in the Swiss Alps, you reminded me of my chalet in Geneva. I have not come across too many African-American women who dream of ski trips to Switzerland. I'm intrigued. You did not have much else mentioned in your profile, but you have definitely piqued my interest. Is it ok for me to learn more about you? I'd be honored to have that privilege.

So maybe I didn't need all of that, but after yesterday's short and blunt message from the panting man, I wasn't taking any chances. I wasn't sure how this website determined similar profiles and I wanted a man who respected me enough to speak to me like a gentleman.

I pressed send and smiled as my screen filled once again with the dancing hearts and arrows and flowers and roses and quivering harps. The message, *"You've been struck by love,"* danced across the screen.

"Berry, what do you think if I had my little nieces and nephews be dwarfs and serve in my wedding party? Do you think seven flower girls and ring bearers would be too much?"

At my old job where I was manager of my department, I had an office with a door that locked and people had to knock to come in. No such thing here. I spun around in my chair and faced Celeste who stood at the entrance of my cubicle.

"Um, yeah, that would be awesome." The harps and birds chirping seemed to grow louder as if waiting for me to respond. Without turning around to look at the screen, I fumbled for a button, any button, on the keyboard to make the shrill commotion stop. I must have hit the volume button because the sound got even louder.

"What's all that, Berry?" Celeste moved her head from side to side as I tried to block the screen. How would I even begin to explain?

"Oh, nothing." I sat blinking and smiling as if it was completely normal for birds and butterflies to be dancing across the screen before the customer service lines went live.

"Does your computer have some type of virus?" Celeste stepped closer as I scrambled for the mouse. *How do I make this stop?* "What are all those arrows and butterflies on your screen? And that music?"

"No... My computer does not have a virus. It's a…viral video…music video…from…"

"Wait, is that some type of online dating site, Berry?" Celeste came fully to my desk and peered over my shoulder. "I think I've heard of this site," she beamed. "You've been struck by the love arrow, that's what this is. Ooh, Berry, someone's into you."

"No, I –"

"Oh, don't be ashamed." Celeste looked down at me with great concern. "Online dating has become so much more accepted than it used to be. If you can't find your one true love in person, there's nothing wrong with taking that one last chance on the internet."

"This is not what it looks like. I'm not some type of desperate women turning to the Web for love." *Why won't this thing stop?* I continued pressing down on keys. I was desperate all right. Desperate to get this thing to stop.

"What's with all the chirping and strings?" Gina entered the cubicle. Naomi and Carolyn were right behind.

"Oh, Berry has a man after her," Celeste beamed.

The other three squealed. "Really?" Naomi clasped her hands. "Do tell!"

"No, this is not –" I tried to explain.

"He's online and he just aimed the love arrow at her," Celeste continued.

"I've heard of that site," Carolyn exclaimed. "Berry, aren't you going to accept? I mean," she came closer and squinted at the screen, "chalet in Geneva, chief legal counsel, Brazil? Wow, he sounds wonderful."

"Sounds too good to be true, if you ask me." Gina's face was a slight shade of red.

Nobody asked you, Gina, I wanted to say.

"I mean, if he is that great," she kept talking, "why is he available and why no picture?" She glared at the profile of Malikai Carter that floated across the screen in a large heart bubble. The place where a picture should be only had a large, gray question mark. The chirping and harp strumming had finally stopped and just the profile and "his" message to me remained, as if all time had suspended while "he" awaited my response. Speaking of time, the call queue was mere minutes from going live.

"Well," I finally had a chance to speak as all eyes – and raised eyebrows – turned to me, "you may have a point about him being too good to be true. See, I actually had this plan to –" I stopped mid-sentence only because a new box of profiles had appeared on the screen. *'Similar to Malikai Carter'* was the header. This is what I had been waiting for.

It took all I had not to start memorizing the list right then and there, especially since the queue was going live in less than three minutes. "Thanks for stopping in, guys, but I need to get ready for our callers." Was there another way to say "get out" so I could salivate over the growing list? *Hope!*

"Wait," Gina shook her head, laughed, and then, to my horror, grabbed my computer mouse to enlarge and re-read Malikai's message. The list of the similar profiles began fading away, almost as if the longer you spent studying an admirer, the more the others disappeared into the background. "He wrote that he's intrigued by you? You barely have a description up about yourself. A thirty-four year-old non-diva who likes the color orange? That's what you wrote? Plus, you don't have a picture on your profile either."

"Oh no, this isn't good, Berry," Carolyn shook her head with that all too familiar and all too old look of pity. "He's probably not real."

"Or he's really ugly and desperate and depending on his resume to win a woman over." Celeste chimed in.

"Or he's the type of man who, once he gets a picture and a longer description of you, won't have anything else to say to you." Gina had a sudden smile on her face that I didn't find appealing. "You know how these ultra-successful males are. They have a certain image in their mind of what a woman they'll date would look and be like. Not that anything is wrong with you, Berry," she quickly added. "It's just that, you know, Swiss chalet? Landmarks in Rome? You're probably not the image he has in mind."

"The image he has in mind? What exactly are you trying

to say, Gina?"

"Oh, Berry, you're such a sweetheart and I just don't want to see you get hurt. All I'm saying is that if he is even real, you may not be his type."

Huh? What was that supposed to mean. "Why wouldn't or couldn't I be his type? Why would you say that? You barely know me."

"Berry, we've been working with you for a couple of years now, so we know you pretty well." This from Naomi.

Yes, I had been working there a couple of years, and I tagged along during lunch breaks and joined the morning gossip huddles – but I rarely talked to them about what was truly important to me. They knew nothing about my weekends, or my mother, or the girls at church. They didn't know that I struggled daily with what to do with my hair or how I was struggling to make it paycheck to paycheck. They knew nothing about me – and yet they thought they knew enough to say I wasn't Malikai's type?

Wait, Malikai is not real, I reminded myself, inwardly embarrassed that I couldn't be seen as desired by a man of my own imaginations.

The nerve!

"I think you're taking this the wrong way. It has nothing to do with your being black," Carolyn stated matter-of-factly as the other women stared at her in horror and then at me with pity. Who'd said anything about my blackness being a liability? "It's just that a successful African-American man such as him, jet-setting around the world and all, might not be into girls like… like any of us call center workers."

She said that like they all weren't managers, like they all had the same title-less nameplate of *Customer Service Assistant* pinned to their cubicles.

The patronizing made me frown even more. "So you're

saying that this…successful African-American man wouldn't be into any of you all either since you, too, are call center operators, just like me, right?" I felt my own eyebrow rising, not sure how my skin color had even entered the conversation.

"Well, he could. But that's different, you know?" This from Naomi.

"No, I don't know. Exactly, how are we different? Please explain. You just said yourself that we all have the same occupation. So, you can't be talking about my career." I crossed my arms and cocked my head to one side without thinking.

"Hold on, Berry," Gina backed up. "You don't have to get all sister-girl on us. I was just saying that, I mean, do you even know how to ski?"

"What, you don't think black people ski?"

"Of course they do, but in the Swiss Alps? You know what I mean, Berry. Stop making us feel awkward with all this race talk. There's no such thing as race in America."

I wanted to point out that they were the ones who'd brought up race, but there was no use. My arms were crossed tighter around me, a bear self-hug.

The four of them lightly laughed as I frowned, but I saw nervousness in their eyes. Did I scare them? If they thought I was angry, didn't they know I was merely trying to hide my hurt at being offended?

I wasn't good enough for a successful black man? And they were? What? Hold on, I reminded myself. I'm getting worked up over a fake man. This dude wasn't even real and I was taking it personal; but I still felt like I needed to keep the whole situation in check.

"Wait," I narrowed my eyes as we entered the final minute before the work day officially began. "How do you even know this man is even black? Remember, there's no picture."

"Oh, Berry, his name is Malikai, spelled M-A-L-I-K-A-I,"

Celeste jumped in. "If that isn't an Afro-American take on a Biblical name, then I don't know what is."

The four of them giggled. Only twenty seconds remained before the queue went live. They all began turning toward their own cubicles, a sign that the conversation would resume at lunch.

I couldn't have these women think I was less than them and undesirable to any successful man – regardless of his color. Shoot, we all worked in the same office and *they* were marrying lawyers and accountants and businessmen. *Their* significant others were all successful men with high pedigrees. Why would they expect my man, if I ever got one, to be any less important or special? Why would they even balk at the idea that I could get the attention of any man they'd even admire?

"I'm going to post my picture," I spoke up to all of them, "and maybe he'll post his back. I bet he's far from ugly *and* he'll find me to be his type before it's all said and done."

"Good for you, Berry," Carolyn shouted from her cubicle, all of us putting on our headsets. "Go for it, but just don't let yourself get hurt. Be prepared either way." I imagined the joint look of pity they'd all give if they found out "Malikai Carter" lost interest in me. As the phones began ringing, I knew what I needed to do before lunch. I nodded to myself as I took my first caller for the day.

This relationship with the fake Malikai Carter was about to get real.

Chapter 5

Kissy lips. Sideways pose. Over the shoulder look back. Doe eyes. Half-smile.

I was in the restroom trying to capture the just-right selfie. Cell phone in hand, gold-framed mirror in my view, I posed, snapped, and re-posed, determined to get one that I could use as my profile pic.

My hair wasn't quite right, my wash-and-go a little wash-and-no; but the rhinestone studded, butterfly pin that pushed part of my hair to the side gave me a sultry quality. Or so I hoped. I'd dug deep in my purse to find the lip gloss I'd used at last year's company holiday party. A shimmering bronze that complimented my caramel skin. I widened my eyeliner, giving my eyes a smokier look. Thankfully, I was wearing one of my favorite dresses – a simple gold sweater dress with a thick, black belt that sat just over my hips. Don't get it wrong. I could work a size twelve, brown clogs, knit leggings and all.

I just needed one shot that worked and I wasn't getting it.

Serious face. Joyful grin. Head to one side. Finger to the chin. No, no, and no. I had to get this right.

My coworkers thought Mr. Malikai Carter would turn away once I put my picture up. They were convinced that once he got one good look at me and read more of my soon-to-be expanded *About Me* section, he would run away and not look back. Well, these little biddies were going to find out just how mistaken they were.

I was going to see to that. Gina had killed my "similar profiles" mission. I shut my eyes, recalling how the list of males similar to the perfect mirage I'd created had faded into nothingness once she started messing with my computer.

Welp. Call me crazy or maybe obsessed, but I was going to teach these coworkers of mine not to count me out. Ain't no reason a successful, gorgeous, wealthy man wouldn't want to know me better.

Lord, what am I doing? I stared at myself in the mirror, lowered my cell phone, and stopped taking shots. *Malikai Carter is a made up man, a pure figment of my imagination.* What's sadder: the fact that my coworkers may be right about my non-ability to attract a man of a higher class or that I was willing to pretend he existed just to prove them wrong?

Prove to them.

Was this really about proving something to *them*?

"Someone still in there?" A loud knock jolted me back to motion. This was the only female restroom on this floor of the office building. Most of the office suites and companies in the building were comprised of female employees, so there was always someone waiting to use the single stall bathroom. I was surprised I'd had this much time.

"I'm coming." I grabbed the paper towel and wiped off the glittery lip-gloss, repositioned the butterfly clip in my hair and dropped my phone back into my purse. I flushed the toilet to pretend that I'd actually been holding up the bathroom for a noble reason and turned the water on and off to ensure that I came off as a civilized citizen.

"Sorry for the hold up." I smiled as I finally came out of the restroom. A black girl who helped clean office suites throughout the building rolled her eyes as she marched past me and shut the door.

Ooo-kay… We didn't really know each other like that. I think I'd complemented her once on her 'fro – a gorgeous mound of jet black curls and coils – but that was about it, so I didn't get the negative theatrics over the bathroom wait.

Seemed like the whole world was dissing me today. But that was okay.

I could feel a fire re-igniting in me as I pulled out my cell phone once again. I had no mirror, no makeup, and my camera may not have been focused, but I took a snap anyway. Guess what?

This picture looked good.

Me.

The real me, slightly off-centered and staring at an unseen, unknown down the hall.

I uploaded it to my email as I re-entered my office suite. By the time I'd sat back down in my cubicle, my picture was waiting in my inbox. I had three minutes left for my mid-morning break, just enough time to complete my fire-fueled mission. I smiled as I put back on my headset.

"Cole Financial Services. This is Berry Jenkins. How may I assist you today?"

***

"Wow! He really did respond!"

"Move over. Let me see!"

"Ooo, Berry, this might be the beginning of something spectacular!"

My four co-workers huddled around the lunch table trying to get a better view of my tablet. We sat at the same table together nearly every day, in the small food court on the bottom floor of our downtown office building. I'd skipped getting in line for my usual egg salad sandwich. Instead, I'd gotten to the table first, logged on, had the dating website pulled up and waited for them to finally join me for our thirty-minute gossip session.

For once, for maybe the first time, I was the center, the main topic, the focus of lunch time conversation.

"As soon as I put my profile picture up and added a few sentences to my description, he sent me an instant message." I don't know why I sat there beaming as if this really mattered. As if this was really real. What horror it would be for them to find out I was the author of both my profile description *and* "his" response. For the moment, the attention from the girls and Gina's hot red cheeks were enough to push back the worry.

Afro girl from the bathroom encounter sat at a nearby table, a packed lunch of cheese, cubed turkey, and crackers in hand. Our eyes met and she rolled hers at me again.

What was her deal?

"Let me see what he said." Gina frowned as she grabbed my tablet. She read the message out loud. "I'm at the airport, waiting for my flight to Dubai, when I see a face so sweet, I feel like I'm already soaring. There's a depth to your eyes that keeps drawing me back, makes me want to search in them more. I can only imagine your smile. Thanks for sharing your picture, BerryLady34. You've made my day."

"Awww. He sounds so sweet." Celeste hugged her hand over her heart.

"I'm still not convinced that he's real." Gina still frowned. "Or that he's a looker. See, still no picture. I'm going to Google him and see what I can find." She pulled out her phone.

"Stop it, Gina." Carolyn grabbed her wrist. "Whether he's real or not, let's let Berry enjoy the moment.

Whether he's real or not? Oh, this man was going to be real, for sure. My brain was already at work, charging ahead. I needed him to be real enough online that even a Google search would shut Gina up.

What am I doing?

"Ladies, Gina," I nodded, "I appreciate your interest and

concern. Don't worry. I'm going to take my time with this. I'll do my research, figure him out. And I will keep you posted." They smiled, all except for Gina, who slowly eased her phone back down.

Dubai? I typed into the instant messenger function to give "him" a response. *Sounds exciting! What's the name of the company you work for as chief legal counsel?* I held up my tablet for them all to see. Even Gina nodded in approval.

"Good start, Berry. Find out where he works and we can figure him out from there."

I felt like I'd dodged a bullet even as sweat beads formed on my forehead and down the center of my back. *What am I doing?* My throat felt dry and my stomach rumbled, and I realized I'd skipped lunch for this foolishness.

"Did he answer back yet?" Celeste asked between munches of her spinach salad.

I stared down at my tablet as if there really would be a response. I shook my head no.

"Well, he did say he was about to get on a flight to Dubai. Maybe he's boarding the plane now," Carolyn answered for me. "My fiancé has been to Dubai a few times. Berry, this is so exciting. Who knows what waits in your future?"

Naomi raised her diet cola. "To Berry, to possibilities, to love."

We held up water bottles and soda cups for a toast. Gina joined in last.

"To the man of my dreams," I added and all five of us smiled. As the conversation turned toward Celeste's wedding plans and Naomi's upcoming baby shower, I noticed Afro-girl shaking her head at me from her table across the food court.

She can't hear our conversation. Why is she looking at me like that? Then again, maybe she was just rocking her head to music. She did have headphones on. And there was no real way to say for sure that she was even looking at me.

Paranoia.

The first symptoms of a lie gone bad.

I swallowed hard, and then refocused on my scheming. I had to make this man real. Immediately.

Chapter 6

"Davis, I need to use your computer."

My brother lived ten minutes away from me and directly on my bus route. He'd bought an old, dilapidated, auto body shop and transformed it into a habitable apartment. Not sure that he'd ever obtained the legal permits and zoning licenses for his residence in the middle of an otherwise industrial area. But, I will admit, once you got past the rusty exterior, his dwelling place was bright, warm, and comfortable, with a stylish earthiness all his own. We called his place The Garage. I don't think I'd seen loft apartments downtown with the same appeal and funktitude that his self-made studio quarters allowed.

"You didn't call." Davis rolled up his front door, a tall, fruit smoothie in one hand and a bottle of Colt 45 in the other. Behind him, a thick, green blanket and mounds of pillows covered his sofa. Candles of various sizes and scents lit the room.

"Expecting company?" I stepped around him. A single flower sat in a vase on his table. I used the word "table" loosely; a painted piece of plywood resting atop two step stools is what he used for dining. Somehow, maybe because of its silver metallic and sky-blue colors, it worked.

"Don't you have a computer? Why are you coming over here to use mine?" Davis shut the garage door behind him, ignoring my question about his plans for the evening. He walked over to the stainless steel commercial oven and cook top he'd installed after finding them at a closing appliance store. I followed behind him. Several pans bubbled on top and amidst the soothing scents of the candles, I caught whiffs of chicken and apples. Something chocolaty baked in the oven.

"I have a computer tablet, but I need to use an actual computer for a project I'm working on."

"Taking another class?" He stirred something in a tall pot. I was known to register for courses at community colleges just to explore interests. "You don't have enough certificates and degrees?" He shook his head as he spoke to me, but he had some nerve.

"Are you starting another business or dabbling in another get-rich quick scheme?" I retorted back. "What will it be this time? Selling tropical healing juice or are you going to make your millions with fake websites?" Wait, I needed to use his computer. Let me bring this back down. "Look, Davis, I'm sorry. I registered for…this business management class online… and some of the assignments are better suited for a workstation and not a tablet. I won't be long. I promise."

He frowned at me a few moments and then shrugged. "Here, taste this." He held out a spoon of a rice dish. "Chicken apple sausage with brown rice. I'm pairing it with a homemade pineapple salsa on pita squares and vintage white wine. What do you think?"

I tasted it, hoping that the gesture would get me some screen time. "It's great, Davis. Mom and I keep saying you should have been a chef. Not that there's anything wrong with your temp job at that warehouse, but…" Oops. Sore spot. I saw his jaw clench again. Quick, change the subject.

"What time is Ertha coming over?" I recalled that Ertha Bellvue had been giggling along with him on the church van last night when I'd gotten him to give me a ride home.

"Ertha's not coming." His jaw relaxed.

"So, you're not having company?"

"Oh, I *am* having a friend over. It's just…not Ertha." He winked and turned back to stirring a pot.

I rolled my eyes and dropped my coat on his sofa. He didn't object. "And that, Davis, is why you're a thirty-nine-year-old bachelor. Always trying to be a player."

"If you're winning at the game, why quit?" He chuckled.

"You're almost forty years old. Do you not have any plans to settle down and get married one day? I'm only thirty-four, and everyone is on my back, worried about when I'm going to walk down the aisle and pop out babies."

"The curse of womanhood. What can I say? If I want to start my family when I'm sixty-two, I can do that. Pass me the salt."

I glared at my brother. Wanted to smack him. Shook my head and groaned instead. "And what about your friend coming over? Is she burdened by this 'womanhood curse' too? Are you just playing into it or does she believe that this dinner you're preparing for her is something real and meaningful and not just an elaborate set-up for a booty call?"

"She can believe whatever will make her happy for the night."

"Really, Davis?"

"Like they say, don't hate the player, hate the game. If you still need to use my computer, go ahead. You won't be disrupting my flow at all. As long as you are gone by dessert, that is." He winked again.

"I'm sick of you." I picked up my coat and headed to a partitioned area Davis called The Control Room. Multiple workstations, a couple of laptops, speakers, an old analog 4-track recorder, and an assortment of subwoofers, broken mixing boards, and other pieces of musical and computer equipment crowded the small space. I settled in front of one of the larger computer monitors and commenced my current mission: give Malikai Carter a digital imprint.

Seemed like an easy enough task.

I just needed to put something up online that made him seem real beyond the dating profile. My plan was simple. I didn't want to make any type of social media accounts that could be discovered and dissected by others. What made sense to me was a website, a company website. There are millions, if not billions of websites out in the virtual universe. A website that had no links to social media or search engines would be more or less hidden, invisible. Only someone looking specifically for Malikai Carter, chief legal counselor of a yet to be named corporation, could actually stumble on it, I figured.

As R&B hits from the 1990s suddenly blared on my brother's living room speakers, I pulled up a website that offered templates and cheap prices to create basic websites. The website creation program had a free trial with no payment needed for a couple of weeks or so.

"I'll have this thing shut down before then," I mumbled as I began building a home page. "Okay, I need something plain, easy, and fast." I scrolled through the template option. "First, I need a name."

What am I doing? I kept pushing the thought back. This was just for fun. I needed to teach those girls a lesson; show them that little old average me was completely capable of landing a drool-worthy man.

A smooth-as-silk tenor voice crooned from the other side of the partition and I listened for a few moments as my brother sung a ballad along with K-Ci & JoJo. I hadn't heard that song since my high school days. That song had been playing during the senior superlatives assembly where I'd learned that I'd won "Best Smile." I recalled taking the stage next to a classmate, Adilson Rodriguez who'd won "Best Hair." He'd been a member of the basketball team, but had kept his near shoulder-length, black tresses flawless and in place, no matter how much he was drenched in sweat.

The flood of memories continued and by the time I heard a knock on Davis's garage door, I had a simple website created for Adilson Enterprises, an international corporation that specialized in creating legal performance enhancers for athletes. It made sense to make the corporation sports-related as I'd written in Malikai's dating profile that he'd previously played ball in an overseas league.

Stay In The Game Without Breaking The Rules! I wrote as a slogan on the home page for my fake performance enhancer website. I made a logo out of circles and triangles, added some color and gave it a pretty border. The website creation program made it all look legit. Lastly, I created one other page for the website, the *Contact Us* page.

Founder and CEO: Dexter Schneider

Chief Operating Officer: Jasper Pearce

Chief Legal Counsel and International Affairs Advisor: Malikai Carter

Director of Sales and Marketing: Vashti McMillan

Included in the free trial was the ability to have a company email account. I went ahead and gave all listed members of this corporation email addresses and added them to the names. Finally, for good measure, I used another free trial program to create a phone number with a San Francisco area code. Malikai had mentioned having a place in San Fran so it made sense that the office for this "corporation" would be based there as well.

"Ooh, this is going to be good." I couldn't stop giggling. I hooked up one of Davis's musical equipment boards to a microphone so that I could create a voice mail message for the number. Not quite auto-tune, but it worked. My voice was not at all recognizable in the message.

"Greetings, you have reached the general mailbox for Adilson Enterprises. Please leave a message and someone will get back to you shortly."

When I played it back, I realized that whatever song my brother had been playing on his loudspeakers at the moment was also in the message.

"You know what? I think it works." I nodded, pleased that the hip-hop/R&B melody playing in the background of the message sounded like a song an athlete would work out to. Upbeat. Positive. Inspiring. World-class.

I settled back in my seat and smiled at my progress. Work tomorrow was going to be awesome.

And then I would shut all of this foolishness down.

"Berry, sorry to interrupt, but I wanted to introduce you to my friend."

I nearly broke the seat as I spun around to face the entrance of The Control Room. "Wha- oh, I, oh, hello."

My brother raised an eye at my obvious and unexpected display of nerves, but he quickly flashed me a smile and nodded at the woman standing next to him. "Berry, this is Li Yan, a friend of mine from the club where I DJ from time to time. She's a bartender there. Li Yan, this is my little sister, Berry."

I stood and extended a hand to the petite, Asian girl who grinned back at me. Her hair was dyed a platinum blonde and she wore a cute, flowery minidress and knee-high, black boots that I wanted for myself. "Hi, Li Yan, nice to meet you."

"Hi, Berry! Davis told me that you were back here working on a class assignment, so I won't interrupt, but I'm glad to meet you, too."

"Same here," I smiled again, but then made the mistake of looking back at the large monitor where my website still displayed. Why had I chosen to use the biggest screen? And why was I so paranoid?

"Business management class, right?" Davis nodded at the screen as now both he and Li Yan studied the monitor.

"Uh, yeah, I… We had to analyze a website of a new corporation to…take notes about…how their website is or isn't…successful for new viewers?" Did either one of them notice that I spoke in question form? Or that whatever I'd just said barely made sense? *And why didn't I just tell the truth?* Oh, right, so I wouldn't look like a fool to my brother and his girl of the day.

"Oh, neat. I had a class like that once," Li Yan was all bubbles and smiles, "but I was majoring in graphic design and we had to re-do the websites if they weren't up to par. It was a win-win situation; we helped real businesses and they allowed us to have real design experiences. We would actually be graded by how many viewers engaged with our redesigned webpages."

"Sounds like a great program. I'm not quite doing that. I'm…" My voice trailed off as I looked back at the screen and reached to click off the *Contact Us* page. What remained was the home page.

"That's a pretty basic site," Li Yan frowned for the first time.

"Yeah, well, dinner should be just about ready." Davis glared at me from behind his date. I was messing with his flow.

"Perfect timing. I was just about to leave." I reached for the mouse to log off, but Li Yan stopped me.

"Wait a minute," she squinted her eyes as she looked over the home page. "That's a revolutionary idea. A legal alternative for athletes who want to improve their performance? Davis, did you see this?"

"Oh, yeah. Interesting." He was bored. He glared at me more. A new song came on, a slow jam. This man had his playlist on a schedule, I realized.

"Okay, well, it was great meeting you, Li Yan." I wanted to shut off the computer, but she had taken over the mouse and was now sitting down in front of the monitor.

"Davis, you know all those pro athletes that come through

the club? I'm sure they would love to hear about this. Some opportunities might exist here."

The sudden flicker of interest in Davis's eyes told me I had to shut this whole thing down immediately. "Well, your dinner's getting cold and all those candles are about to burn out, so let me get on out of your way." I reached for the mouse which Li Yan still had in her palm.

"Hold on, Berry." Now, Davis was reaching for the mouse. "Let Li Yan write down the phone number. This might be something worth looking into." I noticed then that Li Yan had pulled out her cell phone and was adding the San Francisco-based created phone number to her contact list.

I looked at him over her head and shook my head frantically 'no.' He raised an eyebrow. *How do I even explain this?*

"Don't worry about calling them, Li Yan," he shrugged at me and looked at me like I was crazy. "Let's go eat."

"Oh, I wasn't calling them tonight." Finally, she stood. The computer began shutting down. "It's probably already after business hours. I'll dial them tomorrow."

A part of me relaxed. A disaster avoided. Not that it would have been the end of the world if she'd called anyway. I held the power on the other end of the line. She just wouldn't have gotten a call back. At least now, I had until the morning to keep her from leaving a message on the number in the first place – and late morning at that since business hours on the West Coast were three hours behind our time zone.

As I walked out of Davis's garage home, I sent him a text.

Thx for letting me use your computer. Oh, don't let your friend call that number. This company is not what it appears to be. Good night!

Should I have told him that the whole website was fake? Should I have come clean with him and explained my ploy to pretend I had connected with the perfect man and that this webpage was merely my way to legitimize him to my coworkers? Yes, probably. In retrospect, if I knew what was going to happen, I would have been completely up front, and maybe the three of us would have just laughed it all off as the immature actions of a pathetically desperate woman.

But, that night, when Davis immediately texted me back with. "*No problem, she won't call at all,*" I didn't think anything else about it.

I actually smiled when I got into my bed that night, Huxley's bowl scraping along the floor.

Chapter 7

"That's a very plain website," Gina frowned. It was Friday morning and the five of us stood in my cubicle, my creation from last night up on my monitor.

"That just means they are a very successful company," Celeste replied with certainty. "My fiancé used to work for a corporation like that, one which had a very minimal web presence. Some corporations keep a low profile because they can. No need for extra smoke and lights if you're doing business in the millions – or even billions. Attention won't be put into marketing and design because your customers are a given. That approach leaves more money in the company's pockets."

That explanation didn't make sense to me, but everyone else nodded so I nodded along, too.

"Wow, Berry, you may have really scored a winner. Rich, successful, and probably the epitome of a gentleman" Naomi rubbed her bulging belly.

"But there's still no picture," Gina piped in. "I'm getting more and more convinced that he must look like a toad."

"Well, we won't know until he updates his profile, but I did get another message from him." I went back to the dating website and opened the inbox for my profile. There were seven messages waiting for me – six of which came from actual people. I deleted the real suitors quickly and opened the one from "Malikai." My co-workers squeezed in closer to see.

Hi BerryLady34, it's late where you are on the East Coast, but my day is just getting started here in Dubai. I have an early morning meeting and then it's off to Brussels then Tokyo.

Although the next two days are busy for me, I am hoping that perhaps we could schedule time to chat sometime this weekend. Yes, this is an online website, but, honestly, I feel a little awkward about the internet dating thing. I guess I'm somewhat old-fashioned… Not sure how else to ask, but can I call you sometime? Or, if you are not comfortable sharing your number, I will give you mine. Let me know. I know we don't know each other, but I am looking forward to learning more about you. Have a great day!

"I don't know, Berry," Gina rested her chin between her thumb and first finger. "Something about him doesn't feel all the way right to me."

"I hear what Gina is saying," Celeste chimed in. "He seems to be moving pretty fast. You've barely finished your profile and he is already moving to the telephone stage? At least exchange emails first."

"You saw what he said." I pointed to the message. "He's old-fashioned. He wants to come from behind the computer screen and have a regular phone conversation. That may not be a bad idea in getting to know him."

"So, you are going to contact him?" Naomi gasped, her face all smiles.

"I don't know. I think I want to get more information about him first." I closed the website for Adilson Enterprises. *I'll delete that when I get home.*

"Did you find any profiles for him on *Facebook* or *Twitter?*"

"Nope. I checked." I had no plans to put him on those social networking sites. Besides, that would mean creating pictures and status updates and tweets and posts and I barely could keep up with my own accounts.

"It's odd for a man with that high of a position to have such a nonexistent virtual life," Gina voiced.

"Or, maybe because of his position, he's decided to keep a low profile," Naomi countered. "Remember, he's the chief legal counsel for an international corporation. I would imagine he'd be very careful about what information he puts out there about himself."

"What about the company?" Celeste cut in. "Maybe if you do some digging into where he works, you might find out more information about him. Someone at his job is bound to have a *Facebook* profile with company party pictures, conferences abroad, trips, meetings, adventures, something." Celeste had a dreamy look on her face as she played with the engagement ring on her finger. I noticed then that we had not had any detailed conversations about her wedding plans. My fake dating interest had taken over the minds and fantasies of everyone in my office.

I didn't know whether to feel proud or ashamed.

What I did know is that I didn't want any more questions on the matter.

"I'll look into it, but at the moment we probably should get ready to begin the day."

The four nodded and began turning toward their respective cubicles. Everyone except Celeste.

"Berry, see if you can find out where he went to law school. For the type of position he has, I'm sure he probably went somewhere impressive, probably Ivy League. I know it's a long shot, but find out where he went, and I'll get Greg to see if he or any of his partners were classmates with him or know anything about him. I'm really hoping he's legitimate, Berry. You deserve to have the best. I hope this is really your chance at love. He sounds like a dream."

"I just want to know what he looks like," Gina boomed over the cubicle walls. "I still think he's probably ugly. Or really old. Or both. He never gave his age, did he? The moment he posts or you find a picture, text us all."

"Will do." I wanted to smack my own smile off of my face as I settled in my seat and readied to answer the phones.

Law school? Classmates? Pictures?

What had I gotten myself into? Surely, I had taken things too far. I was trying to convince these women that Malikai Carter was real – and that he totally wanted to get to know me better. But why? Why was I working so hard to make this little lie work?

Little…

Was it really a little lie anymore?

I swallowed hard as the phones began ringing. Maybe I should just come clean and 'fess up. I could say it was all a prank. Nothing more.

An email popped up on my screen. It was from Gina.

> *Berry, I'm not sure this man is real. He doesn't have a picture, his company's website looks like anyone could have made it up, and I've been trying to find him on Facebook, Twitter – anything – and there's not a single trace of a Malikai Carter anywhere. I know you want him to be true, but this man is probably some crazy stalker killer dude who likes preying on desperate women. Don't give out your number. I mean, a Swiss chalet? Why is he available? It's not adding up. The way I see it, Malikai Carter is either OLD, UGLY, MARRIED, A KILLER, OR A FAKE!!!!! Just think about it. I'm not saying this to be mean, but if this man is really real, why would he be chasing after YOU?*

Well, why wouldn't he? My eyelashes fluttered in disbelief

as I tried to make sense of Gina's apparent anger and shock that a man of Malikai's supposed magnitude would have an interest in ME. Hey, she used all caps, so why couldn't I?

Desperate women.

The words from her email jumped out at me, swung at me, jabbed me right in the core of my stomach. I felt a part of me bow down in defeat and then stand back up with a renewed, determined arrogance.

The nerve of this woman to think that only a fake man, or otherwise undesirable man, would have any interest in me.

But he is fake, Berry. I punched down the still, quiet voice that whispered through all the inner commotion. I had no time for such thoughts as I re-configured my battle plan.

Yes, this was a war.

This was a fight for the plain, brown-skinned girl who'd been overlooked and unwanted by the rich and beautiful elite. I was going to show the world, well, really, the girls in my office, that my beauty, my worth was enough to get the attention of a man they themselves wanted.

Whatever qualms I'd had about lying had been erased with a single unwelcomed email. I knew right then that this would no longer be a "little lie." I was about to cross the waters into a foreign land of a major whopper: tall ship, captain's hat, cannons drawn and all. Treasure awaited me in that foreign land where lies shaped my passageway, and fantasy intermingled with reality. The treasure I sought was simple: the priceless look on Gina et al.'s faces when they finally had no choice but to accept the fact that little ole me could have better than all of THEM.

The waters would be rocky, I knew, as I would have to make my way through unchartered territories of make-believe and imaginations. I'd have to be consistent with my stories and be prepared to provide whatever proof was necessary to show that my island of lies was on the map of love's realities. There would be unexpected storms and swells, icebergs and ragged cliffs to avoid, I knew.

But I was prepared to fight through the currents and get to my golden chest. Show them all that I was worthy.

I didn't expect to drown along the way.

Part 2:
"Welp, Huxley, looks like I'm all in."

Chapter 8

Friday night.

Most weekends, I spent the evenings experimenting with my hair. Braid-outs, twist-outs, roller sets, deep conditioners, *YouTube* "how-to" videos… I spent hours (and dollars) trying out new products, new styles, sometimes, even new colors. I would then get online and read blogs and articles about celebrity gossip, some politics, get trapped yelling at comment boards, and then unwind with television marathons of my favorite reality shows and 1990s sitcoms. If I really felt like talking to any one, I'd pick up the phone to catch up with a cousin or two, argue with my mom, or harass my brother.

I had a simple life, enjoyed simple pleasures, and up until now, it had felt like enough.

"Huxley, we are on a mission," I announced to my cat. Tonight, he stared at me from a blue beanbag chair I had in the corner of my living room. He curled up into a ball, one ear twitching as I continued to outline my current plan.

"Gina is so concerned about his picture and his online presence that I have no choice but to give him one. Before the night is over, I will have a picture for Mr. Malikai Carter and a profile up on a career networking website. See, he's not on *Facebook* or *Twitter* because he has no time for such trivialities. He's a busy man jet-setting around the world managing international legal affairs. And, Huxley, that's why he's still single and available. He's been too busy building his career to stop for love. But, just like me, the time for relationships is now. Sounds good. Doesn't it, Huxley? And believable."

Huxley's ear stopped twitching. He turned his head away from me and stretched out to sleep.

I was alone in this.

No problem, I nodded, as I gathered the documents and papers I'd printed out. Not wanting to miss something that could be picked apart by Gina or anyone else for that matter, I'd typed up some notes and printed them out to use for reference as I worked on Malikai's career profile. My stories had to stay consistent.

"This resume is incredible," I smiled again at my ingenuity and quick thinking. "Celeste wants to know if her fiancé or his partners went to law school with him. Nope. Not a chance."

Malikai graduated from law school in South Africa, Cape Town to be exact, several thousand miles away from any state-side Ivy League schools Greg and his colleagues would have attended.

"And Huxley, the reason he went to school all the way out there is because his parents were charity workers. He spent most of his childhood in Africa… Huxley?" The cat had long tuned me out. "Botswana to be exact." I decided on the location after checking online to see what countries bordered South Africa. Botswana sounded foreign enough. I smiled.

I wasn't putting all of this on his resume, of course, but I needed to have the context of his story straight in my head to answer any questions. Malikai and I were going to talk that weekend and I would need to fill in everyone on the details. It was a fool-proof plan to have a little fun. They'd all be back to talking about wedding plans before the end of next week, I figured, so I might as well enjoy the charade while it lasted.

Specialist in international business law. Excellent computer and communication skills. Fluent or semi-fluent in many languages, including French, Korean, Russian, and, of course, English. Several professional awards and recognition for charity work. Hobbies include playing the saxophone, gourmet cooking, and mentoring at-risk youth.

I was impressed with this man. I skimmed through the main sections of the resume one last time before uploading it onto a career networking site. I set it up so that he didn't have to connect with anyone, but his resume and profile were public. His business email served as his lone contact information. All that was left to be completed was his picture.

A picture.

Hmmmm…

I pulled up some online stock photos. "No, too easy to find." I figured any picture I could find in mere seconds could be easily discovered by the likes of Gina. For good measure, though, I scrolled through some of the photos on my tablet, admiring the various male models who stared back at me through the screen.

Black, white, Asian, Latino… All the chiseled and buff fellows on my screen looked delish.

His name is Malikai, spelled M-A-L-I-K-A-I. If that isn't an Afro-American take on a Biblical name, then I don't know what is. Celeste's pronouncement dug into me. I needed to make this man racially ambiguous to dispel all my coworkers' misguided theories, I decided – if that was even possible. I wanted any woman from any background to look at him and melt. Not sure why it mattered to me so much, but it did.

Using a feature on my phone that allowed me to manipulate photos, I picked out five photos of men who spanned the spectrum of the skin tone rainbow, then merged them.

"Uh, no." I quickly undid the monstrous looking creature that resulted from the merge.

Cake.

I had to treat my Malikai like a delicate, prized, made from scratch dessert, and not just a box mix pile of ingredients that I plopped together.

A little of this nose, some of these eyes. Hair, eyebrows, chin and lips... I went through the photos and picked out features I liked, no, loved, and then carefully merged them into a single palette of perfection. Bronzed skin tone, full, kissable lips. Bulging muscles underneath a gray dress shirt.

Too clean. Squeaky clean.

Using another photo feature on my tablet, I drew a couple of black lines on the skin just past his shirt sleeve; the hint of an elaborate tattoo. I put a diamond stud in both of his earlobes, completing the bad boy in a business suit look. I wasn't worried about him looking too rough. His resume more than spoke to his ability to carry himself as a well-capable professional.

"I think I'm taking this a little bit too seriously, Huxley." I looked over at my sleeping cat and wondered why I was still up messing around with this foolishness. *It's fun!*

"Mary Shelly ain't got nothing on my skills." I sat back and looked at my creation. Far from the Frankenstein that Shelly had crafted in her nineteenth century novel, my piecemeal creation was now nowhere near monstrous.

Perfect.

Wait, something is missing.

I stared into the deep black eyes of the man who stared back at me and decided to do one more thing to make Malikai's merged photo roots even more untraceable.

"Say cheese, Huxley." I snapped a picture of my cat's light brown fur, enlarged it and then used the brown coloring as the color of Malikai's intense eyes. The softening effect was immediate. Inviting.

"And there you have it, ladies and gentlemen. The perfect man." I smiled at the unsettlingly handsome man I'd made with a few flicks of my finger on my tablet. I used my cell phone to take a picture of the image so that the final product couldn't be picked apart or unscrambled.

And then I uploaded it to his professional profile alongside his resume. I didn't put it on the dating website. I had a good explanation ready for Gina about that omission.

"Oh, if you could be real." I licked my lips at the playful grin, the beckoning eyes. "Um, um, um." I was so caught up in my admiration of "Mr. Carter" that I completely missed the jingle of keys in my front door.

But I didn't miss the sudden voice.

"Berry Martini Jenkins, we need to talk. Now."

"Mom!" I almost dropped my tablet and spilled the sweet tea I was drinking as I scrambled to shut my handiwork down. "What are you doing here and why did you use the key? I gave it to you to only use in an emergency."

"This is an emergency, Berry. I can't play around with this anymore."

"What are you talking about? Did something happen? Is Davis okay?" I noticed for the first time that the tote bag hanging off her shoulder was brimming over with hair products and cosmetics. My alarm level went up even higher. "Wait a minute. What's going on?"

"An intervention." She marched over to where I sat and began pulling out bottles and jars and containers and cases and lining them up on my desk, pushing my papers and knick-knacks out of the way.

"Hold on, Mom, what are you doing? You said there's an emergency."

"Yes." She pulled out a bundle of fake hair and eyed it before giving me the eye. "Did you know that Victoria Smallwood just got engaged?" My mother's eyes were on fire.

"Uh, yes. I talked to Vickie and the other girls at Wednesday night service. She showed us her ring and shared some of her wedding plans." I looked down at the tub of unmixed relaxer, the fake hair, and the flat iron my mother had lined up on my desk. Her eyes darted frantically over the three. "Ma, what is the emergency and why do you have these things on my desk?"

"Victoria Smallwood just got engaged. Victoria Smallwood, Sister Evangeline Willow's daughter, is getting married." She paused between each word and glared at me.

"I know that," I snapped back, "What I don't know is why you are here yelling about an emergency, and thinking that you're about to do something to my hair."

"Victoria Smallwood?" My mother's voice was a sharp hiss. "That little homely looking, bucktoothed grapefruit can pin down a good man and you're sitting alone in this apartment on a Friday night? Are you serious? You really don't see the emergency in this situation?"

"Ma, that is totally uncalled for. Vickie is a sweetheart and she is not *that* ugly." I shook my head, ashamed. "What am I saying? Ma, you know as well as I do – because you raised me this way – that looks don't mean anything. It's all about who you are inside. She is a lovely lady who has found the love of her life. I'm happy for her. Aren't you?"

"Oh, bull crap, Berry." My mother plugged up the flat iron. "You're not in second grade anymore. Leave the fairy tales and feel good phrases alone. We need to fix you up so you can get a man. The last thing I need is Sister Willow frowning down at us at Victoria's wedding reception. She's probably looking up a scripture right now to rub in our faces that you ain't been blessed with a man yet."

"Ma, listen to what you're saying." I pulled out the plug from the socket. "Why are you harping on my relationship status? We're in the twenty-first century. Why are you so worried about me getting married, anyway? What if I'm happy being an independent woman? I'm single and satisfied."

"Are you really?" She opened the hair pack, closed it, and then began measuring out the relaxer ingredients. She pulled out a rattail comb to mix it. I glanced over at my phone. The snapshot of "Malikai Carter" was still on the screen. That was a different issue, though, I told myself. I just wanted to prove that…that what?

"Well?" My mother put down everything and crossed her arms.

I…didn't know what to say. "I've got Jesus. And He's all I need." The words felt empty on my lips. I felt as real as the fakery I'd witnessed at my church on Sundays; as genuine as the parade of charades I'd seen on Wednesday nights.

Something was wrong with all of us.

Did it take my realization of loneliness to awaken to that conclusion?

"It's okay, baby. We are going to do something to that unruly bird's nest on top of your head and everything will be alright. We can lye it, fry it, or buy it, whichever way you choose; but we are getting rid of those naps tonight, so you can get a man tomorrow."

"You are not touching my hair, Mom." Now *my* arms were crossed as I ducked out of my mother's reach. "You may not like it or understand it, but I am fine with wearing my hair the way it naturally grows from my head. It's not always easy to manage and it may not be the status quo, and I'm not saying that there's something wrong with altering it or wearing it the ways you are suggesting. But it's wrong if it's not true to who I am, who I feel myself to be. I'm a naturalista, and any man that wants me is going to fully accept me just as I am."

In my head, I could hear all the blog and *YouTube* stars in the #TeamNatural world applauding, high-fiving, cheering me on.

In my head.

In my face was my mother who was not hearing or having one word of my heartfelt speech. "Girl, if you don't tame that knotty mess, and put some more make-up on, and buy some outfits that got a little flirt to them, you will never find a man worth bragging about. Ain't no man of quality ever gonna be drawn to you looking like somebody's field hand, and that's a fact you will never prove me wrong on."

We stared eye to eye, arms crossed. I felt the corner of my bottom lip tremble. Extra wetness pooled in the rim of my left eye. My mother began to smile. Her arms relaxed. She plugged up the flat iron again, pulled out a small case of foundations and blushes, eye shadows and lip liners.

"You are wrong," I heard myself whisper as she opened a magazine to a picture of a model half my size with long, flowing hair and an airbrushed face. "You are so wrong about a man of quality not giving me a second look."

I felt numbness, complete nothingness as my hand reached over and picked up my phone. My wrist was limp as I pressed a button on the side, brought up the screen.

Brought up the picture.

I held it out for her to see. She stopped fumbling with her impromptu beauty counter and frowned and raised an eyebrow, confused.

"Him." My voice gathered strength. The whisper turned to a full voice. "He's the chief legal counsel for an international corporation, a former pro-ball player. He lives in San Francisco and has a chalet in Switzerland." I stared at the picture, pushed the phone into my mother's hand. "He saw my picture online this week. Me. Natural. No makeup. My old, gold sweater dress. And he wants to get to know me better." My lip trembled again.

I wanted this to be true.

I willed this to be true.

"We've emailed a couple of times. He wants to talk to me over the weekend. Dubai. That's where he is at the moment. He wants to know me better, Mom. I'm enough. He's quality and I'm enough." My voice cracked. Shame. Guilt. Brokenness. "I'm enough."

And it was all a lie.

My mother stared at the photo, the one I'd created in the hour before she'd come. Bronze skin. Hints of Asian, Latin, European. Black. A man who couldn't be pegged in any category, but beautiful.

Delicious.

I stared at the photo anew, marveled at the perfection I'd managed. He looked real. My mother looked up.

"He…wants to talk to you?"

The surprise stung. It was familiar. But still, it stung. I shut my eyes, heard Gina's scorn. Opened my eyes again. Looked my mother dead in hers as I built my lie.

"Yes. I was preparing to *Skype* him just before you came bursting in here."

"Oh." She frowned. "Oh." She began packing up the hair things, the cosmetics. "Well, I guess if he was fine with the way you look…we shouldn't mess with the formula." My mother zipped away the last of the containers. "Berry, don't blow this. I've got a good feeling about this one. His eyes…"

Huxley's fur. I'd used my cat to create his eye color. *Forgive me, God. This is so wrong.* My mother packed up her things, headed for the door.

"Go ahead and call him," she said. "I won't interfere. Just call me in the morning and tell me how it goes. This might be it, Berry. You are due." A smile snaked over her lips. "And there won't be anything Sister Willow can say. Dubai. Um, um, um." My mother was on the other side of the door now, about to close it. "He sounds perfect. Just make sure he's a church man and that he's not crazy or has a crazy ex or something like that."

She started to swing the door shut, but had one more thing to add. "And put a flower in your hair or something. Gives your natural hair a sultry look." She swung the door shut and was gone.

It took all I had in me not to scream. "What have I done, Lord?" I looked up to the heavens.

Silence.

But what really was I expecting? A lightning bolt? I'd just told my mother a bold-faced lie. I eased my phone back onto my desk and then I did something I hadn't done all week, maybe all year.

I cried.

Chapter 9

"The Lord will make a way, won't He, church?" Pastor Beamon roared from the pulpit. Sweat poured off his forehead and dripped down onto his long, red-collared, black robe. "I said He'll make a way, won't He?" He screamed again, punctuating each word with a wave of his white handkerchief.

"Yes, He will!" This scream was from my mother. She hopped up from her seat next to me. Her blue pumps clattered on the floor. "Yes, Jesus! Thank you, Jesus!" She jumped all around the pew, one hand upraised, the other balled on her hip. Her screams and shouts grew louder. An army of ushers came rushing toward us with fans and cups of water. The organist, Deacon Flint, pumped the pedals to match Dejuan Jackson's lively, one-two beat on the snares. "He will do it church! You better believe He will!" My mother shouted.

I grabbed a fan out of the pew and did my part to wave it on my mother as the usual praise break dancers began to join in.

Mother Ethel Thompson.

Sister Rita McClooney.

Brother Thebes Morgan.

Deacon Rory Segellus.

One by one. On cue, in order. Almost as if rehearsed, the mothers and sisters and brothers and deacons of the church began dancing in the aisle along to the one-two beat of the drums and lively chords of the organ. Bystanders shielded their hats, held onto their wigs, tapped their canes and thumped their Bibles.

Pastor Beamon had quieted in the pulpit, his eyes roving over the sanctuary as the shouts and screams, wails and runners reached a crescendo and then slowly ebbed back down.

And then his eyes were on me.

As were First Lady Beamon's.

And then Sister Evangeline Willow's who sat next to her. Wait – the fan in my hand stopped mid-flip – *is everyone looking at me?*

"He did it, church! He blessed my daughter! He blessed her! Thank you, God. Halleluiah! He gave her His best. I believe and receive it! I claim it. He did it!" My mother's voice echoed through the cavernous sanctuary. Her yells and cries became more pronounced as the musical accompaniment of the organ and drums died down.

First Lady Beamon raised an eyebrow.

Sister Willow frowned.

The entire first row of the choir, including Vickie, Pat, and Shaneka leaned forward.

How had the Lord blessed Berry Jenkins? I could hear the collective question forming in everyone's head. My mother was not part of the usual praise break crowd so this blessing must have been a big one for her to jump up and upstage the others.

I began fanning again, this time aiming the airflow at myself as I tried to make sense of my mother's shouts. I needed to have a statement prepared to answer the current congregational stare down.

"Mom?" I whispered as three ushers helped her ease back down into her seat. Her body stiffened into one more loud, long convulsing jolt before she finally gathered herself together and took her seat next to me. Sweat poured down from her hairline, not a light matter considering that she'd just gotten her 'do freshened up last night.

This praise break was a serious one, I realized, as a new

sensation of horror inched up my spine. My mother rarely let anyone get her worked up out of a new hairdo. Yup, even Jesus seemed to take a back seat when my mother had been out of the beauty salon for less than twenty-four hours. I knew this was major.

"Mom," I whispered again. "What are you talking about? What blessing are you shouting about up in here?" I already knew the answer, but I couldn't bear to let myself think it.

"Dubai, baby." She gave me a wink, and squeezed my hand. "God done answered my prayers and given us something way beyond what I imagined. I feel it in my spirit. Praise God."

Like the ball dropping in Times Square, I felt my heart sink down to my toenails. As my mother smirked at Evangeline Willow, a confetti of emotions splattered out of my psyche. I knew a new level to an already complicated situation had just begun.

I saw it in the frown that tugged on Sister Willow's lips. I felt it in the stir of excitement that rumbled out of the choir stand where Vickie and the others sat blinking, mouths agape, eyes on me. Even they knew that such a show from my mother about me could only mean one thing.

"Berry's got a man, y'all." I read Pat's lips as they high-fived and giggled like teenagers. The service settled back down into Pastor Beamon's sermon.

I wanted to cry, but I knew the only thing for me to focus on at the moment was figuring out what to do with the lie I'd let leak from my workplace and infest my home front.

My mother would kill me and probably herself too if she'd known that she sweated out her fresh hair-do for nothing.

"Let the church say amen," Pastor Beamon lowered his voice into the microphone as he squeaked it back into position.

"Amen!" My mother was the loudest.

She tossed a peppermint into her mouth and winked at

me again.

As Pastor Beamon's sermon continued, I searched through my purse to find a pen and scrap of paper. At least I would look like I was taking notes from the pastor's message as I fussed out my mother. All I could find was a yellow sheet of paper that had been the receipt from a cupcake shop by the Harbor I'd sampled a few weeks earlier.

Mom, I scribbled with a vengeance on the back of the pastel paper, *why did you do that? Why are you putting my business out in front of the church? There are some things I need to tell you about this whole situation before it gets out of control.* I pushed the paper in her hand and she balled it up and pushed it into the hymn book holder on the pew.

"I put it out there so you don't mess it up, baby," she murmured in my ear as Pastor Beamon told the congregation to say amen again a few minutes later.

"Stand up and tell three people around you that God is good!" the pastor commanded from the pulpit as he adjusted his notes.

I took the opportunity to release more steam. "Mom," I grabbed her elbow, "what you put out there was so not acceptable. I'm a grown woman, not a little teenage girl with a…childish crush. You don't do this kind of stuff. You and I haven't even talked since Friday night. You don't even know if I called the man I told you about. This might not even be…happening."

"Oh, it's happening." My mother smiled back. "My spirit tells me he's a good guy. I don't want you to mess this up, Berry, and my hinting it to the church is our assurance that you won't. With all these witnesses, you will have no choice but to do all you can to make this relationship work. I want to plan a wedding, and I want grandbabies," she hissed before turning with a pleasant voice to the woman next to her. "God is good, Sister

Angie. I'm a witness."

"Mom," I wasn't finished. I grabbed her elbow again. "We don't…I…we don't even know this man. You said yourself he could be crazy or have a crazy ex. I don't even know if he is real…ly, well, real. Sometimes, something that sounds too good to be true…isn't."

"Oh hush, honey. Stop assuming the worse. You've got to have faith. I feel it in my soul, Berry. This man is the one for you. A chalet in Switzerland and he tolerates your hair? Berry, you better claim this one now. Brother Phoenix," she turned to face an older man in the pew in front of us, "the Lord is so good, ain't He?"

As she hugged him, I felt a tap on my shoulder. "Berry," a twenty-something year-old who I'd helped tutor when she was in high school, stared at me with innocent doe eyes. Whatever God's got going on for you, I'm excited. God is good." She hugged me and moved on to my mother, whose smile had not yet left her face.

Everyone is excited. I groaned inside. Enough is enough. I had to put an immediate stop to this foolishness. I'd had the same thought before, I recalled, but this time I meant it. *The moment service is over, I'll explain everything to my mother.* I sighed as an inexplicable sense of relief washed over me.

I promise that was my plan. 'Fessing up to my mother was my single objective as we finished listening to the sermon, walked around for offering, and lifted our hands for the benediction. I'd played the whole scene of what would happen in my mind: taking my mother by the hand the moment service was over, pulling her into the foyer restroom, crying on her shoulder as I told her that Malikai Carter was a figment of my imagination and a visual creation of my tablet's photo editing app; her wanting to smack me for letting her sweat out her hair because of the lie, then her embracing me as she understood my reasons for pretending he was real.

I was ready. I had my words together, and I even had two tissues clutched in my palm to use for both of our eyes once I finished my confession.

I promise that was my plan.

However, the moment Pastor Beamon said "amen" at the end of the benediction, a crowd of the curious got into formation and marched toward me.

Chapter 10

"Mom, I need to talk to you." The crowd of inquisitors marched closer.

"Wait," my mother's single response. She stood as a proud sentry to the side of me, ready to greet the coming army, answer questions, and ward off any form of embarrassment or defeat.

I saw it in her eyes: her refusal to let me crash and burn her dream that I'd found the perfect man. Leading the charge was Evangeline Willow, followed by Tressa, Vickie, Shaneka, Raina, Pat, and a few other young and old women who looked ready and willing to sop up any spills and details.

"Oooh, girl, we knew you were holding out something from us," Raina spoke first. "You were way too quiet on Wednesday night."

"You must have something really worth bragging about and were trying to stay humble," Pat co-signed. "God bless your humility."

"Oh, she does have something boast-worthy in the Lord." If my mother's smile was any juicier, it would have leaked all over the floor. "Wait until you see and hear about the man who is into her."

"I knew this was about a man," Vickie threw her hands over her mouth and let out a squeal. "Details. We want to know details. Tell us all about him. What's his name?"

"Malikai." My mother was doing all the talking.

"Ooh, strong."

"Biblical."

Everyone was grinning, squealing and smiling. Everyone

except for me and Evangeline Willow, that is.

"Mom, I need to talk to you," I nudged quietly, my two tissues I'd been saving for my planned confession now wet shreds in the palm of my sweaty hand.

"Oh, don't be embarrassed, Berry," Tressa giggled. "Ain't nothing wrong with admitting that you've got some love in your life."

"See, that's the thing." I took a deep breath, braced myself for the coming slaughter. "This man my mother is talking about…Malikai…he–"

"–He is new on the scene," my mother interrupted, "and Berry is worried about claiming something too prematurely while they're still getting to know each other. But the Holy Spirit has already confirmed in my spirit that it is so."

"So, Berry is not actually *in* a relationship." Evangeline almost seemed to exhale.

"Don't get this wrong, Sister Willow. This remarkable man is calling her. Actually, *Skyping* her. From Dubai. This is just the beginning of a God-ordained union sealed before time began. We are just now seeing it be revealed in the physical."

"Oh, a long-distance relationship? Those can be difficult." Evangeline didn't even flinch.

"He doesn't *live* in Dubai. He travels for a living." My mother shot. "This brother is an attorney for a major international corporation and he flies all over the globe and speaks French, Korean, and Russian."

Huh? My head snapped back. *How did she know that?*

"I do my research, Berry," my mother seemed to have read my mind. "I found his career profile online." She dug into her purse and pulled out several sheets of paper. "I printed these off my computer last night," she waved the papers in front of everyone.

His profile from the dating website.

The resume I'd uploaded Friday night.

The picture I'd created and posted.

The girls and women around us snatched at the papers like squawking ducks fighting for food pellets at a children's zoo.

"Oh, my goodness, he's looks divine."

"Chalet in Switzerland?"

"Beachfront condo in San Francisco?"

"Rome!"

"Soul food in Harlem… Sweet."

"I want to go to Carnival in Brazil one day!"

"How did you meet?"

"He is some kind of sexy. Forgive me, Lord."

"Could be on the cover of GQ."

"Does he have a brother?"

The shouts and squeals came all at once as the women spoke over each other, grabbed at the papers, high-fived and slapped backs, and pinched my arms.

God, what have I done? How do I fix this? How do I even begin to explain? I stood frozen, silent, stunned.

Terrified.

"I bet you he ain't even saved." Evangeline had one of the papers in her hand. She glared at it and then began folding it down into a tiny square, pressing firm on the creases with her manicured fingernails. She handed it back to my mom. "I don't see one thing about Jesus on his resume. A man who has the Lord in his life is not ashamed to share it. What does it profit a man to gain the whole world and lose his soul?" The smile had returned to Sister Willow's face. "Vickie's fiancé may not have a private corporate jet – yet – but he has Jesus, so he is soaring high, beyond countries and into the heavenlies. Vickie's Micah may not speak in French or Swahili or Creole or whatever, but he does speak in tongues."

"Oh, Mother, stop it," Vickie smiled and swatted, seemingly

oblivious to the undeclared war simmering between our mothers. "I know Berry wouldn't even be giving this man a second glance if she didn't already know where he stood on the most important matters."

"That's right!" My mother chimed in. "And he *is* saved, Sister Willow. Berry spoke to him the other night, by *Skype* while he was in Dubai. Remember, Berry? You were waiting for me to leave so you could talk to him, and the whole point of the conversation was to confirm his sanity and his spirituality. Right, Berry? Tell us about that conversation."

My mother's smile looked like it would kill me if I said anything other than…what I heard myself say next.

"Um, well, about him…see…he is…he is…" *Not real. A figment of my imagination. A flat out lie.* "He is…saved, sanctified, and filled with the Holy Spirit, Sister Willow." My mother nodded in relief and approval as I continued. "He loves the Lord…so much. He loves Him. All he did in our conversation Friday night was give credit to God for the many blessings in his life. He…is all about Jesus."

I wanted to shut my eyes, back up from the crowd, and spare them from the sudden bolt of lightning sure to immediately crack through the church steeple and land in the center of my skull. I imagined my hair straightening out once and for all as it sizzled with smoke. I pictured my entire body dropping into a pile of black, smoldering ash. I held my breath, waiting for all that to happen. Instead, my mother spoke next.

"Oh, Berry is being so modest. Listen to this: His parents do mission work for a charity in Botswana and he even started a charity himself for African children with the money from his international ball career."

"Wait, what's this guy's name again?" Raina jumped in again. "Drew used to play basketball overseas. He might know him."

"Um, he played ball overseas, but, I'm not sure if it was basketball or another sport. I'll have to clarify that the next time I talk to him." There. That was an easy squelch. My heart raced as I tried to figure out how to end the conversation – and how to throw water on the wildfire I'd started. But the flames were just beginning.

"Malikai Carter and Berry Jenkins." Evangeline spoke solemnly. "I will add the two of you to my prayer list."

A collective "amen" brought the discussion to a close and the ladies began to disperse, join in talks about other things, make plans for the evening, and joke about the coming week. My heart continued to race as I put on my jacket and waited for my mother to finish greeting an elderly woman who had made it out to service for the first time in weeks.

"Mom, I need to talk to you." I finally got a chance to speak alone with her – though I'd lost all words for what to say next. Tears filled my eyes as I tried to woman up, as I braced myself to come clean and figure out how to sweep up the mess I'd made standing on the church's red carpet. I felt a mess, was a mess.

My mother must have seen the tear forming in my eyes because she used the tip of an index finger to wipe it away before it trickled down my cheek.

"Berry, I know I put you on the spot and I'm sorry. I know you don't like being the center of attention, but, sweetheart, you deserve it. More importantly, you deserve love. I know it's scary and awkward and new, but I've got such a good, good feeling about this. My faith, my dreams are coming to fulfillment. I love you so much, Berry. You are so beautiful – all of you." She reached up and touched my hair. "I am proud of the woman you've grown to be and it's your time, baby girl. It's your time, now. I am so, so happy." She looked in my face, beamed a little bit more, then shook her head, smiled brighter, and walked away.

I stood planted to the floor, silent.

How could I ruin this moment for her? For me? It would be too devastating. No, I couldn't tell her Malikai wasn't real. The best thing I could do, I decided right then, was let this "relationship" play out for just a little while longer. My mother would be there to comfort me when the inevitable "break-up" happened.

I smiled at the plan. This was my way to make everything right. Continue like he was real, and then have a break-up and move on.

A foolproof plan.

I smiled as I followed the remaining idlers out of the sanctuary. Nothing left to do but enjoy the attention having the perfect man brought me, and then come up with a way of breaking up that left my dignity – and the lie – intact.

Brilliant.

And there had been no lightning strikes.

I looked up at the church steeple as I stepped across the parking lot to the church van where my brother was ready to take people home.

Maybe God was on my side with this foolishness.

Who am I kidding? God is the Author of truth – not lies, chaos, and confusion. I settled into one of the van seats, trying my best to ignore the uneasiness that gnawed at my consciousness like a dog chewing on a shredded shoelace. I'd opted to get my brother to add my apartment to his route because there was no way I could share car space with my mom right now. I'd almost settled my stomach down as the engine to the van roared to life.

However, on the other side of the window, I saw Evangeline Willow walking to her car with a slight smile on her face. In her hand was a wrinkled sheet of yellow paper that she was smoothing down with her fingers. I recognized the paper as the receipt on which I'd written the note to my mother after her praise dancing;

the note my mom had balled up and left in the pews.

What did I write on that the back of that? I tried to remember my words, growing sicker at Sister Willow's smile. The pit in my stomach widened and I felt myself free-falling into it as I recalled what I'd written.

Mom, why did you do that? Why are you putting my business out in front of the church? There are some things I need to tell you about this whole situation before it gets out of control.

Yup, I conceded, that was enough to give Sister Willow something to smile about.

She knew something was awry.

"The devil is a lie," Ms. Marjorie, a senior sitting across from me in the van, mumbled as she read something on her phone screen. Though I knew whatever she read had nothing to do with me or my current situation, I shuddered at the timing – and the truth – of her words.

God forgive me, I prayed. But how could He forgive me for a lie I intended on living?

Chapter 11

"You don't have to keep staring at the window. Come in, darling." A woman in a glittering white cowl neck sweater and black pants smiled at me from an open door. I hadn't even realized I'd stopped at the window of the small storefront on my way to work.

Zeus Masseuse. I looked up at the sign above the plushy business. The art-deco theme of the high-end day spa looked inviting, but the funds in my wallet and the time on my cell phone told me I could not afford such an early morning splurge. The phone lines opened in seven minutes and my behind needed to be sitting in my cubicle ready to start taking calls. I was just getting off the bus, a few blocks away from my office's building.

"Thanks, maybe later," I smiled and took the postcard the woman placed in my hand. *Throw yourself the ultimate pamper party: The Personal Holiday Package! 90-minute full body massage with heated stones; 60-minute seaweed facial with rare minerals from the Mediterranean Sea; hair and makeup consultation with a celebrity make-up artist; sumptuous mani/pedi including aromatic foot bath with exotic oils and spices; full body wrap and polish; cleansing breakfast, 3 course lunch, and 5 course dinner. Book today!*

"In my dreams," I murmured as I stared at the $800 price tag for the package. "Some people have such different lives." I watched as several women took the cards and then entered the day spa.

"This is such a great deal!" one woman stepping out of a luxury car and wearing name-brand everything exclaimed as she disappeared into the elite day spa.

Five minutes. That's how much time I had left to go one more block, enter the downtown office building, wait for an elevator, get to the fourteenth floor and walk to the office suite where I worked. I knew I'd be pressing my luck with the time, but a part of me intentionally wanted to get there right when the phones began ringing to avoid having to converse with my office mates. They would be expecting a report from the weekend, and although I knew what I wanted and needed to say, the whole thing was feeling a little…tiresome.

It's work keeping lies together, I realized, especially now that I had to balance out my stories and keep them consistent in two different settings of my life.

"Excuse me," a sharp voice echoed in my ear.

I had entered the rotating doors of my office building – but pushed the wrong way while someone else tried to get out.

"Oh, I'm so sorry," I shook my head at myself and put on my most apologetic face. "I'm…my mind is…" I froze in the middle of the turn as I recognized the pair of eyes rolling at me.

"Are you moving? I need to get out." The girl on the other side of the glass rapped with a knuckle.

"Yes," I sprung back to life and we both finished our turns through the rotating doors, me entering, her exiting.

"I love your hair," I shouted through the glass, and then immediately wanted to kick myself for looking and sounding and acting so stupid. The cleaning lady with the jet black, curly afro shook her head, muttered something, and turned away from the building in her usual black and white striped shirt, black apron, gray pants. I wondered if she had worked overnight and was just leaving, or had stepped outside for other reasons.

My answer was offered a few seconds later as she re-entered the building and joined me with the crowd of office workers waiting for the elevator. A bucket of spray bottles and cleaners hung from her hand. I guessed she'd gotten them from a car parked near the entrance.

Maybe it was the clean simplicity of her tasks, the routine in her schedule juxtaposed next to the messy complications of my life that made me notice her more than usual.

That and her rolling eyes.

"Are you getting on?"

Oh, she was talking to me. "Yes, I'm sorry."

I stepped onto the elevator which she'd held open for me. Four or five other people were aboard as well. I watched as she peeked at her cell phone, smiled, typed a message, and slipped the device back into a pocket in her apron. When the door opened for the fourteenth floor, I stepped off and made a point to hold it open for her.

"This isn't my floor today." She blinked, unsmiling. I shrugged, wanting to say something else, but not sure what or why. The door closed.

"Have a good day," I mumbled, hoping that good would apply to both her and to me. My heart began to pound harder as I neared the office suite. It was in full gallop when I finally entered at 8:29. Everyone else was in their cubicles, but I didn't miss the questions on their faces, the smiles they cast my way.

"Well?" Celeste shouted out as I passed her cubicle on the way to my own. I plastered a full smile on my face and gave a thumbs-up.

"An unbelievable weekend," I gushed as I rushed to sit down and put on my headset. A loud beep in my ear indicated that I'd met my goal. My work day had officially begun without me having to offer one single detail about my weekend "phone call" with Malikai.

And then the entire phone and computer system went dead.

"Darn it!" Naomi yelled, letting me know that the shutdown was not exclusive to me. I shut my eyes, knowing that if the system didn't come back up in the next few seconds, it could be hours before we were back to work again.

Hours that would only be filled with conversation.

"So?" Celeste wasted no time waiting to see if this was a temporary interruption to our work tasks. She was in my cubicle before I could even get my headset off. "Did you talk to him? Is he real?"

"Do you have a picture yet?" Gina came in next, her arms crossed.

"Tell us about your weekend before the queue comes back on."

Where was Mr. John, the regional supervisor, when you needed him? He had a habit of popping up for surprise site visits and interrupting the usual flow and banter of the office. I could have used him right then. Instead, I set my headphones down and turned my chair to face them, scrambling to remember what I'd planned to say.

"Yes, I did talk to him, and our conversation was far better than anything I could have imagined."

"Oh, my goodness, so he is real?" Carolyn gasped.

"We *Skyped* late Friday night while he was in the airport in Belgium."

"He was flying to Tokyo, right?" Carolyn's grin grew broader. "I remember all details." I smiled back and shivered at the same time.

I was going to have to take special care to keep my story straight.

"Yes, he's in Tokyo, but will be flying back stateside tomorrow. And before you ask, Gina, here goes." I pulled out my cell phone and pulled up the photo I'd created.

"No need," Gina held up her hand and shook her head. "I found his profile on a career networking website and I saw his picture on it. I just wanted to see if you had it to confirm that it's really him."

"You looked him up?" I raised an eyebrow as the other women took the phone out of my hands and gasped and sighed at the "image" of Malikai Carter.

"Yes, well, I just didn't want to see you get hurt, so I did some more research. He's…really good-looking."

"Aw, Gina, thanks for caring." I flashed her my brightest smile as her cheeks turned a darker shade of red.

"Yeah, sounds like he is the real deal. Congratulations, Berry. I'm glad to hear your conversation went well." She wasn't smiling.

"So tell us more about this conversation you had with him. I want to know more. This is amazing," Naomi grinned.

"Well, we talked for, like, three hours and he was just so sweet and funny. He kept giving me compliments about my hair. He made me feel like I was…interesting and beautiful."

"He sounds like perfection," Carolyn sighed.

I thought about that for a moment and realized I needed to give him some kind of flaw to stay believable.

"Yes, but, uh…"

"But what?" Gina livened.

"He…aside from the fact that I have no idea how or when I will see him, he…had this annoying way of licking his lips and biting them after every other sentence. It was cute at first, but then, I don't know."

"Are you kidding?" Celeste looked flabbergasted. "Sounds like he was nervous. That's a great sign that he's into you! If that's the case, no ocean or country or long-distance flight is going to be able to keep him from pursuing something with you."

So, basically, he sounded more perfect. Go figure.

"Well, it will be kind of difficult to date someone whose job takes them to other countries all the time and whose home is across the country from where you live. San Francisco is a little far from Baltimore, you know." Gina's smile returned. "Not sure what he'll be able to do for you from such a big distance. Talking and *Skyping* are nice, but not everything."

I exhaled, thinking quickly. Or, in retrospect, not really thinking at all. "I thought the same thing, Gina, but then I got a message from him this morning. I'd told him I worked in downtown Baltimore and he wrote that although we couldn't go out on a date anytime soon, he still wanted to give me a good time and a relaxing reprieve from my day. He researched downtown Baltimore and booked me something called *The Personal Holiday Package at Zeus Masseuse.*"

"What?!" Celeste gasped and threw her hands to her cheeks. "Shut up! You mean that wonderful day spa over on Charles Street?"

"That package is $800." Gina was already researching it on her phone. "It's an all-day experience that includes breakfast, lunch, and dinner, and every kind of spa treatment imaginable. Wow, Berry. If he's giving you that as some kind of 'first date,' I can only imagine what else he's got planned."

What else he's got planned.

The words and realization stung, slapped, and shook me silly. *Why had I reached so high? Really, Berry?*

Wait, I'd said he booked it. They'd never know whether I actually went. All I had to do was say I went on Saturday, or better yet, take a much-needed day off, and no one would know the difference whether I had soaked in the elaborate tubs at the *Zeus* or spent the day soaking in my apple-scented bubbles at home.

"Sounds like it's a nice place," I played along. "'I'd never heard of it before. I'll check out the website and book my pamper day when I'm available."

"You should do it soon, Berry. That's a generous offer from him."

"I'll look into it," I smiled and looked back over at the computer. *Is the system back up yet?*

"I have an idea." Carolyn interjected. "Why don't we all go together? My sister gave me a gift card for them which I've never used, and Celeste, weren't you talking about gifting your bridesmaids with a day spa package as a present to them? This could be a way of checking it out." Carolyn was all smiles.

"Yes! That's a great idea, Carolyn. I think we should do that. I'm excited," Celeste giggled.

Wait. Did these girls actually have $800 to throw down on a whim like that? I could feel the corners of my smile quivering. *What have I gotten myself into?*

"I'm in." Naomi asserted.

"Me too." Gina's cheeks were a bright red. Her eyes darted around the room and I saw the lump in her throat as she swallowed.

Shoot, we were both about to go into debt over this foolishness I'd started.

"I was going to say we could plan for a Saturday, but honestly, if these phones aren't going to be working, maybe we could do it today? We could call Mr. John and see what's going on." Celeste was all smiles.

"Uh, yes, great idea." Did I still have a stupid smile on my face? All eyes were on me as I looked down at my desk, glanced at my blacked-out computer and looked at my telephone. "I don't think I have Mr. John's number stored on my desk phone. Hmmmm." I shuffled through some papers on my desk, trying to look like I wanted to find that man's number; trying to delay the inevitable.

"Oh, don't worry about it, Berry. Looks like I'm getting a call from him right now." Naomi put her cell phone to her ear. "Yes?... Yes?... Really?... Oh, okay." When she hung up, the intense smile on her peach-glossed lips made my stomach hurt. *What am I going to do?*

"Well," Naomi said, "our phones aren't going to be operational until after three, he says, so the calls for our region will rollover to the Pittsburgh office for the day. We've got a free work day, ladies, care of Cole Financial Services. I say we celebrate by getting over to *Zeus Masseuse* right away."

I sat frozen at my desk, willing, wishing the phone lines would somehow come to life despite the district supervisor's update. Never did I long so much to have a conversation with a customer about an unpaid bill. *How do I get out of this?*

"I'll call and book appointments for the five of us," Celeste giggled and headed for her cubicle to get her cell phone.

"I'll start shutting everything else down." Naomi left the cubicle.

"I'll get my jacket." Carolyn took off.

Gina smiled at me, her face no longer red; just pale. "This will be great, Berry. I'm going to grab my purse."

"And I'm going to run to the restroom." *And figure out how to get out of this lie!*

I grabbed my sweater, phone, and purse and made a quick dash to the hallway toilet. Thankfully, nobody was in there. After shutting the door behind me, I splashed water on my face and stared at the look of horror staring back at me from the mirror.

Did I really just tell my co-workers that this imaginary man I'd effectively convinced them was real had paid for me to have the most expensive day spa package this side of Baltimore?

Why not just send flowers to myself? Or show them a

compliment-filled email? Or talk about plans of a fake date? *Or tell the truth?*

Tell the truth.

Felt too late for that.

"Berry?" A knock sounded on the door. I could hear sighs and giggles on the other side.

"I'm coming." I turned off the water, reached for a paper towel to dab the tears from my eyes. *How do I get out of this?* I felt stuck, trapped.

"We'll meet you down in the lobby." Celeste shouted through the door. I listened as they continued down the hallway; heard the elevator ding, open, close. Silence.

I opened my purse and took out my wallet. I kept a single credit card for emergencies. Last time I'd used it had been during my time of unemployment after getting laid off from my managerial job.

"I can't believe I'm doing this." My fingers shook as I pulled up the website for *Zeus Masseuse.* My stomach felt like jelly, slime as I punched in my credit card numbers for a gift certificate that was then emailed to me. From *Malikai Carter,* I typed in the subject line.

"I deserve a nice day of relaxation," I said to the still horrified image in the mirror.

Who was I kidding? $800?

I didn't know how to get around this one.

The transaction went through. The email with the gift certificate came. I put my credit card and phone away and headed downstairs for our day spa date.

Chapter 12

5:13 p.m.

"Hey, Berry." My brother plopped down in the seat across from me, and then frowned. "What's up with all the make-up? You look really dressed for a Monday night."

"I… It's a long story," I shook my head and looked down at my newly manicured nails. Between the mani/pedi and the shimmering colors painted all over my face, I knew I looked more made-up now then I had for my senior prom years ago. "I spent my day at a day spa. Every part of my body has been sprayed, plucked, rubbed, heated, and pounded on. Breakfast, lunch, and dinner were included."

"Food, too? No wonder you were so reluctant to meet me here for dinner. Sounds like you already ate – a lot." Davis picked up one of the menus a waiter had dropped down on the table between us. Gourmet pizzas. Homemade sodas. The small diner was part of a new digital café a few blocks away from *Zeus Masseuse.* I'd told him to meet me there when I got his text at the end of my day spa disaster. I'd been curious about this place with its dining area featuring organic food on one side and a row of computers and work spaces on the other. The people in here looked as eclectic as the plates of food being served around us.

"For spending the day at a day spa, you look anything but relaxed," Davis chuckled. "I see they didn't do anything to your hair."

"Trust me, I am nowhere near relaxed." I yanked on my temples. "And as far as my hair, they didn't know what to do.

They washed it and then just stared at it. Some lady sprayed some rosewater on it and called it a day."

"Okay, so that's what I smell." He leaned forward. "Roses and ginger?"

"I got some really high-end treatments today. I'm not sure what was poured and wrapped on my body. And between the duck confit, roasted figs, and octopus soup, I'm not sure what exactly I put *in* my body, to tell you the truth."

I need to tell someone the truth. I exhaled. Maybe this impromptu meet-up with my brother was just the thing I needed. I was certain my brother would not only hear out my confession, but would give me sound advice on how to fix the mess I'd created.

"Sounds like your day cost a small fortune. I didn't know you rolled like that, little sis." Davis chuckled as he took a swig from a bottle of soda.

"Believe me, I don't." *And I'm rolling with even less now.* "Davis," I couldn't hold it in any longer, "I did something stupid and now I need to know how to fix it in a way that I don't lose face – or lose any more money."

"Hold on, Berry. We'll talk, but she's here." Davis put down his bottle, stood to his feet.

"She? Who…what? You were expecting someone else to join us?" I turned around in my seat, tried to see what had him smiling. The waiter had someone behind him. Davis reached out his broad arms and embraced the newcomer, kissed her on the cheek. I recognized the to-die-for black boots immediately. Li Yan.

The sight of her made me nervous, though I couldn't pinpoint why.

"Hi, Berry," the Asian beauty smiled at me as she took the seat Davis held out for her. "Sorry I'm late. Did you guys order yet?"

"Nope. You're right on time. Berry and I just got here." Davis was all smiles.

"Love the make-up, Berry. Violet's a good color on you. Wait, I know that rosy ginger scent. Did you go to *Zeus Masseuse?"*

"All day." My eyes darted between my brother and Li Yan as I tried to make sense of where this evening was going. Why would Davis have me join him on an obvious date with one of his girlfriends?

"I have a cousin that works there. If you got the ginger treatment, I know you spent a pretty penny. That package is what, seven, eight hundred dollars?"

"Eight hundred dollars? Berry?" My brother looked at me like I was crazy. "Please tell me you didn't spend that much. I hope it was a gift or something like that."

"Uh…something like that..."

"Wait, is this related to whatever blessing Mom was talking about you getting? Something about a man from Dubai?"

"Davis, I... We'll talk about that later." I quickly took a bite of some hot wings the waiter put in front of us as appetizers. The spicy sauce sizzled on my lips and my eyes watered. "I already feel like I'm imposing on your dinner with Li Yan," I coughed out.

"Oh, no, not at all." Li Yan passed me a water bottle and I pushed it into my mouth. "I asked Davis to invite you. I wanted to talk to you about that company you were helping for your assignment last week."

Water sprayed out of my mouth like a fountain. "Uh..."

"Over the weekend, I had a conversation with a bunch of the athletes who come to the club where I bartend. Davis helps with the music there sometimes. You should come by when you have a chance. Anyway, there's a real interest among some pro football and basketball players in learning more about the legal performance enhancer Adilson Enterprises created. And, as you said it's a start-up company, there may be some people interested in investing in it."

I looked at Davis. Glared at Davis. "Oh, I…told my brother not to…"

"Don't worry, Berry," my brother glared back at me. "I did my research." His eyelashes blinked faster as he moved in closer to Li Yan. "I told Li Yan I would look into things, so she wouldn't have to worry about calling them herself. That's exactly what I did."

This man was lying, and he didn't even know I knew it.

Our parents should be proud. They'd raised children so desperate to get loved or to get laid, that all manner of truth was thrown out of the window.

"Adilson Enterprises is not a real company." There, it was out. No other explanation needed.

"Now, why would you say that, Berry?" Davis looked ready to cause me physical harm as Li Yan's face twisted into confusion. "Didn't you just hear me say I researched it? Are you trying to call me a liar?" Davis's face lightened as he broke into a loud laugh. "Excuse my sister, Li Yan. She always has jokes."

He kept laughing, but he never broke eye contact with me. "Listen Berry, Li Yan's talking to players with real funds who may be able to help bring this company to a bigger audience. I told her since you've been working with them with your project, you're probably best suited to approach them about how others can help, you know?"

"It's a perfect business opportunity for all of us." Li Yan sat smiling at me. She reached for Davis's hands and squeezed. I didn't miss the gesture or the way he practically drooled over her touch. "You're sitting on a gold mine, Berry, and you can open the doors for a lot of people to succeed."

Had either one of them heard me say that this business was not real? Was the idea of getting money (her) or sex (him) so important that it caused temporary deafness?

"Look, it's all a mistake." I took out my phone, pulled up the website that I had created for the fictional Adilson Enterprises. "This company, these people," I scrolled through the two simple webpages, "they simply do not exist. It's a long story, and I apologize, but–"

"–I'm confused." Li Yan's smile dropped for the first time. She looked to my brother who looked to me. His nostrils flared.

"And I'm not." He snatched my phone from my hand. "I understand exactly what's going on." He used an index finger to start tapping on my screen. "That name right there. The Chief Legal Counsel and International Affairs Advisor. Mom was just telling me about him last night. Your new boyfriend. Malikai Carter."

I looked where he pointed, gasped. "Boyfriend? Wait, Davis. Let me explain."

"No explanation is necessary, Berry. I see exactly what's going on. You're trying to get something going on with one of the executives of this company, and now that you know there may be a way to cash in with Li Yan's friends' backing, you're scared that coming at him with offers of money will be misinterpreted by him, that he'll think you're just pursuing him to get rich. I understand, but you could have just said that and not try to act like this whole thing isn't real."

"Whoa, Davis, you've got this all wrong."

"Do I, Berry? Or maybe, you just don't want me involved so I can't have any claim to your coming fortune. You are always talking about what career I should have gotten into. You and Mom are always talking about my money situation."

"Davis, no. Let me explain." I started laughing because

the whole thing was ridiculous, horrifying, embarrassing, and completely insane. "Wait until you hear the stupid thing I did."

"It makes perfect sense, too." He seemed not to hear a word I said. "The day spa? He paid for that, didn't he? I know you don't have that much money, Berry."

"Davis, it's all made up."

"Don't play with my intelligence, Berry. Just because I didn't go to college like you, doesn't mean I'm stupid. Our mother was in church rejoicing over your new, rich man friend. I know full well you wouldn't have our mother looking like a fool over some fake sh–"

"–Davis, listen to me," I interrupted quickly. Once my brother got started, it was hard bringing him back. Li Yan's head bounced like a ping pong ball between us. Her eyes were wide.

"Come on, Li Yan." My brother nudged her and they both stood. "We're going to connect with this company ourselves, without the help of my sister. Li Yan, you're the one who the athletes trust, and I'm the one with the research. We don't need Berry to make our fortunes. Let's go."

"Nice seeing you again, Berry." Li Yan flashed me a nervous smile as she filed behind my brother. By the time they stepped out of the restaurant, both had phones to their ears. My brother looked irritated. Li Yan looked excited. She rubbed his back and I watched him relax and smile.

Wait a minute. Why was I getting worked up? Why was my stomach turning in knots? This company was completely fictional. Even if Davis or his girl of the week called the phone number, they were just going to get the voice mail message I'd created myself. There would be nobody calling them back. A dead end. Why was I so worried?

And as far as that little spat with my brother? Wasn't the first time we'd had a falling out, and it wouldn't be the last.

A bump in the road.

A minor inconvenience.

I'd already put major money into this charade. If my mother was happy and out of my hair – literally and figuratively – then maybe I should just leave it alone. All that huffing and puffing over nothing. Why ruin a good thing over Davis and his dumb dating moves? Serves him right if he ends up embarrassed. Hey, I told him Malikai Carter and Adilson Enterprises were fake. I did my part to be truthful. If he didn't want to accept the truth, what else could I do? And what could he really do about it?

"Ma'am, is your party ready to order your entrees?" The waiter had returned.

I looked at the plastic menu my brother had left sitting between us. "I'll just take the chocolate cake."

I'd had duck and octopus, massages and treatments, arguments and regrets. I figured the day deserved some comfort food.

"Chocolate cake it is." The waiter took my order and I pulled out my credit card.

I'd already spent $800 I didn't have. What was $3.50 more?

Chapter 13

"Welp, Huxley, looks like I'm all in." I stared at myself in the mirror. New dress suit, black pumps, leather work bag, and for good measure, a sparkling necklace. It was Friday, and I'd spent the whole week looking good. No jeans, no tennis shoes, no flip flops.

All business and all beautiful.

Even my hair had cooperated with me this week as I'd fought to get the perfect twist out and won.

"I don't look like the non-diva today." I beamed at my reflection, admired the confidence it exuded. After getting all dolled up at the day spa on Monday, it had only seemed fitting that the rest of me matched my perfectly polished nails. My face still glowed from the seaweed facial, and the tricks I'd learned from the celebrity makeup artist had been put to good use with the cosmetics I splurged on at a department store counter.

Eight hundred dollars was already on my credit card. What was three hundred fifty dollars more for clothes, shoes, and makeup?

"You look like you're falling in love," Celeste had told me every day of the week as I walked in with new outfits and a new confidence. Not sure why I felt so good, but I did.

Maybe it was the attention.

Maybe it was the text I'd gotten from Gina on Tuesday night.

Berry, I am happy for you. Seems like you've found

yourself a real winner. I'm sorry for being so difficult about it. Wishing you continued good luck in love.

Whenever I had qualms about the whole situation, I reread that text.

Who was unlucky in love now? Not me, boo.

Every day, I offered a new story about a late-night conversation with Malikai. I had new messages in my inbox, new emails to show them. This man laid out all kinds of compliments that would make any woman blush.

Respectful. Kind. Tenderhearted.

Malikai truly was the man of any woman's dreams.

I planted a lemon-yellow flower clip in the soft coils of my hair. Studying my face in the mirror in my foyer, I smiled. My eyebrows were perfectly arched and the liquid foundation I'd applied gave my skin an almost golden hue.

Maybe I really am pretty.

I grabbed my phone before turning toward my door to leave for work. No calls from Davis. I dialed the voice mail message for the company I'd created; no messages there either.

"All that worrying for nothing, Huxley." I patted his head as I headed out. I'd decided against pulling down the career profile and website I'd created for Malikai just yet. What harm could come of it? Besides, it had been a lot of work and effort to pull this whole thing off and I wasn't finished with the act. A couple more weeks, I'd decided, and then we'd begin the breakup. A gentle, but necessary dissolution.

That's when the free trial for the website and profiles ended.

"Berry! Oh good, I'm glad I caught you."

The voice startled me as I locked my apartment door.

"Mom?" I checked my phone. 7:30 a.m. Why the early visit? Had someone died? "What's wrong?" I grabbed my chest, braced for bad news.

"Honey, ain't nothing wrong." My mother's smile was brighter than the morning sun. "This is a glorious day. I'm thankful. I just wanted to catch you before you left for work so I could give you a ride, that's all. They're calling for rain to start any minute now, and I figured you wouldn't want to be out on the bus stop getting wet."

"Oh, okay." Not sure why I felt a little hesitant. There were a few drops trickling down. Why wouldn't I want a ride from my mother to stay out of the rain?

Uh, maybe because my entire life is a lie right now and I've got to spend the next fifteen minutes keeping the lie together in front of my mother? I ignored the pitter patter of nerves that threatened to sour my stomach as I followed my mother to her Cadillac. *Stick to the plan,* Berry, I told myself. A couple more weeks of this, then I'd announce the break-up. No hard feelings, no embarrassment, and my mother would comfort me. Knowing that she finally saw me as "date-able" was enough to keep the charade going.

I was smiling, too, by the time we both got into her car.

"Berry, I'm so glad to see that you're happy. You're looking really good these days, too." She reached over and teased the clip in my hair.

"Aw, thanks, Mom." Now, I'm a thirty-four-year-old grown woman. Why am I milking this attention from my mother like an esteem-deprived teenager? Maybe what I needed instead of a fake boyfriend was a real therapist.

"Listen," my mother continued as she directed the car down Northern Parkway to get to I-83, "I wanted to have a serious conversation with you."

"Okay, what's...going on?" I felt my eyelids flutter. Where is this going? "Have you talked with Davis?" Had he said anything to her about our fight – or that I'd told him Malikai was not real? I held my breath.

When we stopped at a traffic light, my mother reached for her purse and took out a white envelope. With a smile, she handed it to me. "Open it."

I swallowed hard and pulled apart the sealed business-sized envelope. Several fifty and one-hundred-dollar bills were inside.

"Seven hundred dollars?" I re-counted. "Mom, what is this?"

"I priced how much a first-class flight from San Francisco to Baltimore would be. With this whole online dating thing, I figured you two will have to meet in person at some point, and I'm not comfortable with you going across the country by yourself for a first meeting. Tell him that your mother would like to invite him over for dinner and I would like to pay his way." The look on my mother's face looked as crazy as she sounded.

"Uh, that…no. We just started talking a week ago. I'm not inviting him to fly across the country. Plus, saying you're involved would make me sound…I don't know…childish?"

"It's not too early, Berry," my mother spoke while merging onto the JFX. A passing truck splashed a massive flood of water on the windshield and my mother upped the wipers. "In fact, I'd rather you meet him in person early on to know for sure if he's the right man for you. I already know he is – I've claimed it – but I feel like *you* need more assurance."

She turned the wipers back down. "You seemed so shy about it in church Sunday. Before you continue with more phone calls and *Skype* calls, you need to meet face to face to see for yourself that those flying sparks are real. I believe with faith they are, but there's just something about seeing someone in person that confirms what's meant to be."

"Mom, I don't know if you've been watching too many romantic movies or too many late-night cable televangelists." I stuffed the bills back into the envelope and put the envelope back into her purse. "I'm not telling that man to fly out here.

You can keep your money."

"Oh, Berry, what are you afraid of?"

"It's been one week, for one. I'm not going to scare Malikai off by saying my mother wants to meet him. That's ridiculous."

"So, are you saying there has been no conversation about meeting in person? Has Malikai not once said anything about coming to Baltimore to see you?" My mother looked pitiful, desperate. You would think she was the one in this non-existent relationship waiting for dreams to come true.

"Um, we've briefly talked about meeting."

"What did he say?" She gripped the steering wheel. The rain suddenly began coming down harder. The wipers went back to full speed.

"Well, we both agreed that we wanted to take our time, get to know each other better before rushing to meet in person. Besides, I need to really pray about dating someone who lives and works at such a significant distance from me." The set-up for our eventual break-up. I was determined to let my mother's high hopes and big dreams be dashed gently.

My mother grabbed the envelope out of her purse and wacked me upside the head with it, all while changing lanes to get to the St. Paul Street exit.

"Girl, are you crazy? This man has a great job and is into you. Don't you start worrying about how far away he is. You must let this love seed get firmly planted and let it bloom. Tending and caring for it will become natural as it takes root." My mother shook her head. "Berry, don't let this perfect man slip out of your hands because of fear. Be brave and don't let that distance stop you from discovering true love."

"Mom, you're sounding more and more like a *Disney* movie." I shook my head as we neared my office building. "I can't take the money, but don't worry. If and when it's time for Malikai and I to meet in person, I'll keep you posted." I put the envelope back into her purse.

My mother pulled to the curb in front of my building, her face a twisted maze of emotions. She had high hopes for me and my fake love interest. "Berry, please take the money." She took the envelope out again and tried to push it into my hand. "Just take it. I'm not saying you have to force the idea of a trip into the conversation, but if it does come up, let him know I'm excited about inviting him over to dinner, completely on my dime."

I nodded, looked around. Cars were starting to get backed up behind my mother's car. A couple of honks rang out. I looked at the envelope, looked back at the nervous excitement on my mother's face. I didn't have to do anything with the money but take it with me; keep my mother's dreams alive. My mother's face broke out into a smile again as I took the envelope from her hands.

"Deposit it as soon as you can. I don't like you walking around with that much cash."

"Okay, mom." *And I'll return it to you as soon as I "break up" with him.*

"One more thing, Berry," my mother called out while shifting the car into drive, her windshield wipers squeaking. "Promise me that you'll meet him in person before making any permanent decisions about your relationship status with him, okay?" She narrowed her eyes at me. "You promise?"

The honks were growing. One driver flashed his middle finger.

"Sure, Mom." I nodded and slammed the door shut. She drove away.

As I entered the building and headed to the elevator, I thought about that middle finger, the honks, the glares.

I knew I deserved every single one.

Chapter 14

"Berry, wait until you see what's waiting on your desk." Celeste met me at the door of the office, a huge grin dripping off her face. Gina had rolled her desk chair out from her cubicle and the smile on her face had no hint of snarkiness. I smiled back at them both, nodded, and pushed past them to get to my desk, not sure whether to be alarmed or excited about whatever waited.

"Look, Berry. How sweet." Carolyn stood in my cubicle.

Naomi was beside her. "Beautiful!" she echoed and pointed at what sat on my desk. "It was just delivered."

Flowers.

My heart settled back down as I recalled that I'd placed the order online myself Tuesday night, right after I'd gotten Gina's text about my luckiness with love.

Couldn't get you out of my mind after talking with you all night. Hope these blossoms brighten your day as much as you've brightened mine. – M.C.

That was the note I'd entered to be attached to the bouquet. Not quite sure what I was thinking when I purchased the $88 arrangement of pink, white, and red roses and paid the $20 delivery fee.

"It's only been a week, but the two of you seem to be really hitting it off nicely." Carolyn bent down to smell one of the buds. "This is really special, Berry. I'm sure you're excited."

"Yes, I feel like…like I'm in a dream…like I'm in a too-good-to-be-true fantasy." *Y'all just don't know!* My hands couldn't keep still as I pulled on my hair, tugged at my suit jacket, and fingered the necklace around my neck. My nerves were a mess and my body couldn't hold still. Would I be able to sustain this concert of lies for a couple more weeks or would I hit a low note that left me falling flat?

"That necklace." Celeste had joined us in the cubicle. She pointed to the cubic zirconium heart pendant I'd bought that week to match my new suit. "Was that a gift?"

"Uh, actually, yes." I was amazed at how easy an unnecessary lie fell from my lips. "It was in a gift-wrapped box delivered to me last night. I wasn't going to keep it because, well, you know, it feels a little soon to be accepting gifts from someone who was a stranger to me a week ago. But, it just feels right."

"Wow," Gina's eyes were wide. "That must be, what? Close to a carat's worth of diamonds? Where did he get it from?"

The others crowded around me to examine it. I cupped it in my hand and stepped back so they wouldn't look too hard. "I don't know." I stared down at the $16.99 necklace I'd purchased at the mall. I squinted my eyes like I was staring at a blinding jewel. "I didn't recognize the store name on the box. Part of it was covered up by the express shipping label."

"Wow, Berry," Carolyn shook her head. "Flowers, jewelry, late night conversations… I'm surprised you haven't talked about meeting each other in person yet."

"Has it come up at all?" Celeste jumped in. I realized we hadn't talked about her wedding plans all week, nor had there been any mention of Naomi's pregnancy. "I know it's kind of soon, but considering how well you two seem to be hitting it off, and for how much you're talking, has there been any discussion about meeting face-to-face?"

"It's too soon," Gina shook her head. "This guy could be a serial killer or something like that. The more I think about it

– the flowers, the jewelry – it could all be a set-up. Don't meet him yet, Berry." She frowned as she spoke.

"It's funny. My mother was just talking about that this morning." That was true. "She's insisting that we meet at her house for dinner – if the discussion ever comes up."

"So, it hasn't come up." Gina looked pleased.

"Well, not in detail." I stared back at her. Irritation inched up my spine as Gina's smile grew. *Why do I care about this woman's opinion so much?* I looked at the four sets of eyes staring back at me; thought about the promise my mother made me make.

There was no way around it, I decided. I had to somehow meet this man in person before the whole thing cooled down.

But how?

"I don't know, Berry." Gina couldn't drop her smile. "Telling him your mother wants to meet him sounds a little juvenile–"

"–And too soon." Carolyn and Naomi spoke one right after the other.

"I completely agree with you." I nodded, still thinking.

"So, what are you going to do if and when the subject of meeting comes up more definitively?"

"I think what I'm going to do…" I took a deep breath, exhaled. "What I'm going to do is suggest to him that we meet each other halfway."

"Halfway?" Gina raised an eyebrow. "I don't understand."

"If I suggest we meet in a city halfway between San Francisco and Baltimore, then it takes away any sense of obligation for him to feel like he needs to pay my way or for me to feel like I need to stay if I'm not comfortable." *And nobody will be asking to meet him like they would if "he" came to town.*

"I still don't know about this, Berry." Always Gina. "Do

you really think it would be a good idea to meet a stranger in a strange town? I mean, while he seems to be a nice young man, you really have no way of knowing if he's some type of gangster or thug waiting to rob or rape you."

Thug. Gangster. My internal racism radar started pinging. If he had lily white skin, would she have used *those* words? Maybe I was crazy for thinking so, but any time I heard a white person use stereotypical words like thug and gangster to describe a black man, something in me went…well, crazy.

"Actually, Gina," I could hear myself say before I really thought it through, "although it's not really a halfway point, I was thinking of telling him to meet me in Aspen."

"Aspen, Colorado?"

"Yes, Aspen." I was on a mission to break down all kinds of stereotypes and assumptions about all of Black America. Shoot, I think I needed to add a ski trip to Aspen to my bucket list for real. "See, I was thinking we could meet to ski. And as far as my safety goes, a friend of mine from college, uh, Shaniqua –" that was the first name that came to my mind "– my old friend, Shaniqua, owns a lodge where I can recommend we stay. In separate rooms as a safety precaution, of course. And she'll keep an eye out for me, unbeknownst to him."

Dang.

Now, I had imaginary friends, too.

"Oh, that might not be a bad idea," Carolyn chimed in. "Actually, a ski trip is perfect. It could serve as a pre-trip to maybe a future trip to his chalet in Switzerland. Between your friend Sha- Shaquaisha, no, Shaniqua, right? Between her and the crowds of skiers on the slopes, you should be safe."

Carolyn had stumbled on the name Shaniqua, but not on the idea of black girls skiing or owning lodges.

My work is nearly done.

And it was all a lie.

"Berry, before you go anywhere to do anything with this guy, do some more research and get to know him better." Was Gina searching for something to say to bring me down? "It's still too soon to go and meet him alone and so far from home."

"Thanks for your concern, Gina, and don't worry. I'm not going anywhere. Yet."

The sound of ringing phones broke up our cubicle party. As everyone scurried off to their workstations, I looked at the flowers sitting on my desk and patted the fake flower clip resting in my hair. As I thought about all my stories and assertions over the past hours and days, a part of me knew even then that the only thing about to bloom was trouble. I'd effectively planted, watered, and tended a seed of trouble.

All that was left was the harvest.

Part 3:
Oh. My. Goo. Goo. Beans.

Chapter 15

A few days went by with silence from my brother, louder oohs and ahhs from my co-workers, non-stop smiles from my mom.

I skipped church on Sunday.

I ain't that crazy. Just because the lightning strike didn't happen last time didn't mean it wasn't working its way down from the heavenlies waiting for me to cross the sanctuary doors.

I spent the weekend shut up in my house, watching *YouTube* videos, laughing at old sitcoms. Funny, despite all the extra attention I'd been getting from my co-workers and my mother, I was still alone.

Maybe more so than before. I guess keeping a lie together keeps you traveling a solitary road.

"Well, Huxley." I patted his head the following Tuesday night. "Looks like it's still just you and me." And a vase of roses that were now dying on my dining room table. And a fake diamond necklace I had to wear every day that was starting to turn green on part of the chain. And new suits and shoes and makeup that were starting to make me itch. And a near two-thousand-dollar balance on my credit card.

"This sucks." I sat on one side of my bed. Huxley sat next to me, seeming to enjoy the re-runs of *The Wayans Bros.* playing on TV. Well, at least that's what I told myself as I fed him another cat treat from a bag in my lap. I knew the truth, though. Once those treats were gone, so would be Huxley.

"I'm stringing everybody along and pretending it's real."

The envelope my mother had given me a few days earlier

peeked out of my purse at the foot of my bed. Seven hundred dollars in fifties and hundred-dollar bills. That would all be going back to her the end of next week, the following Friday at the latest, I'd decided. I planned to tell her – and the girls at work – that Malikai and I were in the process of making plans to meet when something went awry. Not sure what that thing was yet. I felt like an author penning a book. This was my story to create and I had to decide the ending. Peaceable? Violent? Kill him off? Quiet ride out to the sunset?

"Listen to me, Huxley. I'm lost." And in need of saving, I knew. But how? God wasn't responsible for this mess I'd created, so how could I even pray to ask Him to show me how best to end it?

My phone rang.

"Hello?" I answered, not recognizing the number.

"Berry?" a female voice asked.

"Yes?"

"Oh, good. I wasn't sure if this was the right number. This is Raina, from church."

"Oh, hello." I straightened up, turned down the volume of the television. I'd gotten calls every now and then from the other women at church, usually when one needed a ride. However, since my car had been out of commission for a couple of months, the calls had thinned out. I checked the time. 10:30 pm. This must be important. I suddenly felt nervous.

"I'm sorry to be calling so late, but I leave for Miami in the morning and I wanted to talk to you."

"That's right, your trip with Drew." I recalled her talking about her husband and their plans to club the nights away down in Florida for their anniversary. "Is everything okay?" I held my breath, hoping this conversation was strictly about her. I didn't want to be asked a single question. *What does she want to talk about?*

"Oh, yes, Berry. Listen, I was hoping to catch you in church, but you weren't there Sunday."

"Yeah, I…" had no idea what lie to say to explain my absence. Please don't let this woman ask me about the supposed new man in my life.

"Berry, I'm not going to hold you long, but I wanted to find out if you ever talked to that guy you met online about what kind of professional ball he played overseas."

Welp, there goes my hope that this conversation wouldn't be about him.

"Um, yes, actually, I did." I scrambled for a stack of papers I kept on my nightstand. Copies of the website, career profile, and resume I'd created. I kept them there to use as a quick reference if my mother called. Cheat sheets to keep my stories straight. "Why do you ask, Raina?" I thumbed through the papers, trying to remember everything I'd told my mother and the girls at church about his professional sports career.

"Do you remember me telling you that Drew used to play basketball overseas? He played for several different countries right after college before starting his real estate investment firm."

"Okay," I followed along, waiting to see where this was going before offering unneeded details.

"Well, I told him about the man you met online and when I said his name is Malikai Carter, he said he thinks he might know who he is."

Who he is.

Her last three words sunk like weights on me as I begin treading the waters, fighting against a current that threatened to take me under.

"Hmmm, how about that." I looked at Huxley, scrunched up my face. *Some help, please?* My cat yawned, turned away.

"Well, I…like I said, I'm not sure that Malikai played basketball."

"But you said that you talked to him about it."

"Yes, we did talk briefly about his athletic career." *Um, where did I go from here?* "He didn't go into too many details. I think he was devastated about some injury he received. It wasn't basketball, I'm pretty sure. Actually, I know it wasn't. It was some weird sport I'd never heard of. That's why I'm struggling to remember what it was he said he played." *Why don't I just come clean?*

The reasons I had to keep up the lies flung at me like buoys, trying to keep me afloat in my sea of fibs. I was in too deep. My mother would kill me. I'd spent too much. I just needed to make it one more week or so. That's what I told myself.

"Oh. So, he didn't play basketball, but you don't remember for sure what he played?" Raina paused. "Well, find out, because Drew seems pretty convinced that he knows who this guy is. He wasn't on Drew's team, but from what he remembers, he's not really someone you'd want to be connected to. I'm just trying to look out for you, girl."

"Oh, okay. Um, well, uh, thanks." There was a pause. Was I supposed to say something? "So, Raina, what exactly did he say about him? I mean, the man he thinks is him." This was getting truly ridiculous.

Raina sounded happy to share. "He said he was a total jerk, a complete a-hole who pitted women against each other, broke hearts, and laughed about it. If this is the same guy, he's really bad news, Berry. He doesn't know how to treat women at all. He even punched his mother in the face when she showed up after one of their games and complained about him not making NBA money. He was cut off the team after that."

"That sounds…horrible."

"I know, right? Drew had a bunch of stories about him – if

he's the same guy. His name might be slightly different, but it would make sense for him to change it up a little since he had such a bad reputation."

"I really don't think it's him, Raina." And I hope she hadn't been putting this info out there. My mother would have a fit if Evangeline Willow caught wind of this unflattering news.

"I don't know, Berry, but I think it's worth investigating. Although Drew wasn't one hundred percent sure of his name, after he saw the picture, he's really convinced that this man, Malikai Carter, is someone who played in the same league with him."

As Raina talked, I grabbed my tablet and did a quick Internet search for unusual sports from around the world.

"Berry, I just want to make sure that you're not getting hooked up with some kind of loser."

"Sepak takraw," I blurted.

"Huh?"

"Sepak takraw," I repeated. It had been the first result that came up in my search for unusual sports. "That's the name of the sport Malikai played." I skimmed articles as I talked. "Like I said, we didn't spend a lot of time talking about his athletic career. That's why I struggled to remember the name. I'd meant to look it up to better understand what it is. I'm looking it up now."

Silence.

Did she believe me? Did she have more to share from Drew? I held my breath as the silence continued.

"Called takraw for short…A game like volleyball except hands can't be used," Raina muttered, paused, and then spoke again. She was looking it up herself. "Originating from Southeast Asia, it looks like soccer and martial arts combined to get a rattan ball over a net between two teams of three. It's also sometimes called kick volleyball." She sounded like she was on the same website where I'd landed.

"It's played in many countries across most of the continents. There are hopes of getting it into the Olympics," I read along. I stopped talking, letting her absorb whatever she was reading. I heard several clicks of a computer keyboard through the phone; several long, heavy sighs. I watched the beginning of a *YouTube* video on mute to get a visual.

Is she buying this?

"Uh, Berry," here came my answer, "I don't know about this. I've never heard of this sport, and I bet most of America hasn't either."

"Probably why he had to play it overseas." I held my breath, waited.

"So, you actually believe this? You think this guy Malikai is telling you the truth?"

I could hear the obvious doubt in her voice. If I tried to sound too convincing, she would probably have even more doubt, more questions, and wonder why I was being so gullible.

"You're right, Raina," I chose my words carefully. "This does sound a little too different. I'm going to do more research and ask him more questions. My gut feelings tell me that he is telling the truth, but I'm not going to be naïve about it." A plan on how to deal with this wrinkle was forming in my mind even as I spoke. "Listen, Raina, thanks for the information. I appreciate you looking out for me."

"Girl, you don't have to thank me. That's what we do as sisters in Christ – look out for each other so we don't get bitten by snakes."

"Yeah, watch out for snakes." My voice quivered.

Oh God, these women can never find out that I've lied about it all. What kind of "sister" am I? I swallowed down the guilt, pushed out my next words. "Look, Raina, enjoy your time in Miami. Don't even worry about this situation anymore." *Don't talk about it to anyone,* is what I really wanted to say. "I'll get to the bottom of it. I know how to dig for info."

"Okay, Berry," Raina replied. "And if Drew finds out any more information, I'll definitely let you know."

"Enjoy your trip," I got in before we both hung up. The moment the call disconnected, I collapsed into my bed. My head sunk into the pile of pillows I kept by my headboard. Huxley stepped over me and jumped down to the floor with a loud thud. I listened as his paws clicked out of the room, down the hall, and into the kitchen to his water bowl.

"I am a liar." The accusation and truth of my words hit me anew.

But I was in too deep now. The only way to right this was to stick to the script, work out my plan. In a week, this will be over, I consoled myself as I sat back up.

I knew what I needed to do to address the new twist presented by Raina. I knew what I needed to do, but wasn't sure how to best achieve it.

I reached again for my tablet.

The screen went black.

Dead.

And, I realized, I'd left my charger at work.

I needed a computer. Davis's workstations were not an option at the moment.

It was near 11 o'clock. Libraries were closed. I had work in the morning.

My eyes were beginning to feel heavy and I'd already gotten ready for bed, but I knew I'd have a disaster on my hands if I didn't take care of this tonight.

I grabbed a tote bag, threw a pair of jeans and a shirt into it for my workday tomorrow. I put on some sweats and sneakers for the work I needed to do tonight. Probably wasn't a good idea to catch the bus downtown at night by myself, but coming back on the bus at an even later time when I finished my plan would be even worse. I was prepared to stay the night where I was going.

The new digital café downtown where I'd met Davis and Li Yan for dinner.

It wasn't far from my office building, and, because it sat between a luxury loft apartment community and a swanky hotel, I recalled that it was a twenty-four-hour operation. I remembered their hours plastered on the windows, and the comfortable sofas and dim lighting that filled the interior.

Yup, I was definitely going to spend the night there.

I grabbed my tote bag of clothes, knowing that the casual wear would be a departure from my recent dress clothes and suits at work, but I was tired, and just wanted to be comfortable, and just wanted this to be over.

"Good night, Huxley," I called out to my cat as I left. The next bus was due in three minutes and another wouldn't be coming for another forty-five.

This would absolutely be the last week of this foolishness. I would do the "break-up" now, but I wanted my mother to believe I'd given it a fair chance as I promised. I couldn't wait for the end of next week when all of this scheming would be over.

Chapter 16

My mission is almost complete. Seeing the smiles on these children's faces is worth all the twists and turns of the past few years. Today, at the last day of summer camp, I watched as one boy, age five, charged toward the net, kicking the ball with the back of his foot. The ball soared over the net, and the boy turned to me and smiled.

It was the first time I'd ever seen a smile on the lad's face. He ended up at the orphanage after losing his parents to malaria last summer. I've been told that he has said very little and cried very much.

I've always been a firm believer that sports can bring joy, and teaching these children at the orphanage the skills, athleticism, aerobatic maneuvers, and discipline that is needed for the beautiful game of sepak takraw has done nothing but humble me and showcase the real values of love, giving, and service. Now, more than ever, I am determined to pursue the most lucrative career possible, so I can pour funds back into this charity I was moved to create.

My dream is to give these awesome children in the fast-growing city of Gaborone, Botswana sports camps year-round and for them to learn and experience a sport that is new to them. Most people have never heard of this centuries-old sport, but it is my hope to expand the game to new cultures and ethnicities. My parents came to this city on a mission. I'm adding my own twist to their original goals as I share the love of Jesus through the beauty of sports.

1:37 a.m. I looked at the time on the corner of the computer screen and threw down another gulp of straight black coffee chased by a shot of an energy drink.

I had to stay awake.

The attendant for the computer wing of the café had his eye on me.

The white man with wiry dreadlocks had a sign near his station: *No sleeping still.* Guess the downtown wireless spot didn't want to be mistaken as a hotel for the homeless. I looked over at a woman at the station next to me. Five grimy plastic bags sat on the floor by her feet. We both typed away as I gulped down another shot of my energy drink.

Clearly, this wasn't a well thought out plan. My office, in the building a few blocks down, wouldn't be opening for another six hours and catching the bus back home at two in the morning was not an option. I'd accidentally left my credit card home, so hailing a taxi was off limits, and there was no way I was going to use the cash my mother had given me. It was bad enough that I was a liar. Using the money would make me also feel like a thief.

Nope. My decision to stay at this computer spot until dawn was not a good idea.

However, what I'd created online? Genius.

I looked at the blog entries that I'd written reflecting a two-year time span. Rather than create a new website for a sports team that didn't exist, it made sense to make a blog. It felt personal, a chance for nosy readers to get to know Malikai Carter better. Plus, since I'd put out there that he'd started a charity, I figured this blog would kill two birds with one stone, so to speak, if anyone asked.

Like I said, genius, right?

Having him write out in supposed real time his interactions with orphans and his desire to teach them the sport he'd once played showed his depth of character and compassionate heart.

No mistaking him for whatever jerk Raina's husband once crossed paths with.

It felt like weights were on my eyelids as I struggled to stay awake and focus on my task. The attendant kept his eyes on me. I guess everyone else in the establishment must have been regulars, because he paid them no mind.

Maybe I was just paranoid.

Seemed like I was thinking everyone was watching me these days.

I exhaled and started typing another entry. This one I dated five months earlier.

So excited about my new position. No more traditional law work as I can now fly all over the world, representing a company that is going to change the game for many sports. Performance enhancers that are legal, legit, safe, and effective.

I smiled. Maybe I could show Gina this. Kept typing.

While the income is impressive – giving me significantly more than the funds from my sepak takraw career that helped fund my law school education - what I am most excited about is that I will have abundant funds to pour directly into my work with the orphanage. I want to build a world-class gymnasium on the outskirts of Gaborone. I want to give the youth here a sporting arena that rivals one found in any major metropolis. And that's just the beginning. Together with my personal funds and the money that comes in to support my charity, the youth and young adults in this part of Botswana will be blessed beyond measure.

Perfection.

I re-read all I'd written and then shut the site down, but not before cutting and pasting the webpage address. I'd opened my email account and found Raina's email address from an old church emailing.

Thanks again for calling me, Raina, I'd typed. *Not gonna lie. I was a little – a lot – worried after what you shared. But I did talk to Malikai after getting off of the phone with you and I asked him about his professional ball career. Girl, I am so relieved to know he never played basketball overseas, so he can't be that guy Drew told you about. His sport really was tepak segraw.*

No, that's not right. What's it called again? How do you spell it?

Sepak takraw, I corrected after looking it up again. *And let me tell you,* I continued, *this man has to be about the humblest athlete ever. All he talked about was his experience teaching the sport to some kids. I did my own research, of course, and came across a blog he started a couple of years ago detailing his charity work. Check it out if you want. I pasted in the link. Hope you are having a great time in Miami. Again, thanks for looking out for me. --Berry*

"Done and sent." I smiled as I clicked on the send button. Mission accomplished. No more questions to ask. All answers given.

And by the end of next week, all of this would be over. I bit my bottom lip, feeling a sudden wave of relief wash over me at the thought of wiping my hands clean.

One more week before the break-up that would set me free.

At the moment, however, it was 2:07 a.m., and the only thing I was free of was energy. I had absolutely nothing left in me. I wanted my bed. Any bed.

The lady next to me, with the plastic bags at her feet,

pecked away at her keyboard. Her fingernails were caked over with dirt, her hair matted, and a faint smell of urine wafted from her workspace. I peered over at her screen.

The Recollections of a Butterfly in a Mid-Winter's Night: Book of Poems by M. Easter Muldaney.

Her page count was 502.

I guess she came every night. With no apparent home or bed to sleep in, she must come here from dusk to dawn as a safe way to spend the midnight hours, finding sleep in the daylight.

No Sleeping. I looked again at the sign by the attendant.

I wasn't going to last until the morning. I felt it, knew it.

I gathered my things, dug deep in my purse.

The envelope.

My mother's cash.

With all the wrong I'd been doing lately, I felt the need to do at least one thing right.

"Ma'am?" I stepped up to the woman after adjusting my bag on my shoulder. "Here." I pulled out a hundred-dollar bill from the envelope and pressed it into her hand. "Hope this helps."

The shock and then smile on her face warmed me as she stuffed the bill down her shirt. "God bless you, sweetheart."

I nodded, not finding words to explain that I was in a state far outside of God's blessing. The lies, the deceit, and my unwillingness to come clean at the moment, had put me completely out of favor with The Most High. Of that, I was certain.

Next week, though, I would be back on track. "Forgive me in advance, Father," I prayed as I left out of the digital café. "I promise to get back to doing right by the end of next week."

As I walked out of the café and stared at the empty downtown streets, I had only one thought in my head.

Get in a bed. Any bed. Immediately.

I didn't have a choice. If I could use my mother's money to help out someone less fortunate, surely it would be okay for me to use some of it to secure a safe, convenient place to sleep.

The café was next to a hotel, I remembered. I only needed a room for a few hours; couldn't cost that much. Home felt too far away and the thought of a cab ride only added to my exhaustion. Plus, by the time I would get back home, I would have only a couple of hours before it was time to get back up and catch the bus right back to where I was. Also, I had a change of clothes with me as I'd intended to stay up all night.

Fifteen minutes and three hundred dollars later, I was sinking into an endless mound of white down pillows and blankets at one of downtown Baltimore's best luxury hotels.

Sleep never felt so sweet.

Until it got bitter.

I overslept...

Chapter 17

"Ms. Jenkins? Ms. Jenkins?" A heavy knock sounded on the door. "Ms. Jenkins?"

My eyelids fluttered open as I tried to make sense of what I was hearing. "Huxley?" I ran my foot across the foot of the bed where my cat ended up in the morning. Instead of a lump of fur, I felt…a tote bag?

I sat up. Tote bag. Change of clothes. Digital café. Gabarone, Botswana. Hotel.

Work.

OMG. What time is it? I clicked on the lamp on the side of the bed and fought against the pillows and comforters and blankets to get to my feet.

"Ms. Jenkins?" The woman's voice that accompanied the knock grew louder.

"I'm coming," I shouted as I grabbed the jeans out of my tote bag. I tripped over my feet and fell on the floor as I scrambled to pull them up my legs. I wrestled my shirt over my head. "I'll be right there!" I hollered out again.

What time is it?

The digital alarm clock in the room blinked 12:00, needing to be set. The room phone was off its base due to my purse sitting halfway on it. With one shoe on and my shirt only partially buttoned, I unlatched and opened the door.

"Okay, I'm here. Hello. Hi." I was out of breath as I greeted the woman who had deep crow's feet around her eyes and shoulder length, springy red hair.

She frowned as she stared me up and down.

Oops. My shirt was inside out, I realized, and my hair – oh no, my hair! I reached up and felt that one side was matted; the other side had unraveling twists sticking straight up. My horror increased and her frown deepened as a few feathers fluttered down from my haphazard coils.

Darn down pillows.

"Ms. Jenkins," the woman began, "we've been trying to reach you all morning, but you didn't answer your phone."

"Oh, it was off the hook." I pointed back to it as another feather floated down. "I think I accidentally knocked it off the holder with my purse last night. Sorry about that, I –"

"Check out was at 10 a.m.," she interrupted

"Ten? Wait, what time is it?" My eyes widened.

The woman, her nametag read Dorothy, ignored my question as she continued. "As you did not advise us that you needed a later check-out time and have not responded to any phone calls, please note, per your signed agreement, there is a mandatory fee equal to a full night's rate."

"A full night's rate? Hold on, I'm leaving right now. I mean," I ran a finger through my coils, "I mean right after I fix my hair. Ten minutes. Wait, what time is it again?"

"Ms. Jenkins, I am here to collect payment since we do not have a credit card for you on file as you paid in cash. We also need you to vacate the room immediately so we can prepare it for our next guest."

"I am so sorry. I overslept. Give me five minutes to get myself together and I will be out of your way. Is the late fee negotiable?" *Another three hundred dollars?* I needed to give this all back to my mother.

"You have five minutes Ms. Jenkins before security gets involved. Five minutes." She looked again at my hair and frowned. "Ten minutes. And the late checkout fee is non-negotiable." She held out a hand, waiting for cash.

Well, there went another three hundred dollars.

I watched Dorothy the enforcer walk away with the bills I'd just given her from the envelope in my purse.

All of my mother's money was gone.

Money that was supposed to be offered to Malikai to come to Baltimore in a first-class airplane seat.

I still had no idea what time it was other than knowing it was some time after ten a.m. My cell phone had died, I discovered as I packed up my tote bag. No wonder my alarm didn't go off.

"This day can't get any worse," I shook my head, not even bothering to rush as I fumbled through my purse for a ponytail holder. I was already late for work, already flat broke.

And for what reason exactly?

Seven minutes later, I walked out of the hotel. Jeans, tennis shoes. Hair struggling to stay contained in the yellow elastic rubber band I'd found at the bottom of my purse.

"This day cannot get any worse," I said again as I entered my office building minutes later. An elevator door was already open. I stepped on and immediately recoiled.

"What the?" The image looking back at me in the mirrored elevator walls was a bit more horrendous than I'd imagined.

It wasn't just that I didn't have on a single hint of make-up, or that I had managed to miss the thick crud in the corners of both my eyes, or the trail of dry crust that led from the corner of my mouth to a single stray hair on my chin; it wasn't just that my jeans had more wrinkles than an old piece of aluminum foil and the top I'd pulled from my closet to match it had a brown stain I'd missed on the collar. Any of these things alone would have been enough to make me want to curl up into a ball and rock in the corner of the elevator.

What made everything seven times worse was the cherry topping it all off.

My hair.

There was nothing natural about the way my thick, unraveling coils were coming out from the sides of my ponytail.

Ponytail? Did I say ponytail? What had managed to stay in the elastic band looked more like a bunny tail: a one inch puff of ragged ends. The rest of my hair was all over the place, and not in a cute way. No hat. No gel. No way could I walk into my office like this. If I had scissors on me, I would have cut it all off right then and there, no second thought about it. This was embarrassing, beyond embarrassing.

I was supposed to be representing myself as a regal woman of color. A queen of natural beauty.

Instead, I looked like I had special problems; like I needed a licensed caretaker, a gardener, maybe even an exorcist. I shuddered.

Ain't no way I'm walking in the office looking like this, no matter how late I already am. I was glad that nobody else was on the elevator; glad that when I got to my floor there was nobody waiting to get on. I let the doors close back up and hit 'B' for basement. It didn't light up. Did the button not work? My plan was to go to the ladies' room on the lower level to make myself some type of presentable.

Can't believe I walked down the street like this. I'm surprised the security guard let me into the building. I slammed again on the button for the basement. It still did not light up, but the whir and roll of the elevator let me know that it was heading back down.

I breathed a little easier as the elevator plunged. Each ding of another floor down with no new passengers brought relief. I was going to get to that bathroom and reclaim my sexy. Well, if not sexy, at least I wanted to look sane.

Wait, why are we stopping?

My chest chamber started feeling like a room full of noisy clocks as my heart began to race. The elevator squealed to a stop.

"Second floor," the automated voice announced as the door began opening. *Wait, this ain't the basement.* The 'B' button still was not lit. I swallowed hard and slammed down on it several times as the doors slid open.

And then I wanted to run and hide.

The cleaning lady.

Today, her afro curled and shined like she was ready to step onto a runway. Perfectly outlined ruby red lips; mascara that made her eyelashes extend high enough to tickle heaven. Her flawless face and fierce 'fro made her cleaning apron and khaki pants look couture.

"Uh, hello," I forced a smile, like I looked normal, like I didn't look like a troll emerging from under a bridge. A feather suddenly fluttered down from my tresses. And then another. How many more feathers were hiding in my knots?

The cleaning woman hesitated in front of the open doors. Hey, I wouldn't want to get on with me either. Considering I'd been wearing dress suits and flowers in my hair lately, looking like Business Woman 101, I knew my sudden ragged appearance was startling enough to make anyone question my mental stability.

Then again, with all my schemes and shenanigans lately, maybe I *was* having some type of breakdown.

"Are you getting on?" I didn't use my hand to hold it open as she stood there. I wanted the doors to slam shut. I wanted to hurry up and get to the basement restroom to end the misery. *Why won't the button light up?*

The girl shrugged and stepped on. She moved to the opposite corner and we both stood there with our hands crossed in front of us as the door began to close.

"Hold that elevator!" A voice rang out from the hallway. My heart sunk as heavy footsteps ran toward us. The cleaning lady pressed down the 'hold' button. I wanted to scream. Instead, I looked down at the floor as the new passenger stepped on.

A man's brown dress shoes.

I studied them and the brown slacks that hung over them.

"Thanks, ladies." His voice had clarity to it. Clarity and confidence. "Can you press fourteen for me, please?"

Um, no we're going down, I wanted to say; but speaking would have required looking up. Plus, I realized, we were indeed going up. *What happened to my basement floor stop?* Everything about this elevator ride was going wrong.

We reached the fourteenth floor and brown shoes stepped off.

"Isn't this your floor?" the cleaning lady called over to me.

Yes, it was. But, no, I was not getting off. Not like this. Especially not with company. And why was she so concerned about my floor anyway? I didn't answer, didn't budge.

However, Brown Shoes had stopped walking. He was holding the door open for me, I realized.

"Uh, thanks," I said, my head and eyes still down. I stepped off, ready to break out into a run for the bathroom to fix all that was wrong with my life. Only reason I didn't was because I figured someone really would call for psychiatric help if I started running down the hallways.

"Excuse me, ma'am? Do you know where I can find suite 14D2?"

Was he really speaking to me? I kept my eyes down, walked away as I answered. "There are no letters on the suite names, just numbers. I'm not sure what to tell you."

"Wait." The man seemed to be checking a message on his phone. "It's 02, not D2. 1402."

"Oh, that's where I work. Cole Financial Services." *Darn it,* I wanted to kick myself. How foolish would it look for me to say that and then walk away to the bathroom without showing him where it was?

And how foolish did I look already? I still had my eyes to the floor, head down. Another feather floated down from my hair. Was I rolling on those pillows last night? Digging my head into them like a power drill in my sleep? "Um, I can show you where 1402 is."

"Great, I'm here to check out your computer system. I understand there have been some issues."

A computer geek. I exhaled. He probably hadn't even noticed how terrible I looked or that I'd kept my head and eyes down like I had some type of social disorder. Equations and formulas and programming codes were probably filling his mind. I smiled. And, then, I finally looked up.

Chapter 18

Oh. My. Goo. Goo. Beans.

I wanted to turn inside out, roll up into a ball, and kick myself down the hallway.

The man in front of me was without question one of the most beautiful creations I'd ever seen. The full lips, chiseled cheek bones, and milk chocolate smooth skin made him look lickable. Yes, I said that. Lickable. Though he wore a suit and had a black book bag over one shoulder, I could tell this man had the physique of a weightlifter, the finesse of a lightweight boxer, the smoothness of a step dancer.

But his eyes, though.

Was this some kind of joke?

I'd used the color of my cat's fur to create the seductive brown orbs of my Malikai Carter. This man in front of me? I swear, same eye hue.

Those eyes of his glittered like bronze gems.

"Uh, is the office this way?" His eyebrow was raised, his finger pointing down the hall.

"Oh," I snapped back to attention, realizing I'd been staring at him, mouth agape, for several seconds. "I'm sorry. I had something in my eye..." *Yeah, you.* "…and I…well." I started digging in one corner of my lids to prove that something was there, forgetting that, yup, something was there. A large ball of runny crust. It came out on my fingertip.

I wanted to die.

Die, die, die, die.

"The office is right this way." I spun around on my heels

and headed toward my office. I heard his steps behind me and willed myself not to turn around and get lost in those beautiful, brown eyes again.

And then I remembered how bad I looked. I wished I could evaporate, forget this moment; have him forget this moment of seeing me at my worse.

"Right here," I said, opening the front door of the suite for him. I stepped away from the door, hoping that he would walk in and block whatever view my coworkers had of me. The moment he was in would be the moment I could finally run down the hall to the bathroom to fix myself.

But, of course, he was a gentleman. He motioned with his hand for me to go first.

Could I really be mad about that?

Um, yeah.

"Berry!" Celeste saw me first. "Oh, my goodness, did someone attack you?" She shrieked and charged out of her cubicle. Carolyn and Gina came right behind. Naomi came out of her cubicle and jumped when she saw me.

"Oh no!" She grabbed a box of tissues, a handful of paper clips, and some antibacterial hand gel and ran toward me. Not sure what she had in mind to do. "Do we need to call the police?" Pure terror was on her face.

All four women crowded around me. Brown shoes stood unnoticed to the side.

For the moment.

"I… I'm okay. I…" Really, what was I supposed to say? Standing there looking at all those eyes looking back at me, what the heck kind of story was I supposed to present to explain my roughed-up appearance?

"Goodness, Berry, we've been worried about you." Carolyn held a hand over her chest. "We've been calling your cell phone, your home phone, texting you, emailing you. It's not like you not to answer or be this late."

"And now you show up looking like this." Gina had not stopped gasping. "Should we call for the police or an ambulance? Is that blood on your shirt?" She pointed to the brown stain on my collar. "What happened to you?"

"I just… Last night… My phone…"

"My apologies for not realizing your distress." Brown Shoes finally spoke up. "How can I help?"

"Wait," Celeste was the first to finally notice the man who had come in with me. "Is this– Are you–"

"Malikai Carter! Those eyes!" Carolyn's hand went from her chest to her cheek.

"Excuse me?" he asked.

"I'm sorry, that was rude of me." Carolyn let out a nervous laugh. "I'm Carolyn. This is Celeste, Naomi, and Gina. We work with Berry," she nodded and winked at me. "So, I assume that you are Mr.–"

"Just call me Kal, please," he interrupted. "I can't stand my name. To this day, I don't know what my mother was thinking, especially the way she spelled it."

"Oh, like Berry." Celeste piped in. "Even though they can be a little archaic, at least biblical names sound strong. Names like Isaiah, Jonah, and Malikai have such strength to them, but Berry? Who names their child after a fruit?" She giggled.

If I wasn't holding my breath, I would have said something – not sure what – to defend my parents' craziness. But the attention was off of me, and I was fine with that. The man was finer than good wine and my grandma's fine china. I could not blame these women for losing all focus of me with that man and his golden bronze eyes lighting up the room.

But like I said, he was all gentleman.

"Berry?" He looked back at me, concern etched on his chiseled face. "Are you okay? Is there anything I can do to help?" He seemed completely oblivious to all our swooning. He had completely missed the questions and assumptions about his name.

"Uh," I squeaked out, resisting the urge to pat down my hair again. Didn't want any feathers to come falling out. "Oh, I'm fine… Just been a crazy few past hours, Kal. As far as helping, I guess you can get started looking at the computers."

"Yes, of course." He started digging in his book bag.

Gina narrowed her eyes, tilted her head, squinted. Aside from the eyes, he didn't look much like the photo I'd created.

He looked better.

"Wait a minute," Naomi whispered to me as he began walking toward the cubicles. She pointed to a sheet of paper sticking out of my tote bag. "That receipt. Skylight Suites? So, you two met…last night?"

Carolyn's face was a big 'O.' "Already?" she whispered. "Berry!"

"I understand that your system crashed again for the second time this month?" He called out to us, completely oblivious to the shock and awe of my co-workers.

"Uh, yes, it did." Gina scratched her head and eyed me as he dug deeper in his book bag. He entered Naomi's work area. Gina pointed and mouthed, "This is really him?"

None of this added up or made sense, I knew. What could I say or do?

"Do you need one of our passwords?" I yelled out as I tried to figure out how to clean this whole situation up. Saving face, maintaining a lie, and trying to get the attention of an actual real man while looking like a junkie was proving to be a bit difficult. Why did he have to be so fine and why did he have to come on a day that I looked my absolute worse?

Gina's face had taken on two extra shades of red. "Mr. John said someone would be coming in to fix the system once and for all, but we didn't realize…*you* would be coming."

She looked at me as she walked to where he was. "This is really him?" she whispered. The doubt and disbelief was palpable.

I pretended not to hear her. Considering that there was only one picture of him online, it wouldn't be completely impossible for him to look somewhat different in person. *Wait, what am I doing? What am I thinking here?*

"Yeah, I didn't think I'd get out here this soon, but I was able to catch a midnight flight, so I let your boss know that I could come today. Don't worry about providing any passwords. I have what I need." The man named Kal spoke as he began typing in codes into Naomi's workstation. He plugged up some fancy looking equipment, played around with some buttons and keys.

I had no idea what he was talking about. My co-workers had no idea what he was saying. He had no idea what they were thinking.

And I had to somehow come out of this in one piece.

"So, you *did* stay at the Skylight Suites?" Celeste looked from me to him and back. His focus was on the computer screen, but he nodded his head.

"Yes, nice place. I always stay there when I come to Baltimore. Actually, can you try and enter your password?" He directed Naomi.

As she complied, Gina started whispering at me again. "Dang, Berry what kind of night did you have?" She winked as she studied my raggedy hair and wrinkled clothing anew.

"I didn't get much sleep," I said, then quickly bit my lip. I wasn't telling a lie, but I knew my co-workers had a completely different take on my words.

"Oh, my." Naomi looked a little disturbed. "That was… pretty quick …You two…"

A sense of shame washed over me. It was bad enough I'd been lying, but now to look like a little fast-tailed hottie within my lies? God, I'm sorry. What kind of witness am I for you?

"So, you fix computers? We thought you were into law and performance enhancers." Gina had more questions for Kal. I crossed my arms and held my breath. *What am I supposed to do? How do I stop this?*

Kal appeared to be too engrossed in whatever he was doing at the workstation to catch all Gina had just said. "Our company does a little of everything. Not sure what all our branches do, but right now I'm discovering my love for computer systems. Working on an extra degree in it, too. Been flying all over helping companies like yours that have sites throughout the States. Even been able to travel abroad with some of my projects." Kal didn't miss a beat. "Speaking of which, I think your system is all set."

"Wow, that was quick," I said, anxious to get him out of there before more questions were asked. Forget my hair, my clothes, and my dignity. I looked a mess, but I would be viewed as an even hotter mess if too much more info about who he was not came out. "Thanks for your speed. You're awesome, Kal." What was Kal short for anyway? I wondered. My question was about to be answered as I saw him fishing for something in his book bag.

It was a business card.

"My pleasure," he had the card outstretched in his hand. "If any more issues come up, don't hesitate to call me." I reached him first and stuffed his card into my pocket. "We most certainly will, Kal." I started walking toward the door, hoping that he would follow. He did.

"So, you're leaving already?" Celeste frowned as the man put his book bag back on his shoulder and grabbed the door knob. "I think all of us were excited about learning more about you. You really seem like an amazing person. With all of your travels and experiences, seems like you'd have a lot of interesting stories to share." Celeste looked genuinely disappointed.

"Uh…" A look of pure confusion took over his face as he stared at the grins and batting eyes of my officemates.

I jumped in. "He's so humble. You have another flight to catch today?" My question was a gamble, but the man did seem like a frequent flier. I needed him to be a frequent flier.

"As a matter of fact, I do. I've got a flight to Cleveland late tonight. Another assignment is waiting for me first thing tomorrow."

"But you *are* going to go out before you leave, right?" Gina had a sneaky smile on her face. She winked at me again.

She was finally a believer.

I didn't even bother to keep patting my hair. The crazed, messy look was working for me, apparently, even if it had in some way changed my coworkers' perception of me.

"Yeah, I do have plans," Kal gave a sheepish grin just as he stepped out into the hallway. "I'm supposed to meet up with my fiancée for dinner."

Fiancée.

The word burned, stung, slapped, and threatened all at the same time. There went any fantasy I'd had that I would talk with him again – on a day when I looked better, of course. There went any act I could hold together to keep my co-workers believing they'd just met Malikai Carter. I tried to think of a comeback, an explanation, something, anything that would keep my lies intact once the door closed behind him.

"Speaking of which, where do you think we should go? I haven't had a chance to look up the restaurants around here."

"There are some nice places in Canton," I blurted. I forced myself to blink and swallow; prayed that he wouldn't expand on anything else about his fiancée or his dinner plans with her.

"Ok, I'll check that out. Thanks, Berry. Nice to meet you all." He waved to the rest. "I'm sure I'll talk with you all again another time. And Berry," he gave me a once over with a sympathetic smile, "I hope tomorrow is a better day for you."

I wanted to melt under his gaze, feel soothed from his smile. But I knew I looked a hot mess and that his sincere wish for me came out of a place of pity. I shut the door behind him as he finally headed down the hall. I looked at the wood door a few moments as I thought about what to say once I turned around.

No, I hadn't lied and said he was Malikai Carter, but I hadn't stopped my coworkers from thinking it was him. But now this bit about a fiancée? How did I explain this?

Turns out I didn't have to.

When I turned back around, all four of my coworkers were staring at me with their mouths wide open.

"Fiancée?"

"Did he propose?"

"The first time you met in person?"

"And you slept with him?"

"Has it even been two weeks?"

"Are you crazy?"

"It's like a fairy tale."

"I guess it can happen."

"My grandparents met and married in two days back during the Depression and they lasted fifty-seven years."

"I guess when you know, you know."

"Berry, I don't know about this."

"Oh, my goodness."

They talked over each other, questioning, affirming, deciding, concluding.

I didn't stop them.

Not because I wanted them to believe an outrageous lie. I just didn't know what to say. How did I even begin to tell them the truth?

"Wait, where's the ring?" Gina.

All the questions stopped. All eyes turned to me.

I never said Kal was Malikai. I never said we'd actually spent the night together. I never said we were somehow ridiculously engaged.

I hadn't said any of those things, so I technically had not lied. But now, a story was necessary, if this fiancée talk was to be the new twist. Did I really want to go there?

I'm not that crazy.

"Look, y'all," I shut my eyes, opened them, took a deep breath, prepared to come clean – a little. "About Kal, he… He's not… We…" All four pairs of eyes blinked at me, their collective breath held, waiting, heads leaning forward. "Now, y'all know good and well we're not engaged. That would be foolish, agreeing to marry a man I just started talking to two weeks ago."

Relief, confusion, disappointment filled their faces.

Too much disappointment.

This was crazy.

"But," I quickly added as everyone turned to their respective cubicles, "we did kind of joke about marriage. I mean, we both know that is something we want for ourselves down the road, and we…we laughed about it a little. That fiancée bit just now?" I sucked in a deep breath. "It was an inside joke. That's what it was. An inside joke based on our conversation."

The smiles returned on their faces. Well, Gina had more of a smirk than a smile.

"Sometimes, you just connect with someone immediately. There's no explaining it, but it's…right." I watched as all four of them exhaled, smiled.

"That's good news, Berry," Celeste had a 100-watt grin. "Sounds like the past twenty-four hours have been really good to you."

I swallowed hard and nodded, still not that comfortable with what I knew these women thought I'd done last night.

Or that they thought that man was the fictional Malikai Carter. *What if he comes back again?* Clearly, I had not thought this out.

I was such a fool. Was it too late to come clean?

"The phone lines will be on in a few minutes. Good thing the system was down so you don't have to worry about clocking in late today, Berry." Naomi headed for her cubicle. "We will keep this lateness to ourselves. Don't worry about HR," she winked.

"Yes. Thank you." I smiled back and nodded. I saw my reflection in the window. My crusty face. The wrinkled clothes.

My hair.

Who was I kidding? I was a mess inside and out.

I finally ran to the restroom to tidy up. Wasn't much I could do with my hair at the moment except put it into two thick cornrows.

Clean out my eyes.

Splash water on my face.

Hate the woman staring back at me in the mirror.

I was a fraud, an immature, stupid fraud, caught in a web of lies that felt too thick and sticky to free myself from.

The business card.

I pulled it out from my jeans pocket as I headed back to my desk.

His name.

Kalypso Delano.

Kalypso. Yeah, that name was a little different. I don't

think I'd ever have to worry about him sharing his name with anyone.

Just the same, God, please don't let that man come back here ever again. It was the first prayer I'd prayed in a while, though I'm not sure I could classify it as a true prayer. Would the Most High really be giving ear to any plea from me?

The phone lines were about to go live. I tucked the business card into the deepest corner of my purse and put my headset on.

"Good afternoon, this is Berry." I exhaled at this first normal act of my day.

That's when I realized living lies had become my new routine.

Chapter 19

Three texts messages, four voice mails, and six emails.

I waited until I was home to plug up my phone. As my phone chirped to life for the first time all day, all thirteen notifications buzzed, dinged, and whistled.

Thirteen.

I didn't like that number. I had no desire to see what calls and messages I'd missed.

Anyhoo, I was home now, my work day over, my phone and tablet chargers were accessible and my lies were still intact. More importantly, my bed waited. I was exhausted. I wanted nothing more than to get in my shower and let hot water purify me, then collapse into the comfort of my own sheets.

I'd deal with my hair and grooming in the morning. I just wanted the day to be over with. Now.

"Huxley, here's your food." The food pellets clanged into his metal bowl. I watched for a few seconds as he dumped his entire face into the dry cat food and crunched away.

"This has become my life." I shook my head. "I have a supposed boyfriend with houses in Switzerland and San Francisco and yet the only person I have the most authentic conversations with is my cat."

My phone let out one more chirp. An email notification. No need to delay the inevitable, I decided.

Time to check the messages.

An unexplainable feeling of dread took over my gut as I settled into my living room's blue beanbag chair. Then again, the feeling was perfectly explainable, I admitted to myself. I normally had this many messages total for the week. A day away from my phone and this many notifications was bound to be bad.

Or maybe I was just paranoid. For starters, the emails could just be a bunch of junk mail, ads for cheap vacations or health newsletters I'd forgotten I'd subscribed to.

My heart quickened when I saw the first email waiting was from Pat from church. Actually, all seven new emails were from my church friends: Pat, Tressa, Vickie, Shaneka, and Raina. Looked like they were all responses from an email sent first by Raina. I thought about her phone call last night, her insistence that Malikai Carter was some doofus from her husband's b-ball days. Had she said anything to the others about it? Did she even get my email with the link to "his" blog?

I couldn't stand the answer to either one of those questions, so I skipped all the responses and opened the original email from Raina first.

There was nothing written. Just a picture attached.

A positive pregnancy test.

I exhaled, relieved that her focus during her Miami trip would only be on the good news she'd just discovered. There was no way she'd be thinking about me and my fake man, or talking about it with the others.

Congratulations, I typed, adding my response to the others' warm words. That was what all the other emails were, congratulatory messages.

"All that worrying for nothing, Huxley." I exhaled again, even let out a chuckle at the fear that had been thundering through me moments earlier. I pulled up my sent emails and confirmed that my message from last night had gotten through. Yup, I nodded, the link to his blog had successfully been sent to Raina.

I clicked it open myself, reviewed what I had written,

smiled at the good heart of my Malikai.

And then I frowned.

There was a comment at the bottom of his last blog post entry. I'd dated the blog as five months earlier. The comment had been added today, around noon.

Hey there! Sounds like an awesome thing you're doing for the children of Botswana. Do you have any more recent updates? Have you begun building the gymnasium? –GinaBean88

GinaBean88.

The username bothered me. Was this Gina? Like, Gina from work? I swallowed hard, trying to assess the situation. I didn't really want to respond and get another stranger caught up in my fantasy world of lies, but if this was really Gina from work, I *had* to respond.

I logged into the blog and typed the first thing that came to my mind.

Hey, GinaBean88, thanks for asking. The money I've been able to raise and contribute myself has been great, but the price for shipping all the supplies and materials needed to begin construction is very staggering. I set high goals of building a true state of the art facility but had severely underestimated the costs of getting it done. I'm pausing for now so I can focus on my job. I should have enough saved in another year or so to get it started. I'll post pictures once construction begins!

"That will never happen." I smiled as I pressed 'submit.' I was determined to be done with this whole charade by the end of next week. I'd been thinking a gentle break-up, but shoot, I might just have to kill this man off to end it all completely.

Kalypso Delano.

Yeah, it would be a bit of problem if he showed up at the office after I announced the death of Malikai Carter; but I wasn't too worried. In the three years that I'd been working for my company, we'd only had onsite computer repairs twice. The odds that Kalypso would be the assigned agent if and when it went out again were slim to none. He was too much of a jet-setter, meaning to me that he'd probably move on to other jobs and opportunities the moment he could carve one out.

That was the message I told myself as I read and re-read the comment from GinaBean88. The thought that this really could be Gina from work bothered me more than I realized.

I still had other texts and voicemail messages waiting, but this Gina business was about to drive me crazy.

Always Gina.

I pulled up a bunch of social media apps on my phone and searched them for users with that username. Someone who found my blog was likely to have an online presence elsewhere, I figured, and Gina did come off as Internet savvy.

Bingo.

I found a GinaBean88 from Baltimore, Maryland on a videoconferencing app. I clicked on the name to get more details…but the phone started ringing.

Oops! Didn't mean to dial. If this wasn't her, how would I explain? If it was her, how would I explain? I scrambled to hang up, shut it off, make it stop.

"Whew!" I rubbed my temples as the ringing stopped. "That was close." I leaned back in the beanbag chair, glad to have averted a near certain disaster.

But keys rattled in the door and then it was swung open.

"Mom," I groaned. "I told you that key is only for emergencies."

My mother burst in, her eyes narrowed at me. "When you

don't answer my phone calls or texts, it is an emergency." She frowned as she studied me in the beanbag chair. "I've been trying to contact you since last night. It's not like you to avoid me, Berry. Where have you been? Why haven't you answered any of my calls?"

"I'm sorry. My phone was dead and I didn't have my charger with me…at work today."

"Please tell me you didn't go to work looking like that.

I looked back down at the big, brown stain on the collar of my shirt; ran my fingers through the hurried cornrows on top of my head. "Look, if you came all the way here to criticize how I look, um…" What was I supposed to say?

"I didn't come here to say anything to you, Berry. If you'd listened to your messages, you would know that I came here to take you to Wednesday night Bible Study. Fix yourself so we can go." She glared at me like I was a heap of garbage.

Maybe, in some way, I was living up to her low expectations of me.

It hurt to even think that of myself.

"Mom, I don't know that I'm going tonight." Last time it had been because of the fakery of everyone else. Tonight, I had my own fakery issues to deal with.

"Oh, Berry, we've got to go. Evangeline said she was going to have some kind of announcement to make about Vickie's wedding plans. I need you sitting right next to me so she can't get too carried away with herself and her crooked teeth daughter."

"Seriously, Mom, I'm not sure that's a good reason to go to prayer meeting and Bible Study. I just don't see God being pleased with showing off." *Or lying, either.*

My rare show of knowledge on spiritual things must have had my mother feeling some kind of way because she sucked in her cheeks and took a deep breath – and looked ready to blow.

But before she could get one word out, my phone made a noise I'd never heard before.

A notification?

Another message?

I didn't recognize this ding.

Oh, it was the videoconferencing app I'd just shut down.

Someone was calling me back.

GinaBean88.

I read the username as it flashed across the screen.

"Are you going to answer that?" my mother looked annoyed as her foot tapped. How old was I again? Why did my mother insist on talking and treating me like I was twenty years younger?

Or maybe I truly did act twenty years younger.

"I'll check it later." I blinked and stared, as if the alarm of cymbals and drums came from nowhere and meant nothing.

"Oh, please," my mother snatched the phone out from my fingers. "If you don't answer it, it's just going to keep going and going and going, and we don't have time for all of that."

She hit the answer button and shined the camera on me so that I could see my image in a box in a corner of the screen.

The rest of the screen was a full body shot of – you know it - that darn Gina.

"Berry, I thought that was your name and picture. You just called me?" She wore a t-shirt, had a towel wrapped around her hair, and chomped on what looked like a bowl of cereal. Seeing her out of context felt a little unnerving.

"Yeah, I uh…I called…I called to…" Um, not sure what to say here as she chomped and my mother blinked impatiently.

"Who is that?" My mother whispered as she held my phone up to face me.

I shrugged, shook my head, tried to figure out how to get out of this new twist.

"Hey, aren't you supposed to be on your date?" Gina's head tilted to one side as she chomped on another spoonful of cereal.

"My…date?" I raised my eyebrow, saw the sudden spark of interest on my mother's face as she continued holding up my phone. I was happy not to have to explain my call to her, but...uh,oh...

"You have a date?" my mother mouthed. "With who?" Concern, maybe anger, colored her cheeks. Nope, she wasn't going to let me let go of Malikai Carter without a fight.

"Yes, you know, your date at a restaurant in Canton?" Gina moved closer to the screen, as if she was trying to figure out who else was there and where I was. "Isn't that where you and Kal are supposed to be? It's so great that we got to meet him today."

My mother's foot started tapping, her eyes widened. "What is she talking about?" she whispered.

"Wait – is someone with you?" Gina gasped. "Him? Are you at home? I'm sorry, am I interrupting?" Her mouth dropped open again before forming into a devilish grin.

"Interrupting what?" my mother's whisper was harsh, but still out of Gina's earshot. "What is she talking about? HIM? As in Malikai? You have a date with Malikai Carter? He's in town?" She started looking around my apartment, as if he was about to step out of the closet, the bathroom, or my bedroom.

"No," I whispered back, "I mean…" I quickly lowered my voice to ensure that Gina couldn't hear. "Look, I'll explain in a moment."

"Berry, I'm not going to hold you." Gina winked and smiled. "Sounds like you're busy. Just keep us posted and tell us all what happened at work tomorrow. We are all excited for you."

"This is one of your co-workers? Wait, your co-workers

met him and I haven't?" My mother looked astounded as she continued holding the phone to face me.

"Wait, are you still going to try and go on a ski trip with him? I thought that was your plan." Gina's questions came out the same time as my mother's.

"Yes, I mean…" I forgot to whisper as I answered my mother. Gina heard my "yes" too.

"Oh, Berry, that's awesome. When are you going? You don't think it's too soon? But then again you two already seem to be getting to know each other pretty well." She winked again.

"I'm confused," my mother's whispers grew louder. "What is she talking about? Are you planning a trip? What's going on? Where is he? I want to meet him."

Too much going on. My eyes bounced back and forth between the two of them as they continued to speak at once, Gina from my phone, my mother standing behind it.

"Gina, I'm going to go now." I had to end this call like two minutes ago.

"Wait, right now? You're leaving for the ski trip right now?" Gina threw her hands over her mouth as her eyes widened even more. "Are you sure about this? What about work?"

"What is she talking about, Berry." My mother's whisper became frantic. "Are you going somewhere with this guy? I haven't met him yet."

"Gina, I'll talk with you later." *Can I please just get off the phone?* Was there another way to say goodbye?

"Make sure you text one of us during every step of your journey so someone knows where you are. Better yet, use this app so I can see that you're okay. Malikai seems like a genuinely nice guy, but you can never be too careful."

"Gina, I've gotta go. Bye." I waved into the camera and reached for it to shut it off, but my mother turned it around to face her.

"Hi," she beamed into the lens, a plastic grin on her face. "I'm Frederica Jenkins, Berry's mother. Did I hear correctly that you and Berry's co-workers met her new friend, Malikai Carter?"

"Oh, we did. He stopped at our office today and he is amazing."

"I can't believe he's in town and I didn't get to meet him myself." I didn't miss my mother's glare at me and then her smile back at Gina. "Berry told me a little about him, but I wanted to meet him in person to make sure he is who he claims to be."

"Oh, he seems like the real deal, Ms. Jenkins. We're all excited for Berry."

Wait a minute. Were these two grown women giggling and carrying on like schoolgirls? What had I created? Really? All this because they thought I had a man?

I wanted to roll my eyes, but I knew more pressing matters were at hand, such as, HOW DO I KEEP THIS FROM FURTHER EXPLODING?

"Well, I thought Berry would be on her date with him right now." Gina continued as I wanted to evaporate into the atmosphere. Too late to come clean? How to come clean? Did I really have a dumb smile on my face during this whole exchange?

"Oh, Berry, were you supposed to be going out? What's going on?"

Now, both my mother and my nemesis stared at me, waiting for a response, an explanation.

"Well, I…yes, we were going to meet, but then…well… I know it sounds crazy, but we really did start talking about skiing…so…it's kind of impromptu, but…"

"No. I know you're not going on a ski trip with a man you just met. I'm all about the excitement, but I don't know about this." My mother looked at me like I was crazy.

She just didn't know.

"Berry, you said something about a friend from college having a lodge where you could stay safely. I'm assuming that's still your plan, if you're really going through with this?"

Gina, Gina, Gina.

"I don't like it." My mother narrowed her eyes. "Are you talking about Keisha or Leilani? Or is it Meeka? Those are the only friends of yours I remember from your college days. One of them owns a ski lodge now? Really?"

"Oh, it's Meeka," I blurted without thinking. Meeka was such a free spirit, I knew my mother wouldn't put it past her to move to a snow-covered mountain somewhere and set up shop.

"Meeka?" Now, Gina's eyes narrowed. "I thought you said it was a friend named Shaniqua?"

I didn't like the way her eyes narrowed. I could see the questions, the doubt that was always trying to battle its way back into our conversations. Maybe that's why I became so insistent on making this sound believable.

"Right, her name is Shaniqua. Meeka Shaniqua." Even I knew that sounded ridiculous. However, I had no choice but to carry on. "Since she moved out that way, she's been going by her middle name because it flowed better with her business name: Shaniqua's Chalet." This was so stupid. Really? Did I really expect either one of them or anyone else to believe this foolishness?

"Berry, you didn't say anything about packing up for a ski trip when I came in here talking about going to church tonight." I could tell my mother wanted to cross her arms, but she was still holding out my phone.

"Of course, I didn't say anything." I kept talking off the top of my head. "I knew you wouldn't approve. He's a stranger to you and, well, it wouldn't sound too Christian of me to be sharing a room with a man who's not my husband. I knew you would have concerns with this scenario."

"Yes, I do. You are grown woman, but you are still my child and –"

"–And –" I cut in – "that's why I'm staying at Shaniqua's Chalet. She has five bedrooms so we'll be in separate rooms on different floors from each other. She'll be there to keep an eye on me for safety, and some of her guy friends will be around for safety sake, too, in case Malikai really has another agenda. I don't think he does, though. It's a quick getaway, but we'll really get to know each other better."

"I mean, does having separate rooms really matter now?" Gina.

I heard her question, but thankfully, or maybe, terribly, my mother had a question of her own.

"Wait, where is this lodge?" My mother's face wrinkled up.

"Aspen, Colorado."

"Oh, heck no." She shook her head.

"Mom, you've got to trust me. I've planned everything around my safety."

"Berry," Gina chimed in, "I'm on my computer and I don't see a 'Shaniqua's Chalet' in Aspen."

Gina and her darn Internet searches. Could this girl just leave *Google* alone?

Nope, and you won't find it anywhere online either." I spoke fast. "She runs a very select, exclusive place with visitors only referred to her by word of mouth. She's a single woman living out in the middle of the mountains. Unless you are referred to her personally, she won't even return your call for reservations.

"Well, I guess that's smart. That Meeka was a wild child, but I do remember thinking she had a good brain on her." My mother looked pleased. "What happened to her fashion design dreams?"

"That's how she ended up there." The lies continued. Now, I hadn't talked to Meeka in three or four years, but with her penchant to travel to off-road destinations, who was to say she wasn't running a ski lodge in Aspen? Shoot, the last time I'd talked to her she was considering starting a retreat center in Arizona and was emailing me pictures of adobe buildings for sale. So, a ski lodge, I guess, wasn't far off from the realm of possibilities.

Oh, the lies I wanted to believe myself.

"Meeka started working for a company that focused on winter clothing and she found her niche in snow suits and outerwear. The chalet was an outgrowth of her interests. I think she still does some designing, but, to tell you the truth, I'm not completely sure." My show of doubt seemed to make my story more believable. I exhaled as my mother and Gina both nodded.

"Sounds like you've put a lot of thought into this." My mother tapped her lip. "And you're leaving tonight?"

"We didn't go on our date as planned so I could come home and pack."

"He does seem like a nice person, Ms. Jenkins." Gina piped in. "I've been looking him up online and I came across his blog where he's been detailing his charity work in Africa."

"Yeah, I –" *Oops, caught myself.* I'd almost said, 'Yeah, I wrote you back. Did you check?' I quickly course-corrected. "Yeah, I think he's awesome. He's compassionate and giving."

"Well, although I wanted to meet him first, I guess I'm excited about him for you. I keep telling you, Berry, that God is saying he's The One. I respect the fact that he's respecting the boundaries you've laid out for him with this trip. That says a lot. I only have two requests." My mother beamed. "You better stay in touch with this video app which I'm going to get you to download on my phone right now."

"Of course," I nodded furiously. "As soon as I meet him at the airport, I'll let you both know."

"And second," my mother talked right over me, "Let me take you to the airport so I can at least meet him for a moment."

"Uh..."

"What time is your flight, Berry?"

"I, uh..."

"Berry," Gina was back to her cereal crunching and chomping, "I'm going to go so you can pack and work out the details with your mom." Here she was talking to me like we were best friends and this is the first time we'd even talked to each other outside of work.

And this "newfound friendship" was all based on a lie.

Jesus, is it too late for my soul's salvation? I had a big ole smile on my face as I disconnected the phone and tried to figure out how to finagle my way out of this new, sticky spot.

My mother was going to be outraged when the truth came out.

No, *if* the truth came out.

I couldn't let it. Forget another week. Poor Malikai was not going to survive the next few days, I decided. A lot can go wrong on a ski trip.

What kind of monster had I become?

I swallowed hard as I smiled and prepared to tell my mother another bold-faced lie.

"Mom, I appreciate the offer for a ride, but my flight's not until later tonight. This was such a last minute, impromptu trip that I had to accept what was left. It's going to be a while before I finish packing, plus I'm going to be running to the store to pick up some things."

"The store?"

"Yes, um, I have to...you know...get a snow suit...and..." What did people get for ski trips? I had no idea. "Oh, and some new boots. And toiletries and stuff. You know, travel-sized lotion, etc."

"You've got to do all that and pack? What time is your flight again?"

"I don't remember the exact time. I have to check my email again."

"Well, I'm taking you so driving around is one less thing you'll have to worry about. Pack what you have now, and then we'll go to one of those sporting goods stores to get the suit and boots and all."

"Mom, no."

"Berry, I'm taking you and that is all. End of discussion. Now, where is your suitcase?"

Her arms were crossed, her feet squared and planted. There was no getting out of this one.

Unless I come clean and 'fess up.

Yes, I knew that was the reasonable, logical, righteous thing to do, but my momma was missing Wednesday night Bible Study and Prayer Service for this foolishness. What's a girl to do? If I told her the truth now, there was liable to be death and destruction in my living room.

My mother would absolutely kill me if she learned that I knowingly and willingly lied. To her face. At church. And repeatedly. And then the people at church? Sister Evangeline? I shuddered at the very idea of my mother trying to explain to Evangeline Willow that I was psychotic or delusional or just plain evil for pretending to have the perfect boyfriend and a whirlwind romance.

"Your suitcase, Berry?" My mother's head tilted to one side. "You need to start packing, right? And didn't you say you also need to check when your flight leaves? I want to get there early enough to at least say hello to Mr. Carter."

Yeah, that.

Meeting him.

In person.

I'd cross that bridge when necessary. For the moment though…

"Okay, Mom. Just sit tight for a moment and I'll throw some things together."

"Nope. I'm helping you. I know your style and there is no way you are going to blow this once in a lifetime opportunity by looking homely on the ski slopes." She headed to my room. I heard my closet door screech open. Huxley burst out of my room and ran down the hallway.

Chapter 20

Chicago. Dallas. Orlando.

Those were the three transfer cities I had to choose from if I expected to get to Aspen, Colorado before dawn. No matter which route I took, however, the destination was the same.

Insanity.

Yup, the only way I could explain my choices and actions right now was that I was having some type of mental health breakdown.

Sitting in the passenger seat of my mother's Cadillac while she ran around a sporting goods store, I tried in vain to remember how and why this madness started. I was in too deep now to wave it all away.

What color ski goggles do you want? A text from my mother popped up on my cell phone screen. There were other messages and notifications waiting from others, I remembered, but just the idea of going through them sickened me.

My gut told me there was nothing good waiting for me in the rest of the waiting messages.

Red, I typed onto my cell phone screen. I re-read my mother's text to which I was responding. *No, yellow and pink,* I added. I hoped she never found any. I hoped that color combination didn't exist. I didn't want my mother to spend another cent on this elaborate scam I couldn't seem to end.

Honestly, my plan had been to lay low in my apartment and hide there for a couple of days, while on my supposed ski trip. But with all the time, money, energy and mouth my mother had expended, I felt like I had no choice but to actually go somewhere. The alternative – telling the truth – felt lethal as I eyed the rows of shopping bags piling up in the back seat. Each new name brand, plastic bag pushed the truth further and further out of reach. How could I not board an actual plane with the amount of money my mother was putting out?

"God, I'm sorry." My cell phone still in hand, I went back to the screen I'd pulled up before my mother's text came.

Plane tickets.

I used my credit card yet again while my mother was in the first store. I'd told her I needed to stay in the car to finalize my trip plans. Good thing I'd set up Huxley's self-feeder and cleaned out his litter box. With all that my mother was buying for me, I felt like I at least owed it to her to actually go to Aspen for a few days.

I know.

I'm a terrible daughter and a terrible person. I deserved to go further into debt booking last minute flights for what I was putting my mom through. As horrible as I felt, I tried to comfort myself in knowing that the snowsuit and boots would be put to actual use.

Even if by myself.

And, I promised myself, I was going to pay it all back. Every cent my mother spent on this sham would come back to her.

I'm really spending my own money, I told myself as I stared again at the row of bags that lined the back seat. I would take care of every dime and penny.

After I killed him off.

Who was I kidding? I was truly a despicable person…

Chicago.

I locked in the round-trip ticket which included a layover at O'Hare Airport both coming and going.

"Oh, my Lord, what am I doing?" Tears filled my eyes as

the enormity of the situation settled on me anew. "I'm going into debt over this to spare hurting my mother with the truth, and why? Why exactly am I in this situation?" I grabbed one of the plastic shopping bags from the back seat and dumped it. A travel-sized toothbrush, toothpaste, and deodorant bounced onto the floor. I took the emptied bag, held it up to my lips, breathed in, breathed out. Wasn't that how you treated hyperventilation?

"Okay, Berry, unlock the door!" My mother's voice boomed from nearly two car lengths away. Her arms were filled with more bags and her face was filled with pure joy.

"Let me get those for you, mom," I hopped out of the car and grabbed what I could to add to the back seat. New outfits, dress boots, snow boots, scarves, hats. "Mom, really, you didn't have to get all of this. Remember, I already packed. I just needed the snow suit and we got that at the first store."

"Oh, hush." My mother still beamed as she jumped into the driver's seat and started the car. "I saw what you packed, and, believe me, you needed a little more wardrobe options for this trip."

"Mom, are you serious? You're doing all of this and you… don't even know this guy I'm supposed to be traveling with."

"Berry, God spoke to me a dream last night and confirmed that this is the one for you. I believe it wholeheartedly. I know this seems like a lot, but faith without works is dead. Your mother is just working it out, amen?" The giggle she tacked on at the end made me wonder who was having the bigger sanity issues, me or her?

"I haven't even tried this stuff on. We're going to have to take it all back. Just leave these bags in the car, and I'll return everything on Monday."

"Nonsense, honey. I gave birth to you. I know what size you wear and what clothes and shoes you need. You are going to have an awesome time, and a holy one, at that." She gave me 'The Look' like I was twelve years old, but then followed it up with a smile. "Berry, I love that he respected your wishes to stay at your friend's place and in separate rooms. That says a lot about his character. This is really good, Berry, and I'm so happy and honored to share part of this journey with you. Falling in love is a precious thing, and that's really what you deserve right now."

What I deserve.

I could think of a few things I deserved at the moment. Love and new clothes and my mother's approval were not any of them.

"So, you said your flight leaves at 11:30, right?"

"Yes." I couldn't even fake a smile.

"Well, when we get to the departures gate, I'll put my blinkers on and we'll dump all the old stuff out of your suitcase into the trunk, and put all the new bags in. That will give some time for Malikai to come out and meet me without us having to worry about being shooed off by the security personnel."

"You've got it all figured out." I swallowed.

"Of course, Berry. You did already text him to let him know to come out and meet me, right?"

"Yes, of course." I looked down at my phone, glad at the realization that this would be an easy hurdle to cross. My mother wouldn't be able to stay at the drop-off point forever, and as far as I was concerned, Malikai would be stuck in a security line somewhere in the airport.

Like I said, easy.

I settled back in my seat as my mother switched on an AM gospel radio station.

"Amen," she murmured as the smile stayed on her face. She began humming along in her rich alto voice and my eyelids began to get weighty. We were about ten minutes away from

BWI airport.

Her phone ringing jolted me awake.

"This darn system. I never know how to use it." My mother pressed a button and her phone system switched to the car stereo. My eyes began to close again, but the name on the dashboard's caller ID jumped out at me.

Davis.

My eyes opened fully as I swallowed hard, sat up, and prepared myself for whatever words were going to come out of the stereo system.

"Hello," my mother practically sung the greeting. Way too happy.

"Mom," Davis spoke over the same AM gospel station. He must be driving the church van home from prayer meeting. "We missed you tonight. Everything okay?"

"Oh, yes. Was it a good service? Was Evangeline Willow there?"

I could tell from the smile that curled up on my mother's lips that nothing was going to break her good mood. She was ready and prepared for anything anyone at church could say, even, especially, Sister Willow.

"Yes, she was there, but listen," Davis continued. "Have you talked to Berry? I've texted her a few times and left a couple of messages, but she hasn't gotten back to me."

I looked down at my phone. Notification symbols were all over my home page, but apart from the comment Gina had posted on Malikai Carter's blog, and the chain of emails from my church friends congratulating Raina's new pregnancy, I hadn't bothered to see what other messages were waiting.

I hadn't talked to Davis since that ugly dinner meeting with Li Yan. I figured that his silence meant our beef was over and he'd moved on to another matter, another girl.

What if he hadn't?

My heart skipped two beats as my mother looked over at me and grinned. "Berry's right here with me." Her sing-song voice remained. "We're on our way to the airport."

"Hi, Davis," I sounded out at my mother's beckoning nod.

"What's going on at the airport? Are you two going somewhere?" Irritation spiked his tone. "Nobody tells me anything."

"Davis –" I jumped in, wanting to say something, anything to keep the conversation from going where I feared it would go. "I've been meaning to ask if you want to go to a Wizards game. We're due for a DC trip, big bro."

"It's easy for me to get tickets from some of the people who hang out at the club where I DJ, but I'm trying to figure out what trip you're going on with Mom right now."

"Oh, *I'm* not going anywhere, Davis." My mother was all smiles. "I'm taking Berry to the airport so she can go on a well-supervised ski trip with Malikai Carter."

"So, he is real." It wasn't a question. Davis said it like it was a bona fide fact. "Berry, I don't understand why you said he wasn't."

"Davis, what are you talking about?" My mother frowned. "Berry never said he wasn't real. Her co-workers even met him today."

"What? That's messed up, Berry. Why would you tell me he's not real and not return any of my phone calls or messages this week?"

"You called?" My voice was weak. I felt like throwing up. I looked at the bags piled up in the backseat and looked down at all the notification symbols that filled the home screen of my phone.

"Yes, I called. I wanted to talk to you some more about that company he works for, but you've been blowing me off all week."

"No, Davis, it's not like that at all. I can explain everything." *Could I really?*

"You're phony, Berry. I get it. You're determined to make sure I never get a break. No matter what I plan or how hard I work, you still act like you are entitled to be the family's only success story."

"Davis, no, listen –"

"No, both of you listen." My mother no longer smiled. "You two are grown adults. I refuse to listen to you bicker and argue like you're teenagers. Now, Davis, I'm sure Berry had her reasons for telling you Malikai wasn't real, but bottom line is that he is. I'm about to meet him, and I'm proud of both of you."

"Mom," I heard myself say as I braced myself for the hurricane volcano tsunami earthquake that was about to explode inside that Cadillac as I prepared to come clean. *I'm going to tell her the truth, right now.*

But Davis cut me off.

"Berry, look, I'm sorry for getting on you like that. I'm sure you have your reasons for not wanting me to get involved with your new friend. I get it. You're trying to get a relationship established and you don't want your big brother interfering. But I need you to understand this is purely a business move that will benefit us all. Please listen to my messages when you have the chance and then get back to me with your thoughts about what I'm proposing. I'm going to go for now. I'm parking the van back at the church lot."

He hung up and that was that.

"Berry, go ahead and let Malikai know we're almost at the departure gate."

It was as if that whole conversation with Davis hadn't happened. My mother had moved back to her happy place and the fantasy was back to reality.

My terrible, lying reality.

We were at BWI, heading directly to the terminal.

I should tell her I'm sick.

I should tell her I'm scared.

I should tell her I'm lying.

I should tell her something, anything to turn around.

But…all those clothes, and bags, and boots in the back seat made me feel worse, like I needed to put out my own money to actually take this trip since my mother had already invested so much of hers.

I promise, I'll pay her back every cent the moment I can.

How on earth could I come clean now? My plane reservations were sitting on the screen of my phone. My co-worker was probably spreading the news of my trip as I sat there.

Nope, couldn't do it. Wasn't time to come clean yet. Not like this. It would make me look like a complete fool at a minimum; hurt too many people at a maximum.

And that was a pretty high and likely maximum.

Stick to the original plan, Berry, I told myself. Let everyone off the hook easy by ending it in the coming days. Sure, there would be grief over his sudden death, but grief over what could have been seemed a better alternative than wrath over what never was. At least I'd be able to cross something off my bucket list. A ski trip. Whatever. I wanted to kick myself two times over for even bringing up Aspen to anyone. I knew nothing about the place.

"Okay, mom, I'm ready. I'm sending him a text now to meet us here while we switch my luggage around." I smiled at my mother before punching some random keys on my cell phone.

My mother was already getting out of the car. She popped the trunk and began unzipping my suitcases, rearranging my clothes and packed supplies.

"Where is he?" I frowned and narrowed my eyes at the terminal after a few moments had passed. "He should have been here by now."

My mother said nothing, just glanced up and around.

"I'm going to text him again and see where he is," I said a few minutes later.

"Yes, do that. That officer is looking over at us. We're not going to be able to stall much longer."

"I'll let him know." I typed again, carefully holding my phone just out of my mother's view. This time, I checked into my flight as I pretended to text. Finally, "Oh, Mom." I shook my head. "He was randomly stopped by a TSA agent since he got out of line to head over to us. There's no way he's going to get out here to meet you before you're asked to move. I'm sorry."

"Oh, I'm sorry, too." My mother didn't hide her disappointment. "I really wanted to meet him before you took off." She shook her head. "Oh, well, it wasn't time yet. It's all in God's hands, so I can't even worry about it." She looked up at me, a weak smile on her face, sadness in her eyes.

Wow, this whole charade would truly break my mother's heart if she ever learned the truth.

"Berry," she reached out a hand to touch my cheek, "I love you. I know you'll have a great time. I'm proud of you for planning this trip in such a safe, virtuous way. Have fun, enjoy, and take lots of pictures. Send some to me so I can see that all is well, like my God is telling me it will be." She pecked my cheek before turning toward the driver's side of her car.

"I will." *Pictures!* I hadn't thought of that. Ugh. "Love you, Mom. I'll be back on Sunday morning. I'll get a cab so you don't have to miss church."

"Don't you worry about that. I'll be here." She smiled

again as she opened her door.

"Yes, of course." I smiled back and then adjusted my carry-on bag and rolling suitcase to prepare to enter the airport.

This was pure ridiculousness.

"Oh, and Berry," my mother called out just before sitting down in her car, "do me a favor and let Davis in. Whatever it is he's talking about, give it a chance. Malikai Carter might just be the blessing our whole family needs. Keep an open mind, okay?"

"Yes, of course," I repeated, the stupid smile still sitting on my face. "I'll check Davis' messages once I get a chance."

"Great. Proud of you for looking out for your big brother. Bye, now." She blew a kiss, got into her car, and joined the other vehicles honking and stopping in the departure lanes.

I watched until she disappeared around a bend and then I headed for the terminal entrance. "Why didn't I make this trip somewhere tropical?" I sighed to myself. I was going to have to call out for the rest of the week. This whole fiasco was going to eat into my hard earned, but limited paid vacation time. "This is my vacation. And I hate cold weather."

Figures, but I deserved to be miserable right about now. There was no justifying my evil deeds.

"Hey, you have a flight out tonight too, huh?"

Huh? Was someone talking to me? I turned around to see who just tapped my shoulder.

"I almost didn't recognize you, but good to see you again. And you look like your day has improved. By the way, your suggestion for Canton was spot on. Thanks!"

He walked past me, heading toward the security screening line, but my feet, my throat, my brain completely froze.

Kalypso Delano.

Though I had a slight recollection of him saying that he

was flying to Cleveland tonight, I'd never expected to see him ever again.

The fact that he was real, and present, and believed to be my new man by my coworkers, but already claimed by a real fiancée, troubled me on so many levels and disturbed my already tormented sense of peace.

I knew then that the colloquial fan was spinning above my head and the contents of my rumbling bowels were ready to hit it.

I knew that even before I ran into him again on the other side of the security line.

He walked down the corridor toward the same gate area where my plane took off.

And the woman who was his real fiancée now walked beside him.

She saw me even before I saw her.

"What are you doing here?" I heard her ask and saw her eyes roll before I registered the magnitude of my self-made disaster.

The khakis were gone, the cleaning apron removed, but the perfected coiffure was still in place.

Afro-girl.

Part 4:
#BerryWrong

Chapter 21

"What are you doing here?" Afro-girl asked again. Her hand was locked in Kal's as the three of us rode a moving walkway.

Of all people.

Of all places.

Of all things.

"I…have a trip, well, of course. I mean, we…are in an airport…and we all are…flying somewhere." I tacked a smile onto the end of my stammered speech, trying to make sense of what thee heck was happening. *They're together? That beautiful man is with the moody cleaning lady?* "Where are you off to?" I realized I was staring. Had to say something to not look as crazy as I felt.

"Jamaica," the young woman giggled as she squeezed Kal's hand and smiled up at him. "This is so last minute, but so necessary."

"Yeah," Kal smiled at her as the three of us stepped off the walkway. "I was supposed to fly to Cleveland tonight, but over dinner we both realized how stressed out we are with wedding plans and our jobs, so we decided to just drop it all, forget everything and make our own way."

"We're getting married. Now. No fuss, no frills, no family or friends to tell us what to wear or what kind of flowers to get." The girl shook her head. "I've been so stressed out lately I realized my entire attitude has been stank. I can't live like that. This is what we have to do. I've never been happier – freeing myself from everybody's timetable and expectations."

Freeing myself from everybody's timetable and expectations. Her words haunted me.

I'd never realized how straight her teeth were. I guess because I'd never really seen her smile. She must have really been stressed and now she must have really been okay.

"Wow, congrats." I looked around for my gate. "I didn't even realize you two were together."

"Well, that's good. We didn't want our relationship to be obvious so we took extra steps like getting on the elevator separately, not talking much in the office building. Can't take any chances."

We'd stopped moving. The gate for their flight to Montego Bay was just behind them.

"Why the secrecy? Just curious." I really was. Was this big time, cross-country traveling computer pro embarrassed to be seen with the cleaning lady or something? And she tolerated that?

"Conflict of interest, really." The girl shrugged.

"What do you mean?" Now, my eyebrow was raised.

"The contract my business has with the office building managers specifically states I can't refer close family, friends, or associates to other businesses in the building, and, well, your computers are fixed aren't they?" She winked.

"As are the ones in office suites 907, 1231, and 608. My girl's been getting me business all throughout the building. She keeps giving me a reason to come back to Baltimore and see her." Kal nodded. "Hush, hush."

"Wait, *your* business?" I felt my other eyebrow rise as I looked at the woman and latched on to something she'd just said.

"Uh, yes, my cleaning business." The eye roll came back. "Oh, you thought I was just working for The Man, cleaning up his mess?"

"Oh, no, I mean, there's nothing wrong with, I mean, I didn't realize that–"

"–That I'm the CEO, founder, and president of The Ultimate Office Cleaners, LLC and that I have twenty-four employees who are the cleaning specialists for four different downtown office buildings?"

"Wow, that's really impressive. I had no idea. I just see you with your cleaning apron and your cart and–"

"–And that's exactly why I proudly wear my uniform and why I spend the first half of my day modeling excellence for my workers, cleaning right beside them. There's no shame in the work I do, with the business I run, or the tasks we get done. I have a bachelor's in art history and a master's in business administration, but if I ever got caught up in appearances, or worrying about what others think about me, I would have missed my opportunity to own my own business. And exactly who are you again?" She crossed her arms, standing next to her luggage for Jamaica and her delicious fiancé. A rock bigger than Celeste's gleamed from her ring finger.

I guess she took it off at work.

Caught up in appearances.

Worrying about what others think.

"I'm sorry. I meant no disrespect. And you're right. We've never been officially introduced to each other." I wanted to lighten the mood, change the subject. Leave. "I'm Berry. Berry Jenkins."

And my officemates think your fiancé is my new man. I swallowed hard as I extended a hand.

"I am NaTosha Lipton." She glanced down at my hand, looked back up at me with narrowed eyes, stared at me like she could see right through me.

I took a step back.

"Ladies, ladies," Malikai, I mean, Kal finally spoke up.

"Look, we're all here to go on trips and have a good time. Tosha, you promised to let the stress and attitude go, and Berry, after whatever kind of morning you had earlier today when I first saw you, you deserve a break too, right? Can you two just call a truce and we all move forward with our respective trips?"

He had an easy smile that I had to force myself to look away from. Why did this man have to be so pretty? And why did he have to be with her?

Whatever thoughts she had running through her mind must have been just as inflammatory as the ones I had because her face was still wrinkled up into a frown.

But then her face softened.

"I'm getting married," she spoke softly, "and I will not let the devil steal my joy. Come on, Kal. They're about to board." She turned away.

Wait, did this chick just call me the devil?

Well, I wasn't exactly an innocent party, I had to admit. And she really had no idea of the depths I'd sunk to.

God, how do I make all things right? The smile on my face quivered. "NaTosha, congratulations." I called after her. "I'm happy for you. Enjoy your trip." I bit my lip, shrugged. Still felt wrong on so many levels.

She paused, turned back around. "Thanks. I hope you enjoy your trip as well." A slight smile.

"Here, let me get a picture of you two together before you board, the before picture before you become Mr. and Mrs.," I offered.

NaTosha smiled and fished for her cell phone as a new group of passengers were called to board their plane.

"I'll just take it on mine and share it with you. Your pre-wedding photo." There wasn't really time for discussion as I held up my cell phone and snapped a shot of the two standing next to each other, smiles overtaking their faces.

Did I mention how fine that man was?

"All right, I got it." I lowered my phone. "Your flight is boarding. I don't want you to miss it, so go. I'm sure I'll see you around the office when you get back. I'll share it with you then."

"Sounds like a plan," her smile continued, though I didn't miss the caution in her eyes just before they turned back and hustled to the gate.

The caution alarmed me.

What came up on my phone alarmed me even more.

Chapter 22

Text me when you land, but I also found Meeka's phone number in case I don't hear from you.

I read and re-read the text from my mother as I boarded my flight to Chicago. Shoot, I didn't even have Meeka's phone number anymore. How was I supposed to fix this? I hoped that girl with all her free-spirited moves and whims had her number changed three or four times over since whenever my mom had gotten it from me.

My brain wrestled with reality and possibilities during the entire flight and my layover in Chicago. I needed to have this planned out before I landed, because I was certain my mother would try to reach out to Meeka if she didn't hear from me in a reasonable time frame after I touched down in Aspen.

I probably really didn't need to fly all the way to Aspen, but it had felt like the right thing to do initially since my mother had spent so much on me. Plus, I needed to kill Malikai off and I needed real ski slope pictures to pull my plan off.

Two more days and this nightmare will be over, I told myself as the plane prepared for takeoff.

But if my mother tried to call Meeka… Or if Kal shows back up at the office with NaTosha…

Okay, focus on diverting one disaster at a time, I resolved.

By the time the plane touched down, I knew what I had to do about my mother. Standing alone in the terminal, I lifted my phone up, took a selfie. I studied the pensive look on my face, the seriousness in my eyes. I took another picture, full smile, brighter eyes.

We're here. Meeka says hi. Don't worry about calling her. I'm not 2 years old. I'll check in often myself. Thx. Love you.

I looked at what I'd written. Then, I swallowed and looked at the picture I planned to attach. No, not my selfie, but the new picture I'd just created with my selfie. I hadn't had the benefit of *Photoshop,* but I must say that my phone's photo editing system was pretty darn good. My selfie in the plane terminal? Yeah, I merged it with the picture I'd taken of Kal and NaTosha – minus NaTosha. Yup, I put myself right over top of her. The final product looked nearly flawless. I'd only included our faces, my head tilted toward his. The background was a necessary and acceptable blur.

Sending the picture was a necessary and acceptable risk.

It was only going to my mother who would never even meet him. I'd figure something out to address the potential of him showing up at my job. At the moment, I needed to make this "trip" work.

I had an elaborate death to plan.

First things first.

I didn't know a thing about Aspen, ski lodges, slopes, or anything of that nature. I had no idea that the room I'd *Googled* and booked while waiting for my first plane was two hours away from Aspen's airport and that the shuttle that would get me there would cost nearly a hundred dollars and not the $25 I'd budgeted for a cab ride.

I didn't realize that the room, after taxes, fees, and some other nonrefundable incidentals, would run me nearly two thousand dollars for the three nights I needed it.

I also didn't know that it was spring break season and

concerts by rock bands and country bands I'd never heard of would be performing every night, all night to drunken crowds.

I knew nothing about ski lifts and trails and snow reports and mountain information.

What I did know was that I was maxed out, overspent, in too deep.

And stupid.

And for what?

"Jesus," I mumbled, half praying, half begging as I gathered my luggage and headed to where the shuttle was supposed to meet me. It was cold, late, wet, and snowy.

And I was miserable.

And for what?

He is too cute. I'm so happy for you, baby. Have fun.

My mother's text dinged through.

Fun.

Whatever.

This trip was an insane mistake. I knew it, felt it, and would just have to deal with it.

I thought about the other messages waiting for me from my brother that I still had yet to check.

Whatever.

I didn't feel like dealing with any of it, truth be told.

I shut my phone off, not caring what I missed or didn't miss. I was at the bus stop and a line of drunk co-eds were locked arm in arm singing songs from The *Wizard of Oz* while the shuttle parked in front of us.

"God, what have I done?" I shook my head as a pimple-faced, pasty-looking frat boy put his arm around me and sung a sloppy and slurred rendition of something related to rainbows and tigers and monkeys.

Oh my.

I headed straight to the back of the bus in an attempt to have some peace and quiet for the two-hour ride. Daylight was just breaking and, with the exception of a few zzz's I'd managed on the plane rides, I'd been up nearly all night.

And this was just the beginning of my ill-planned ski misadventure.

"Rosa said you can sit in the front of the bus," pimple-face bellowed from the front seat back to me. The whole bus of intoxicated college students roared with laughter.

A black girl with short braids who sat with the group laughed the loudest. "Jeremy, you are too funny."

I rolled my eyes, prepared to shut them to get a little bit more sleep before the day fully began. Just before I did so, though, I didn't miss the man who got on our shuttle bus last.

He didn't look college-aged. He didn't look drunk. He didn't look that attractive. And he was looking straight at me.

Gave me all kinds of creeps.

Yup, Malikai's death was going to be quick and easy and over with before the day was done.

I was so ready to go back home and get my life back on track.

Chapter 23

Brown plaid jacket. Dark eyebrows. Brown hair swept to one side. Crisp, blue eyes.

The white male who had gotten on the bus last caught my attention not only because of his rugged appearance – he looked more logger than skier – but because he stared right at me before he took his seat at the front of the bus. Something about him disturbed me, though I couldn't figure out exactly what it was. Maybe *the way* he stared at me when he boarded the bus?

As I sat in the back with my eyes closed, debating my next move, I could not get out of my thoughts those crisp, blue eyes that had penetrated mine. Maybe because I was alone in a city I'd never visited before, and he looked like someone off a *Dateline* special? For all the wrong I'd been doing lately, seemed like I'd been getting away with it all. I hadn't been struck by lightning yet. Was this man the dark cloud before a violent storm?

"C stop!" The bus driver's yell woke me up. I hadn't realized that I'd fallen asleep and that two hours had passed. The bus was nearly empty as the shuttle was almost finished its rounds. The man at the front of the bus was one of the passengers who must have gotten off at a previous stop. I exhaled, aware that his piercing stare had permeated what little sleep I'd just had.

"You need help with your bags, ma'am?" The bus driver was anxious to loop back around. All the other remaining passengers had already disembarked as I fumbled around with my carry-on, still trying to fully wake up. I felt like I was in a fog.

No, a mist.

A cold mist filled the mountain where the lodge was located.

I didn't like it.

"Thanks for the hand." I offered a couple of dollar bills to the driver who hadn't waited for my response and simply grabbed the rest of my luggage from the bus storage area and laid it all on the snow-packed ground.

"No problem." His voice was gruff as he took the money and hopped back on the bus. A thick plume of exhaust washed over me, leaving me coughing as I tried to shake off my sleep fog.

I was alone.

The remaining passengers had already disappeared on the winding path that led to the main entrance. I picked up my suitcases and started toward the entrance myself, my footsteps crunching in the snow. I enjoyed the quiet of the morning, anxious for the comfort of my reserved bed, knowing that I would need a couple more hours of sleep before I could work out the next steps of my plan.

I was almost at the entrance when a second set of footsteps caught my ear. A chill went over me without me even turning around. I quickened my steps to get to the registration desk and even then, I didn't look behind me. So unsettled was I, that I didn't flinch as the attendant explained that there was an additional $50 per day resort fee and a $500 refundable deposit that would be retuned at check-out to cover any incidental fees, room credits, and cleaning expenses.

"Spring break, you know? We take extra precautions because of the parties." The girl at the desk smiled as I signed off on all the paperwork, bracing myself to turn around and see who was behind me in line.

Yeah, it was him.

Brown plaid jacket dude.

Not sure why he gave me the heebie-jeebies, especially since this time he hadn't even looked my way when I did finally turn around. His attention was on the resort guide he had open in his hands. I needed a copy myself.

I was not comforted to learn that the large resort had several different lodging areas – sprawling chalets to condos and townhouses to plain old log cabins – and the one I'd paid nearly two thousand dollars for was of the plain old log cabin variety.

"I see you opted for our rustic experience." The desk attendant smiled as she checked all my signatures on the security deposit and advanced fees page, and then pointed to what looked like a pile of sticks on an expansive map on the wall behind her. "If you go through the doors to your left, one of our assistants will be happy to escort you to your cabin. Here's your helmet." She whisked out what looked like a black bowling ball, but was really a snowmobile helmet.

"Um…." I stared down at it before patting my puffy hair. "A helmet?"

"Yes, your location is easier to get to by snowmobile and one of our assistants will take you there. There's a sled attached for your belongings."

"Wait, I need a snowmobile to get to my… cabin?" No helmet was fitting over my unstable afro.

"You most certainly can walk, but it's a pretty good distance."

"So, I'm getting a ride there, but if I want to leave…"

"You did opt out of our snowmobile rental package," she pointed to one of my signatures, "but we most certainly can add it on for an extra $200 dollars."

"Two hundred dollars? I don't even know how to ride one

of those things."

"You can have a private lesson for three hundred. We have an opening at eleven this morning. Would you like to reserve that time?"

Oh, heck, no. That's what I wanted to say. Shoot, it's what I was about to say.

But brown plaid jacket man still waited behind me in line and the thought of being somewhere out in the middle of nowhere with nothing but a long walking trail back to civilization was not acceptable.

I'm telling you, I've never felt so paranoid in my life.

"My credit card…" I fingered it in my wallet, certain that I was way past my credit limit. "I'm not sure I can…"

"We would be more than happy to open up a line of credit for you through our financial partner. In fact, we can transfer the balance of your room, the fees you signed to, and the snowmobile rental and lessons to your new card. Also, we can add a dining voucher, spa treatment and a ticket to our exclusive bluegrass line-dancing extravaganza for just an extra four hundred dollars."

"I…you…the… What?"

"And you will also get a surprise gift for opening an account today."

I looked behind me. The man with the creepy blue eyes and *Dateline* stalker jacket had finished thumbing through his pamphlet and now tapped his foot as he stared out the wall-sized window, waiting his turn.

Our eyes met for a moment.

"Okay. I'll do that. I'm sure my boyfriend – who will be with me –" I said this extra loudly " – will be excited at all of these options." Humph, that man was not going to think for a second that I was here alone.

"Oh, you have a guest with you?" Smiley lady began

pecking away on her computer keyboard. "We didn't know that. That's an extra five hundred dollars."

"Five hundred –"

"And an extra two-fifty to add him to the incredible package we just booked for you." She smiled and pecked and smiled and pecked.

"So, that's an additional seven hundred and fifty dollars?"

"We can add it to your new credit account. You've already been approved, Ms. Jenkins." She looked up at me, blinking and smiling. And then she frowned. "Is everything okay? Your boyfriend, I'm certain, is helping with this cost, right? Or is this too much?"

"Oh, no, it's not too much at all." *What, did she think because I was black I couldn't afford this? Was this a question she asked everyone who checked in?* "I glanced back at the man before continuing. "And, yes, of course my boyfriend can help me, but it's…his birthday…so I'm surprising him. He's taking me to Rome for my birthday." See, we can do it. Don't let the skin color fool you!

Wait, am I really this crazy?

"Okay, well enjoy your weekend. Do you want us to add the birthday surprise package to your reservation? We'll deliver balloons, champagne, and the rest of the items on this flyer." She pushed a flyer across the counter toward me. "Just seventy-five dollars more."

"No. Yes." My eyelids fluttered. How was I supposed to turn it down?

Yup, I really must be this crazy, I concluded as I penned my signature on another form.

This trip was costing me close to $4000 of money I didn't have, I reminded myself as I sat on the rear seat of a snowmobile minutes later. The route was curvy, wooded, and not kind to my behind. I hadn't felt bumps like that since riding in the back of yellow buses on elementary school field trips.

Airfare. Cabin. Birthday package. Rentals. Lessons.

I hadn't even had a single meal yet so the money spend was not over.

Did I say $4000? I swallowed hard as the snowmobile made one final turn and the "cabin" that was supposed to be my home for the next three nights came in view.

"What?" I gasped. I mean, really? *This is my $4000 experience?* That woman wasn't lying when she said I'd booked their rustic accommodations. "This thing is how much a night?" I gasped again as the driver untied and set my things down in front of the hewn logs that made up my cabin.

"People pay top dollar for this kind of experience this time of year. There is no price tag that you can place on the challenge of surviving the wilderness."

"Surviving the wilderness?"

"Oh, yes. You know there is a storm coming tomorrow morning, right? We'll probably get another foot or two before it's all over. Good thing you came today, because this time tomorrow, nobody is getting in or out."

Um, so this is how I was spending my paid time off? This is what I was going into debt for? A wilderness experience and a snowstorm?

"You'll find some complimentary water bottles inside as well as some fishing poles under your cot. You can get your fire started in a designated spot right behind the cabin. The lake is about a quarter mile east from here. Just follow the path when you're ready to catch some fish, but be careful if you do go down there. A couple of bears around here like those fish-filled waters too."

My eyes widened. "Did you just say bears?"

"Oh, I was kidding, ma'am."

"Okay," I exhaled.

"Well, kind of. Hope you brought some guns. Alright, I'm heading back." He turned away.

Wayment. *Me, too.* I started to follow right after him. The only reason I didn't was because my feet were paralyzed and my legs felt like stones. *Snowstorm? Fishing poles? Guns? Bears?!* What kind of place was this?

"Wait," I found my voice as the man turned toward the path. "You're not taking the snowmobile?"

"Nope." He checked a sheet of paper. "It's your rental."

"So how do you get back? Are you walking?"

"Of course not. I've already called for my ride."

"Wait, your ride?" I raised an eyebrow.

"Yes, we have a team of snowmobilers here who are able to pick up guests who don't want the rental package. Just call them, day or night, and they come."

"Wait, you don't have to rent a snowmobile? You can just call for a ride?"

"Well, you already signed the contract, so the rental is yours for the next few days whether you use it or not. Your teacher will be here at 11 as scheduled for your lesson."

"But…I could have called for a ride?" I couldn't get off that point.

"Sure. Just would have needed the phone package for ten bucks. Phones are not included in the rustic experience and the reception out here is horrible. Have a great stay, Ms. Jenkins."

A snowmobile skidded to a stop in front of the man. Another man attached the sled that had carried my things to the new mobile. Before I could make sense of what just happened, both men and the new mobile were gone.

"I could have called for a ride? For ten bucks? Are you freaking kidding me?" I yelled out into the frigid air. And then I realized what else the man had said.

Something about the rustic experience having no phone

service.

I ran to the door of the cabin and used my key to get in.

"Are you freaking kidding me?" I yelled again. Forget the fact that there was no phone. There was nothing period. No TV, no comfortable furniture, no heat. No darn electricity.

My expensive cabin in the back woods of the mountains was a small room with a dusty floor, a cot in the corner, and what resembled a metal chamber pot for a toilet and a spigot hanging from the ceiling as bathroom accommodations.

"I…no. No, no, and no." I picked up the folded sheet set and rolled up towel that had the nerve to be artfully placed on top of the cot with a piece of beef jerky tied up in ribbon. "Who does this?" I picked up the jerky. "I don't believe this. This is not happening. This is not real." There was absolutely no way I could stay in these conditions. I had no cell phone signal, no Wi-Fi, nothing.

"Bears?" I remembered the driver's words again. "Oh. My. God. I don't want to die. I don't want the end to be like this. No one will ever know what happened to me."

Oh, no!

My mother!

She was expecting me to text her and send pictures during this whole trip.

I sat down on the cot, rocked myself back and forth. "Wait a minute, didn't he say something about needing to start a fire? No, no, and no. This is not going to work." *When the snowmobile teacher comes, I'm getting out of here.* No doubts or questions about it.

I was rocking, moaning, and weeping when a soft motor filled my ears. The crunch of footsteps sounded near the door. Everything in me froze as a vision of that man in the brown plaid jacket filled my imagination and took over my common sense. Eleven a.m. was still an hour and a half away, so I had no idea who would be coming to my cabin. It certainly wasn't housekeeping or room service with these accommodations.

I held my breath as a soft knock sounded. My eyes darted around the room, searching for something that could be used as a weapon if need be.

The fishing poles under the cot.

I reached down to get one as a soft, shuffling sound replaced the rapping on my door.

"Jesus, be a fence. And food, and fire, and a phone." I shut my eyes, quivered from my head to my toes. The shuffling stopped, the motor started up, roared away. I opened my eyes. A white sheet of paper had been slid under my door.

It took me fifteen minutes to get myself up from the cot to see what it said.

> *Due to overbooking, your snowmobile lesson has been changed to 11 a.m. tomorrow morning. Sorry for the inconvenience. Enjoy your stay.*

"Wait, no, NO!" I flung the door open, ran toward the path. "Wait, come back! Please!" Nobody, nothing.

I'd let my imagination run wild and my fears take over to the point that now my one hope for salvation from this wilderness had come and gone. I stared back at the cabin; saw the cot and the simple shower spigot through the door.

Bears.

The thought that they could be out there was enough to send me running back inside. I bolted the door with the... rusty door latch. Really? This little unstable latch and hook was all there was to protect me from dangers seen and unseen?

And that's when I started laughing. An uncontrollable fit that to my own ears sounded like a cross between insanity and panic.

"I hate you! I hate you, Malikai Carter! I hate you!"

Chapter 24

God wasn't in this. Nope. He wasn't in this at all. He was far, far away, curled up in a comfortable place where I'd last left him.

Though I had a front row seat to nature and creation, how could I pray to my Creator? He wasn't the one who'd created this mess.

This was all on me.

At least that's the conclusion I came to as I sat there, several hours later. Having gnawed away at the beef jerky stick, I knew I needed to make my escape from the personal prison cell I'd locked myself into. Mentally, physically, emotionally, I was bound, baby. Bound, bound, bound.

It was midafternoon now and the thought of the coming darkness and the potential of a severe snowstorm meant I needed to act.

I garnered my strength, gathered my bags, and headed back outside.

The snowmobile.

I stared at the massive machine, plopped my bags onto the ground next to it, and pushed, pulled, and tucked my hair back under the helmet.

"What...how..." I studied the levers, buttons, and handles. "Where can I even put my things?" I shrugged, accepting that I would have to address one catastrophe at a time. First things first, I needed to figure out how to make this mobile work. "Well, here goes nothing." I decided on a lever and...the entire machine, jumped, jolted, sighed. And stopped. "God, what am

I doing? How did I end up here?" I looked to the heavens, wondered if God was even bothering to pay me any mind considering my nonstop foolishness.

"Whoa, hey there." A voice.

"Um..." I studied the sky a bit more, trying to make sense of the voice.

"Berry Jenkins?" The voice sounded closer.

I looked back down and saw a man approaching me from a parked snowmobile. Everything about him was orange. Orange mobile. Orange helmet. Orange ski suit. He walked up to me, pulled off his helmet, and orange hair plopped down to his shoulders. "Hey, I'm Mitchell. I'm your snowmobile teacher. Sorry about the confusion. I know you got a message that I wouldn't be coming until tomorrow morning, but I was able to get my schedule changed to meet with you today." He looked at my awkward pose on the machine. "Glad I got here. I see you're trying to get it started."

"I am trying to get back to the check-in desk. I'm not worried about the lesson. Can you just take me back? I absolutely cannot stay here."

"Oh, no. Don't give up so easily. I'm sure you're frustrated, but I can help." He gave me a smile that revealed a few chipped teeth. Sharp stubble covered his chin and cheeks, and the breath that rolled out of his mouth smelled like tuna. Not exactly the image I'd had of salvation, but he was close enough.

"No, I'm not frustrated. I'm just ready to go home. This is not the vacation I was expecting at all."

"Wow, I'm sorry to hear that things are not going the way you planned. Before you totally give up, perhaps I can give you a quick lesson. You might actually enjoy this."

"Take me back. Now. Please."

I could tell he wanted to say something else, but he could

tell I wasn't playing.

"Alright, but I don't have a sled attached, and I can't leave my snowmobile here to use your rental."

"I'll leave my things here. I don't even care right now. I need to go." I meant it. New boots, new coats, new clothes. If I had to sacrifice it all to get out of this crazy wilderness experience, I'd deal with the consequences later.

Mitchell shrugged. "Okay, I'll take you back and we'll see if we can make arrangements to get your stuff." He got back on his snowmobile. "Hop on and hold on."

Getting to the cabin had been one thing. Holding onto the waist of a stranger who smelled like tuna and drove like he had a death wish was another.

"Can you slow down?" I managed to scream. My request was lost in the loud roar of the high-powered mobile as we began down the trail that led back to the main resort area.

"Woo-hoo! Short cut!" he yelled as we turned off the main road. "Hold on!" he yelled again as the mobile dipped and soared, jumped, and went airborne again for a few seconds.

Maybe I would have been safer with the bears, I thought, as the snowmobile bounced and jostled at top speed as it landed.

"Now, you're really going to like this!" The man roared, apparently oblivious to my horror as we began bouncing down a steep incline. "Woo-hoo!"

I shut my eyes as the mobile went airborne again, waiting for the hard thud that would signify we'd landed.

But we were still flying.

And still flying.

"Uh..."

"Here comes the landing!" my escort yelled. "Lean to the left!"

I heard his words, but they didn't register. My eyes still

closed, I dug my helmet into his back and felt my body tilt hard right.

"Whoa, that was close!" He yelled. "We could have crashed. Keep your body to the left. We've got some rough terrain up ahead."

Oh, this had been the smooth part? I felt my eyes widen and my grip on his midsection tighten.

And then an idea.

My phone had no signal, but the video still worked. I braved one hand off his waist and fished for my phone in my jacket pocket.

Record. I pressed the button and managed a video selfie. All you could see were my terrified eyes and my head pressed against his red suit.

"Aaaeeiiiiii!" My scream was no act as the snowmobile whipped through several sharp turns, crackled through thin tree branches, twisted and flew over bumps and small hills. Thirty seconds of sheer terror.

Thirty seconds of perfect footage.

With my shaky hands and terrified face, it would be easy to make my story convincing. Especially with the last hard landing we made just before I tapped off the record button.

"We're here," Mitchell announced as we turned back onto the trail. The main building where I'd checked in just hours earlier was in view. A new shuttle bus was parked nearby and the throng of spring breakers had thickened.

"Woo-hoo!" Mitchell yelled one last time as we skidded to a stop in a shower of snow. "Tell me you didn't enjoy that! You sure you want to leave?"

I didn't even stay around to respond. The moment I could put both my feet on solid ground, I was off. I marched into the building, stormed over to the registration desk.

"I'm leaving." I slammed my stack of registration papers

on the counter so hard, the woman jumped back.

"Oh? Something go wrong with your surprise plans for your boyfriend?" She looked at me sympathetically.

I laughed.

"Everything has gone wrong. Everything. I'm done."

"Oh, we're sorry to see you go, but we do need your signature on this form since you are checking out early and forfeiting your stay."

I had no idea what she said, what I was doing, what I signed. I just wanted out. Maybe I could have asked for another room, an upgrade, but that would have meant more money, more money, and more money.

Enough is enough.

"I'm out." I nodded at the new crowd of drunken college students who filled the property. A different snowmobile with an attached sled carrying my things stopped in front of me several minutes later. I was too shaken to express my gratitude at the sight of my belongings. "Y'all can play in the snow, get caught in the storm, fish, dodge bears, and party to your hearts delight," I mumbled to myself as I boarded the shuttle heading back to the airport. "I'm leaving this foolishness alone." As the bus roared away, I pulled up the video I'd just made while on the snowmobile.

Perfect. I uploaded and shared the thirty-second clip of me screaming in horror. Wow. Didn't realize I'd been that loud. My *Facebook* status update: *The things I'll do for love. SMH.*

Post was up.

Phone was off.

The stage was set. This was act one of Malikai Carter's grand finale. I already had plans for act two. There would be no act three, as far as I was concerned. The curtain was about to drop once and for all on my elaborate performance.

I couldn't wait to be done with this mess. This was the

worst relationship experience I'd ever had – and it wasn't even real. Sheesh. If a relationship that stemmed from my fantasies could get this messy, what would I do with – if I ever had – a real man?

Back at the airport, waiting to board the plane I'd just booked, I noticed a group of couples walking through the terminal. They caught my eye, not because of their professional equipment, big smiles, and sense of purpose. Rather, my attention was roused because with all their specialized, expensive equipment, loud laughs, and big plans to hit the slopes, they had skin like me.

A group of African American men and women, arm in arm, looked ready to face the thrills of something I still had yet to experience, despite my huge investment. Ski.

"Wells Lake Community Church Couples Retreat." A private driver greeted them with a sign and pointed them toward a waiting charter.

So, I guess black people really do ski and I didn't have to make up stories to prove it.

Yeah, I know, my mind is simple, my view limited. I don't know. Maybe I had some skewed racial perceptions in my own head that needed challenging. Seeing that group of brown-skinned travelers in person did something, stirred something inside of me.

Hope.

Hope that maybe my fantasies and dreams of love and acceptance and a life larger than I knew were possible.

That was, of course, if it wasn't already too late.

Chapter 25

"Berry... Berry!"

Pounding on my front door.

"Beeerrryyy!"

More pounds.

My eyes struggled to open as Huxley walked over my face. *Where am I? What day is it?* I forced myself to think, to wake up.

"Berry? Are you in there?" The voice continued. My mother.

I wiped the corners of my eyes, swung my feet to the floor, and grabbed my slippers. Huxley ran past me, out of my room.

"Berry? Open this door right now or do I need to call the police? Oh God, let my baby be okay."

I heard desperation in my mother's voice. I pulled a sweatshirt over my head, tightened the drawstring on my pants and readjusted my slippers. With every step to the door, my focus came back into view.

As did my memory.

Lord, I think it's Sunday morning. The clock in my kitchen said 9:53. I'd been holed up in my apartment for two days or so. Too exhausted to think, too ashamed to show my face anywhere, and too uncertain of what the collateral damage of the past few weeks was, I'd done nothing but fade in and out of sleep since I'd come back home. I rented a car to get back home from the airport in the wee hours of Friday morning using the credit account I'd opened at the ski resort.

My phone was off, my brain hurt, and the last person I felt

like coming back to reality with was my mother.

But she was pounding at my door. I opened it.

"Oh, thank God! You're okay!" My mother squealed and threw her body weight on me, her heavy arms nearly squeezing the breath out of my lungs. Her hair was gone, cut down to a teeny-weeny afro and dyed a rich, dark red.

"You've gone natural," I gasped, partially because I was shocked, mostly because my mother was still squeezing the breath out of my lungs.

"Oh, dear God, I've been worried." She finally let go and wiped tears off her cheeks. "You haven't responded to any texts or calls since Friday morning. I saw your snowmobile video on *Facebook*. And then your posts stopped. You didn't send me any more pictures. I couldn't get a hold of Meeka, but her voice mail said something about a sweat lodge in Arizona. I didn't know if I had the right lodge or the wrong destination in my head. I didn't know what to think or what to do." My mother was gasping for air herself, still wiping away tears. "And then you weren't at the airport when I came to pick you up this morning. I was scared, Berry."

What kind of daughter am I to give my mother this much genuine anxiety and panic?

"When I sat down and thought about it," she continued, "I realized that Malikai really is a stranger to us, and I didn't know if something bad…" She shut her eyes, couldn't get out the words. "I didn't know if… Well, praise Jesus, you're okay." She blew out a long breath.

And then she crossed her arms.

"Now, what happened that you didn't feel the need to call and let me know that you were okay?" The tears were gone. Her foot tapped on the floor. Any hint of fear and anxiety that had been on her face turned over to anger and irritation.

"Mom," I struggled to remember what I'd rehearsed for

this moment, what I'd been waiting to say at this very scenario. I'd crafted a plan starting with the quick video of me riding along on that wild snowmobile ride. *Oh, yeah, I was killing this dude off.*

"Mom," I started again, taking her hands in mine, "I'm sorry I didn't call you. My phone was off. On purpose. These past few days... Wow, how do I say this?" I exhaled for dramatic effect. "Listen, Mom, some things happened that I didn't know how to talk to you about. I –"

"Oh, I see," she interrupted and winked. "You must have been having a really good time for you to go off radar like that. I mean, in a holy, godly way, of course, as Sister Willow and I would expect nothing less from you. Romantic dinners, holding hands in front of a cozy fire..." My mother smiled, nodded, and squeezed my hand as her eyes drifted off into space.

What is happening? I needed to hurry up and tell her about the tragic snowmobile accident that killed Malikai, that killed her every fantasy for my love life.

"Um, mom?"

"Berry, I can't even be mad at you right now," she continued before I could finish my story. "I am so happy to see that you are okay and that you had a great time." She let go of my hands and raised both of hers. "I'm ready to get to church and get my praise on. You need to come too, but I think everyone will understand why you aren't there. You've had a long, full trip, and so much excitement over the past few days."

"Mom, listen."

"Berry, I know you have so much more to tell me." New tears washed down her cheeks. *Seriously?* "I'm already late, so you'll have to fill in the details later. Dinner. My house. After service. Ooooh, Berry, this is so wonderful." She wiped her eyes and then clasped her hands together before heading to my door.

"Mom, wait!" I jumped up after her. "Let me tell you what happened. It's not what you–"

"–Oh, I can't wait to hear it all, but I got to get to service first, baby. I've got too much to thank Jesus for – and tell Sister Willow about. You get your rest. We'll catch up later. I just had to make sure you were okay. And you are. You really are. We'll talk soon, love. Hee, hee."

"Mom, wait!" I called again. "I need to tell you something. It's important. Things with Malikai are not what you think!"

My mother was already heading down the steps. All giggles and halleluiahs. Yup, she was only going to hear what she wanted to hear, even if I was shouting in a bullhorn next to her eardrums.

"My house after church. Details. Don't forget!" She called out just before walking out of the apartment building.

"No. This cannot continue one second longer." I'd been through too much, wasted way too much money for Malikai Carter to live one more minute. I'd had no plans to go to church, but right now, I didn't have a choice. "I should have held her down and told her my story." I shook my head at myself as I did the only thing left to do.

Sweatpants, messed up hair, tennis shoes and all, I headed out the door.

I needed to catch my mother before she made matters worse.

Ten seconds too late.

The back of my mother's red shoe slipped into the church doorway just as I put the rental car in park on the church parking lot.

I still had about seven minutes to catch her, I knew.

Though my mother was late for service, she always kept the same routine upon church arrival, regardless of the time. Stop in the bathroom. Stop at the water fountain. Stop back in the bathroom to check her hair and makeup. With her new hairstyle, she'd probably be in the bathroom even longer before making her sanctuary debut.

I exhaled, bracing myself to break the news to my mother. A part of me felt excited – and relieved – that I was now officially seconds away from being free once and forever of Malikai Carter. I wasn't worried at all about running into anyone there while looking so ragged. My sloppiness fit the story I was ready to tell.

The foyer was empty when I entered. Morning service was well underway.

"God has been so good to me." Sister Daphne Brooks' somewhat soprano voice echoed off the walls. The last note was just off, all wrong, but that was not my concern as I headed to the bathroom to find my mother. Brother Fitzgerald tried to hide Daphne's sharp note behind a fancy piano run, but there wasn't much that could be done with that broken ending. I shook my head as Brother Fitzgerald suddenly began shouting, effectively putting the whole song to an end. His moans and wails and hollers would soon be tended to by one of Sister Brooks' lace hankies. His loud wails turned into sporadic whimpers, the telltale sign that the whole act was going as I'd predicted. Was I the only one who'd caught on to their weekly routine?

The one and only time I could recall him calming down on his own was when the head nurse, Sister Bertha Mae MacIntyre, came rushing to his aid with a fan and some smelling salts. He'd been on the floor motionless longer than usual, seemingly passed out in the spirit right at Sister Daphne's feet.

"I'm certified in CPR," Sister Bertha Mae had yelled in her bass voice, pushing everyone out the way and nearly knocking

Sister Daphne over as she knelt to help wake him up. "You push down on his chest, and I'll breath into him," Bertha Mae directed Daphne. Well, Brother Fitzgerald's eyes popped open before Bertha Mae's other knee hit the ground. He leapt up and broke out in a holy dance.

Like I've said. Fakery.

I looked down at the wad of tissues I'd packed into my palm, ready to be used for the tearful talk I was about to have with my mother.

Did I just say something about fakery?

I guess I was in the right church. Was I not the epitome of pretending right now? I shook my head and pushed open the bathroom door.

"Mom, it's me. We need to talk." My voice echoed through the small, cavernous space. "I need to tell you about my trip… what happened." I stared at the red high heels on the other side of the single stall door. "Mom?"

"Sister Berry Jenkins, is that you?" The toilet flushed and the door of the stall opened.

Evangeline Willow.

Where's my mother?

"Your mother has been talking about you all week, at Bible Study, leadership phone conference, prayer chain – every moment of every fellowship possible. I praise God things have been going well for you."

Okay, there was no way I could kill off Malikai Carter and Sister Willow be the first to know. My mother would be devastated times two. "Sister Willow, good to see you." I smiled as she washed her hands and used the hand dryer.

The look on her face, the singular stare as if she could see right through me, gave me chills.

"I understand you went on some kind of trip with the young man you just met a couple of weeks ago. That's a pretty big risk to go running off with a stranger, and –" she lowered her eyes "– a pretty big temptation to be off alone in another state with a man you're attracted to. I pray you maintained a testimony of purity. It would be a real shame if God has blessed you with one of His kings, and instead of carrying yourself as a queen, you lowered yourself into harlotry."

"Uh, no, it wasn't that kind of trip. No such thing happened. In fact…" I remembered the story I was planning to tell my mother. Though I had no desire to break the tragedy to Sister Willow first, I needed to be consistent with my wording and my tearfulness. "In fact," I began again, letting my voice break as if about to burst into tears, "some things happened that caused me to really lean on the strength of the Lord. I can't get into it right now. I need to talk to my mother about it first."

Nope. Those weren't the right words. I knew it the moment she smiled. Her ears seemingly perked to full attention.

"Well," she almost seemed to grin, "I hope whatever it is, all is well. I'd hate for the big surprise to be ruined for you."

"Big surprise?" *What is this woman talking about?*

"Oops. I didn't mean to let the cat out the bag, but let's just say that all of us here at Rock of Life Church support you and the ministry of your new-found king from God. See you in the sanctuary."

She gave me an up and down, frowning, as if just noticing my sweats and sneakers ensemble. Then, her face broke into another delicious smile as she headed out the door. "Thank you, Father, for giving me the gift of prophetic discernment," she whispered as she exited. Her voice then transitioned into a wave of tongues.

Big surprise?

I felt like a chunk of my throat fell off and landed in a pit of acid in my stomach. My feet froze to the floor. When I did finally lift them, my toes felt like lead trying to maneuver over a magnet.

I had to get out of there.

The past few days had been the worst of my life and I was in no mood or desire for any surprises. Especially one that involved my "new-found king from God."

I bolted out of the bathroom and headed back through the foyer to get to the exit. I was almost at the door when I heard a squeal.

"Berry!" Vickie came out of the sanctuary. "You *are* here. Your mother said you weren't coming, but this is great!"

The shrill in her voice gave me more chills. This was not going to be good. I swallowed as she continued.

"So, I know you're just getting back from Aspen and you probably just want to get home and rest, but you need to come in the sanctuary first."

My heartbeat quickened as no response came to mind to get me out of this.

"Don't worry, nobody cares how you look right now. Just come on in the sanctuary and then you can leave and go rest." She was all smiles as she walked over to me and grabbed my hand. Like a sheep headed for slaughter, I followed behind, no fight, no words.

We entered the back of the church just as the praise and worship part of the service was ending. Brother Fitzgerald was stretched out across the front pew of the choir stand, his head being fanned and mopped by Daphne Brooks, of course. Pastor Beamon stood on the pulpit, ready to give some announcements, but his face lit up and he smiled as Vickie walked me toward the front. She pointed at me and mouthed something I couldn't understand.

My mother beamed from the front row.

Sister Willow grinned from the opposite side front row.

"Well, welcome Sister Jenkins," Pastor Beamon boomed

from the pulpit. Very rarely did he greet late worshippers on his microphone, so I knew this was going to be awful. Awful, awful, awful.

"We weren't sure if you were going to make it today, but we're glad to see you. Come up here, dear heart. God is good and the people of Rock of Life have really responded to His goodness." He turned to face the audience. "God is amazing at how he can use people and circumstances to build unity and to build His kingdom. I am awed and filled with wonder at how He has seen fit to use our little, sweet Berry as a conduit for great blessing. Come on up, Berry. Brother Jackson, can you go ahead and start the video?" He motioned to the sound man.

Video? I swallowed hard, willing myself to disappear, to melt away, to not exist. No, this was not going to be good at all.

"Hi, everyone." The projector screen had rolled down from the ceiling and Raina's face and voice filled the sanctuary. "First giving honor to God, Pastor Beamon and all those assembled, I am down here in Miami, excited about what we have been able to accomplish as a church over the past two days. It's nothing short of miraculous."

The camera panned out, showing her and her husband sitting on a bench. Clear blue water and sand filled the background, along with the rising sun.

Where is this going?

"Many of you know the struggle Drew and I have had trying to start a family. We recently learned that our dreams are coming true. To show our gratitude to God for this beautiful miracle, it made sense to celebrate someone else's miracle, because it is more blessed to give then receive. As a congregation, we've been praying for God to move mightily in one of our favorite member's life, Sister Berry Jenkins."

Um, favorite member? People were praying for me? For what? Wait, so me landing a man was equivalent to…a miracle?

"The same way God is allowing Drew and I to begin a new life, it appears that Berry is beginning a new life, too. To celebrate our miracle, we wanted to sow into Berry's and I am so excited that so many of you yielded to the call for donations."

Donations?

My eyebrow rose as I looked over at my mom. She grinned harder and winked at me.

A voiceover came next while pictures of a foreign land flashed on the screen. *"I want to build a world-class gymnasium on the outskirts of Gaborone. I want to give the youth here a sporting arena that rivals one found in any major metropolis. And that's just the beginning. Together with my personal funds and the money that comes in to support my charity, the youth and young adults in this part of Botswana will be blessed beyond measure."*

Uh, oh. I recognized those words. They were from the blog I'd created while sitting in the digital café the other night. I'd emailed the link to Raina as proof that Malikai was not the jerk athlete her husband had known from his overseas ball days.

I guess my plan worked – and a little too well, based on what was unfolding in front of me.

Pastor Beamon filled the screen next. *When did they have time to create this video?* I wondered.

"Congregation, through the emails and phone calls initiated by Drew and Raina," he spoke solemnly into the camera, "I'm pleased to say that so many of you stepped up to the challenge to raise money for Brother Malikai Carter's charity. It has moved my heart to see the way our congregation has been united in this project. My hope and prayer is that Brother Carter will be able to see our heart for his ministry, and perhaps partner with us to use his influence and substantial assets to assist us with our own ministerial needs. We've been talking about our building fund to build a new sanctuary in our city, but perhaps God wants us to think bigger, nationally, internationally. This is just the beginning, church. This partnership, courtesy of Sister Berry Jenkins, is a singular answer to multiple prayers."

Oh, wow. Raina saw miracles. Pastor Beamon saw dollar signs. And I saw my life flashing before me. Was this the end of it all?

"Amen, church!" Pastor Beamon took hold of the microphone as the projector screen rolled back up. "I am excited, and amazed, and thrilled, humbled, and honored to say that in two days alone, we have raised $6,025 to contribute to Brother Malikai Carter's Christian-ministry athletic center in Botswana."

The sanctuary roared with applause. Brother Fitzgerald found his way back to the piano and began hammering out some "get happy" music. My mother danced in the aisles and Sister Evangeline Willow narrowed her eyes at me.

Dizziness. Lightheadedness. Nausea.

"I…I gotta go," I pushed away an usher who came to walk me up to the pulpit. Pastor Beamon had a check in his hand, a smile on his face, and a look of pure delight in his eyes. "This seed money to Botswana is going to grow us a harvest right here in Baltimore. I believe in my spirit that as we help him, Brother Malikai will be helping us with his resources." Pastor Beamon let out a cheery shout as I began walking the other way.

No, running.

My mother tried to catch up with me in the parking lot. Tried. "Berry," she yelled after me, "where are you going?"

"He's dead, mom," I couldn't hold it in any longer. I shouted it out in the wind. "I came back early because he died. That snowmobile video..." Real snot dripped from my nose. Tears streamed down my cheeks. "Malikai Carter is dead."

"Berry, what? What are you saying?" My mother was still five cars away from me. I didn't know if she heard me or not. I didn't care. I just wanted to get away from there, get away from her, get away from it all.

So, I did.

Chapter 26

Federal Hill was one of my favorite places in Baltimore. A towering hill that overlooked the Inner Harbor, most of the city was in eyesight from the benches that lined its grassy slope.

I needed to get away, to sit somewhere that allowed me to have a big picture view. I needed a moment to rise above where I was and make sense of the broken details of my life.

Details I'd singlehandedly broken myself.

It was an unseasonably warm Sunday and every bench was taken. Children toddled on the hilltop playground, leashed dogs sniffed the ground, and couples giggled around picnic lunches. Solitaires of all ages stood and sat quietly studying the waters, buildings, trees, and stadiums below. After circling around a couple of times, a bench at the forefront of the hill finally cleared. I sat down in the middle of it, hoping that nobody would have the nerve to ask me to scoot over and make room for them to sit as well.

I needed a moment.

I let my mind go blank as I studied a cannon from the nineteenth century that was nestled on the ground just in front of me. A little rusted, greatly worn, but still there. That cannon had survived decades, no, centuries of trouble and trials, even if the trial was just a rainstorm and not a bloody war.

It survived and was showcased and was part of the scenic setting. Maybe there was hope for me. Hope. The thought rose to the top of my mind again, much like it had when I saw that group of couples headed to the snow-covered hills in Colorado.

Hope that everything would be okay. That nobody would

get too hurt because of my lies. That I would have a legitimate chance at love, despite my awful attempt at pretending I'd found it.

"Hey there, can I have a seat?"

A man in front of me gasped for air. He wore a black jacket and running pants that looked like something a championship-level marathoner would wear. He was out of breath and chugging down a bottle of water. I knew it would be cruel to not let the man sit down.

Okay that and he was cute, too.

Not a "knock your momma senseless" cute, but a "make you warm inside", "make you smile outside", "make you feel like everything is okay" kind of cute. Subtly handsome.

Hope.

"Please, have a seat." I felt myself move over a little too quickly to give him space. "Looks like you've been running for a while."

"From Lake Montebello." The man, though sitting, began a series of stretches.

"Whoa, that's far. That's what, a couple miles or so?"

"Five miles to be exact." He reached for his feet, pulled and stretched, before taking another swig from his water bottle. "You look familiar. Do I know you?"

"I don't believe we've met." Was this his weak pick-up line? I kept talking to see what he was about. "What are you, training for a marathon?"

"No." He spoke matter-of-factly, hadn't even cracked a smile.

This was no pick-up attempt. Hold on, was that a little disappointment I felt? I guess he'd really come just to…sit down and rest a moment. It *was* crowded up here. No other benches were free.

"I run three times a week," he continued. "My longest run

is on Sunday."

"Five miles is no joke. You must really love running."

He shrugged. "I used to weigh three-hundred fifty-seven pounds. I ate terribly and didn't even try to take care of myself. It's who I was, how everybody saw me. Then, one day, I realized that wasn't who I was; that I wasn't being true to the man I knew was me. I knew I was a health-conscious athlete before I even looked or acted like one. The three-hundred fifty-pound version of me was a lie I was presenting to the world."

"Sounds like you have an inspiring story."

"No, I have an honest one." He looked out over the Harbor before continuing. "Being honest about who I really was, that was the hardest thing I ever did. It required hard work, discipline, and letting go of all the lies I'd been living that created who I was not. I had to line up every part of my life and daily routine to the true version of me. It was hard, but it was freeing, and now there are no questions from anyone about who I really am. Now," he smiled, and for the first time, he looked me square in the face, "who are you?"

I smiled back. "I'm Berry."

"Okay, but who *are* you?"

I felt my eyelids flutter. My smile froze in place. How did I even answer that question? What was the truth of who I was? A liar? A desperate woman? A fool?

"I'm Berry Jenkins," was all I could get out.

"Well, that's a start."

We sat there in silence for a moment as he took another swig from his water bottle. Looked like he was about to get up. *Was this it?*

"Nice talking with you," I blurted as he rose to his feet. "Enjoy the rest of your run. Wait, what's your name?" I couldn't help myself. He had dimples.

"Kai," he nodded before re-lacing one of his shoes. "Kai

Peters.

I felt the color drain from my face. Welp, this just wasn't meant to be, I knew immediately. This had to be God getting the last laugh for my terrible Malikai Carter plot. I was a terrible person and here in front of me was my punishment.

The probably perfect man for me who would never be mine.

"Nice to meet you…Kai," I pushed back tears as the weight of the past few weeks settled on me anew. "Thanks for sharing your story. Your honesty. You've given me my sermon for Sunday morning. I'm missing church today." Well, really, I'd been missing it for months.

"Ah, church. Haven't found the right one for myself, yet. I can't deal with fakeness and that's all I've seen everywhere I've gone." He shook his head.

Fakeness.

This man would totally get me, get where I was coming from.

Though I no longer knew what was real myself.

"I listen to the Bible while I run," he continued. "That's been my church lately, but I'm open to fellowship once I find the right place. Guess I should get serious about looking."

I just wanted to look at him. There was an authenticity about him that was as refreshing as the new spring air.

"I hear what you're saying, Kai. I'm tired of the fakery, too. I just want my life and all parts of it to be genuine, starting with my relationship with God. No games, no acts, no drama."

"It's nice to meet someone who is committed to being real." His smile deepened, but then his head tilted to one side and his eyes narrowed. "Hold on, I just realized why you look familiar to me. You're that girl from the picture, aren't you?"

"The picture?"

"Yes, the Berry Wrong girl?"

I raised an eyebrow. "I'm sorry. I have no idea what you're talking about." I let out a small giggle as I tried to make sense of his words.

"Yes, this is you, isn't it?" He scrolled through a mobile phone he'd taken out of his jacket pocket. "I'm sure you know about it. It's gone viral." He held up his phone and now I was the one gasping.

The picture I'd created of me and Kal.

I'd snapped the photo of NaTosha and Kal in front of their airplane gate and then replaced her face with mine from my airport selfie. It was the picture I'd texted to my mother on my way to Colorado.

What was it doing on Facebook? My mom had said something about seeing the snowmobile video I. It hadn't dawned on me that she actually was on *Facebook*. She probably posted this picture I'd texted her and tagged everyone she knew. It must have gone viral from there. That was my suspicion, anyway.

I looked at the caption under the picture.

My fiancé. Her face. She cut and paste. What do you call that? #BerryWrong.

I didn't even have to see the name of the poster as I immediately recognized that beautiful afro in the profile pic.

"It's been trending on *Facebook* and *Twitter* all morning," he explained, showing me a series of other pictures from social media users which featured my face pasted into various scenes and scenarios – from the silly to the obscene. #BerryWrong followed each post and picture. Like the #IWasThere memes of anchorman Brian Williams, my face had been cut and pasted into every kind of scenario imaginable. Yup, #BerryWrong was one of the top trending hashtags on *Twitter* at the moment. I'd never imagine that I'd become a meme.

I felt beyond horrible and he looked beyond amused.

"Hey," he said, "can I get a picture of you? Let's get #BerryRight trending."

I didn't even answer. Didn't even say goodbye. My feet hit the pavement and I broke into a quick sprint as if I was the one making a five-mile run on a Sunday morning.

"You're running away from me?" he called out. "Now, that's #BerryWrong."

Oh well, so much for me being real and genuine and honest. Here I was condemning the folks at my church, and I apparently was the poster girl for fakery. The meme for make-believe.

I dodged between children, walkers, dogs, and a host of other obstacles that separated me from the relative seclusion of my rental car.

My phone had been off all weekend. There'd been unchecked messages on it even before I got to Aspen, I recalled. My unwillingness to face reality had kept me from, well, facing it. In the process, my name and image had gone haywire.

How many of my lies had been exposed? And to whom?

And my church members had raised all that money. Guilt swallowed me in a way that left me feeling complete indigestion. My stomach felt like it was going to explode.

Sitting in the front seat of the car, I knew it was time to face the truth. I dug in my purse, looking for my phone so that I could finally turn it on and check the long list of text, phone, and email messages – and social media alerts – waiting for me.

Chapter 27

"Message three, received on Wednesday at 4:40 p.m.: Berry, it's your brother. Call me as soon as possible. We need to talk."

"Message four, received on Wednesday at 5:19 p.m.: Hi Berry, it's Celeste. The girls and I came across something pretty exciting and we wanted to ask you about it. Call me back as soon as you get this message.

"Message five, received Wednesday at 6:31 p.m.: Berry, yo, what's up? It's your brother again. Hit me back. Text me if you can't talk."

There were six more phone messages waiting, ten text messages, and over seven hundred total new comments, tweets, and inbox messages on my *Facebook* and *Twitter* pages. Tears streamed down my cheeks as I tried to make sense of it all.

All this because of what again?

I listened to the next message.

"Hi, Berry, it's Celeste again. Sorry to keep harassing you, but as I was working on my own wedding plans I discovered that this really nice place near D.C. has a rare opening. They're a great venue for engagement parties and receptions. I wanted to have my own there, but they were booked solid for the next fourteen months. You said on Tuesday that you and Malikai had kind of joked around about getting married one day. I know it's a little premature, but if you're serious, you might want to consider looking at this spot for an engagement party or reception, or even a bridal shower. Ok, I know I'm sounding crazy, but I am so excited for you and I wanted this place for myself, but it didn't work out. For a man like Malikai Carter who's probably used to the best of the best, you really should check this out. Okay, call me back."

Next message:

"So, Berry, sorry to call back again so soon, but this venue is about to be booked up by another person. Like I said, it's rare they have an opening, but a cancellation happened and it sounds like they're going to go with the highest bidder. Gina, Carolyn, Naomi, and I really, really want to see you have something there if you think there's any chance you'll have wedding bells in your future soon. Okay, please, please, please call back. Please."

My heart sunk as I listened to the next message, also from Celeste.

"Soooo, this might be crazy. Okay, it is crazy, but we had to make a decision for you. The four of us put together to book the place. The opening is not until October, which is seven months away. Of course, by then, we'll all know if you and Malikai will be together for good. I know, I know it's crazy, but we all have such good feelings about this and we're excited for you. The deposit was nonrefundable, but we think it's worth the risk. This could be for your bridal shower, or engagement party, or just even a bachelorette party dinner. The sky is the limit, Berry, but you will be one of a select group of women to say that you had an event at this place.

"It was too awesome of an opportunity for us to let it go. Call me. Oh, and I'm texting you a link to the website so you can see how awesome this place is. I am too excited. Yes, we are absolutely crazy and out of our minds for doing this, but sometimes you just have to take those big steps. Call me."

Was I going to go to jail? Or was someone else going to go to jail for killing me? Between my mother, my co-workers, and now even my church, thousands of dollars had been spent needlessly. All because I was determined to show what? That nothing was wrong with me as is? That a man of many women's dreams would find me desirable? That I was enough? That I was love-able?

Worthy?

I swallowed hard as I opened the text message Celeste had sent me with the link to the D.C. venue. Wow, my eyes widened at the elaborate hall. My co-workers had actually put their money into this, for me.

Non-refundable.

God, how do I fix this? New tears flooded down my face as I struggled to catch my breath.

"Jesus, I know I created this disaster, but…help. Please, help." My voice was a tiny whisper. Would God really help me after all I'd done? After all I'd cost my friends, relatives, and coworkers? They'd all been so willing to help me, but would they be willing to forgive?

Could God even forgive me?

"I'm sorry." I shivered in the car seat. "This whole thing is stupid. Crazy stupid." The window was down. The sound of laughter, kids playing, and dogs barking wafted in the air. I was parked in a residential neighborhood next to Federal Hill. I watched as Kai Peters, the healthy running man, made his way down the slope's path. He ran past my car, down the street, out of view.

Out of my life.

Yup, I did this. I'd created the mess that was making me miss my blessing.

"God, how do I fix this?" I prayed aloud again, wondering if I was even being heard. I couldn't fix anything, but I was too afraid to ask *Him* to fix it. Was it really God's job to fix my self-created issues?

There were more messages, more texts and notifications. I

felt weak, hoping there wouldn't be more fall-out, sensing I'd only scratched the surface. I clicked on the text message that followed Celeste's.

It was a notification for a new email message for an email account I didn't recognize. I followed the link.

Nope. This didn't look good either.

My heart sunk down to my toenails as I realized it was the email account I'd made for Adilson Enterprises, Malikai's fake employer.

There were six messages waiting in the inbox.

The first was from my brother.

> *Dear Mr. Carter, I am representing a group of professional athletes, entertainers, and other investors who are interested in learning more about your company and providing funds and collateral for your performance enhancing products. We understand that you are a relatively new start-up operation, but have heard positive stories about your international reach. At your convenience, please call or email so that we can schedule a conference call to discuss this opportunity further. Best, Davis Jenkins.*

It occurred to me I hadn't checked in days the voicemail inbox of the phone number I'd made for the company. Sure enough - I sighed and shook my head - my brother had left a voicemail message with the same request. I had recorded the voicemail greeting using some of Davis' equipment. My voice had been unrecognizable, apparently completely unrecognizable.

No worries, though, I told myself. "Malikai" never contacted Davis and this message was a few days old. Once Davis realized there would be no call back, I was sure he would just leave it alone. This group, or whoever it was he called himself representing, would move on as well. Knowing my brother, he at most had rounded up the dead beats, potheads, and other tagalongs that made up his DJ'ing crowd. I seriously doubted that actual pro athletes were involved.

But then the next voice mail....

"Greetings, Mr. Carter," a deep voice sounded in my ear. Sounded a little familiar. "This is Montray Louis. I'm a wide receiver with the *Baltimore Ravens.* I heard about your company from a group of investors who want to support it. I would like to talk directly to you about your product. Please give me a call back as soon as possible." He left both his cell and home phone numbers.

The man was a hometown favorite, the leading sponsor of a local fast-food joint. His wide grin was on billboards all up and down I-83.

"Oh, no..." I could barely breathe.

Things continued to spiral as I listened to and read the remainder of the voice and email messages. A rising rapper from West Baltimore. A homerun record breaker from Baltimore's baseball team. A D.C. basketball player. A few college basketball coaches. A businessman who said he had offices in the Cayman Islands.

My brother had rounded up quite a group – and word was spreading. Even as I sat there stupefied, my phone buzzed another text notification of a new email for Malikai Carter. The message was more of the same. I read the new inquiry written by another pro-football player, another Baltimore ball hero.

Looked like the connection between Malikai's fake existence and #BerryWrong had not yet been made.

Do I sigh in relief or scream in horror? First things first. I needed to get to a computer to shut the whole operation down.

"I'm sorry, Davis. Mom, Celeste, Raina, NaTosha. Everybody," I mumbled to myself. The list of the wronged was too long for me to wrap my head around. Church members. And now, apparently the entire Internet. At the moment, nobody knew the extent of my crimes and I didn't know the extent of the consequences. I just knew that I felt like crud.

As I sat there contemplating where to go for computer access, something else caught my eye that surpassed any feeling of horror I already had.

A brown plaid jacket.

Is that the same man I saw in Aspen that gave me the heebie-jeebies? I squinted to make out the man leaning against a light post a half block down the street. A sensation like spiders crawling up my spine landed at the base of my brain and blocked out any thoughts or plans I'd had.

Wait, I'm being irrational. There is no way that man had followed me to Baltimore. I shook my head and started the engine. Had no idea where I was going and I knew I was freaking out for no good reason. Just the same, I wanted to get out of there. It took all I had not to push down on the accelerator, but a part of me knew I had to get a better look. As my car passed by the light post, the man looked up. Our eyes locked.

It was him.

I was sure of it.

I already felt low and guilty, but now a new, disturbing feeling joined the mix.

Fear.

Who is this man? Why is he following me? I had no doubt that he was tracking my movement. What else could explain his presence in my life in two different states?

I wanted to call my mother. I wanted to call somebody, anybody. But really, who could I call? As I raced down Pratt Street, all the people who I'd wronged – and they didn't even know it – over the past few weeks, entered my mind.

As I turned on I–83, heading who knows where, to do

God knows what, my phone rang.

My mother.

"Berry," my mother spoke the moment I answered the phone. "I assumed you left the church because you were exhausted and overwhelmed. However, Evangeline Willow informed me that you needed to talk to me about something very important and I couldn't hear what you were shouting in the parking lot when you left. I don't know what's going on, but does it have anything to do with this Berry Wrong business floating around the Internet?"

A sharp edge, laced with hurt, cut through her voice, pierced through the phone line, and jabbed into my throat. She was angry and she didn't even know the extent of my wrongdoings. I swallowed hard, blinked back tears, and heard my voice come out in a weak whisper.

"Mom, I need to talk to you. In person."

Silence.

"Mom?"

More silence.

Then, "I'm not going to like this, am I, Berry?"

"I… We… Davis needs to hear this, too."

"He wasn't at church. He didn't even make his church van pick-ups. A number of people were upset about it, but I figured he was probably just a little jealous of all the attention you and your new boyfriend are getting. You know how immature Davis can be."

If you think your son is immature… "Mom, let's meet at his house. Fifteen minutes." I looked in my rearview mirror. Wondered which car in the sea of cars behind me was being driven by the brown plaid man. Everything in me screamed that he wasn't far behind. "No, make that ten minutes." I floored the gas, hearing the fear in my voice.

Should I call the police? And say what, exactly? Maybe I

was just being paranoid. Maybe my eyes were playing tricks on me. I strained to remember the man's face, both in Colorado and just now.

"Okay, Berry. I hope whatever it is you have to tell me isn't too dramatic." She sucked her teeth, sighed.

I just hope you don't kill me, was what I almost said. She hung up, leaving me to my thoughts and my rampant imagination as I tore up 83.

Chapter 28

Red and blue flashing lights.

Not a good sign.

My heart was already racing as I approached my brother's garage-turned-living quarters. A block away from his place, all I saw were police cars, emergency vehicles, and, wait, was that a SWAT team? I looked in the rearview mirror as I approached the scene, not sure exactly what to look for behind me. Shoot, between that man following me and the confession I was about to make to my mother, I could probably use some police protection right about now.

Not a comforting thought.

"What is going on?" I pulled up as close as I could, which was about a block and a half away from Davis' garage. I jumped out of my car and joined a small crowd that stood watching. "Excuse me, do you know what's going on?"

A man with a small machine in his hands and ear buds in his ear shushed me. "Not so loud. I'm listening to a police scanner."

"What's happening? Can you tell?" My heart quickened its pace as I saw my mother's car approaching the scene from the opposite end. I saw the look of horror and concern as she stepped out and stared at the officials surrounding Davis' house.

"From what I can make out, sounds like there was a money scheme targeting professional athletes and entertainers and the FBI was able to track it back to this garage."

"So, the authorities think…someone was running a scam…out of…this garage?" My eyes widened. "Wait, are they arresting someone?"

Oh, dear God. I could see panic settling on my mother's face as she started walking toward me. Several police cars filled the space between us, my brother's pad in the middle. My knees felt weak and my head faint. I was two gasps away from passing out.

"I don't think they have anyone in custody yet." The man had thick, red glasses and black hair gelled up into a single spike, and he was completely unaware of my pending breakdown. "That's a commercial garage, but it looks like someone has been living there," he continued as he fiddled with some buttons on the contraption in his hands. "Sounds like one of the investors is inside demanding answers from the owner. The police are treating it like a hostage situation."

I could barely breathe. "What?"

The man adjusted his earphones. "From what I'm hearing on the radio frequencies, sounds like they traced everything back to a single computer on the premises."

Davis' computer.

I had created Malikai Carter's fake business, Adilson Enterprises, in The Control Room, the area of Davis' home where he kept all of his computers and electronic equipment. I shut my eyes, feeling tears between my lids, as I recalled the night he and Li Yan discovered me crafting that website.

And now…

My mother could not get to me. Despite the cars and commotion between us, our eyes managed to meet. I could see the fear and confusion on her face as she stood in a position I'd never seen her in. Frozen.

"I have to fix this," I murmured more to myself than out loud. The man with the radio had walked away. Pulling on wires, twisting on buttons, I assumed he was trying to get a better signal to hear exactly what was going on at my brother's house.

I needed to get one of the officers' attention. I walked up to a cop on the edge of the action.

"Excuse me, but I need to talk to someone. This is my entire fault and I've put my brother in danger."

"Ma'am, you're going to have to back up." If he'd heard anything I'd said, he either wasn't interested or didn't care.

"No, see this is my brother's house and I–"

"–Ma'am, I'm not going to repeat myself. Move away from the scene." He began talking into a walkie-talkie. A static-filled voice responded back.

"I lied and said that I'd met a man and then I created this whole online thing with a website and a dating profile and I made up a blog about his charity and–"

"–Ma'am, if you need psychiatric help, please go to the nearest emergency room. This is not the time or place to deal with your imaginary fantasies. I'm giving you one last warning to back up from the scene. Immediately."

"But I–"

"–Do you want to be arrested for refusing to comply with my directions?

"No, I–"

"–Then move back right now." His voice got louder.

"But my brother, no, my fake boyfriend...I–"

"–Ma'am, I'm going to have you arrested for disobeying an officer."

Something told me that getting arrested would lessen my chances of being heard and fixing it all. I took a step back. The officer walked away. My mother was still on the other side of the scene. I had to get to her. There was no way around.

I could walk to another street, go up and come back down to meet her. I waved at my mother, motioned that I was going to circle the block to swing around to her side. She nodded.

Whether or not she understood my chaotic hand movements was another story.

I broke into a quick trot, turned on a side street and made a right onto another street that ran parallel to where my mother was. I just wanted to get to her.

The street I was on was like the one where Davis' garage was located: a commercial zone with old warehouses, junkyards, dilapidated buildings and vacant businesses. This street, however, felt even more desolate. Off the main strip, I ignored the lump that formed in my throat, focused only on my determination to get to my mother. I had to tell her the truth, apologize, and get everything right. I quickened my pace, looking for a way back to the street where my mother stood. I hadn't realized that a large part of the block was fenced off and abandoned. Trashed lots stood between the two avenues.

Brown plaid.

My eyes are playing tricks on me, I told myself as I kept my eyes focused forward. My eyes thought they'd seen someone in a plaid jacket walking in tall weeds not far behind. A chain link fence was on the other side of the street and the lot it surrounded looked like it hadn't been tended to in decades.

Nope, there was no reason to think that someone was walking in that field behind me.

Just the same, I hurried up even more, looking for a path, a walkway, anything that would get me back to the main road. Turning around was not an option. I couldn't go back, not if that man was back there.

My eyes are playing tricks on me, I told myself again, wanting, willing myself to believe that was true.

But my ears weren't lying.

A couple of dogs barked in the distance and the sound of breaking glass or falling metal sounded from the field across the street.

I forced my head to turn, my eyes to look back, focus on what was causing the noise.

White man in a brown plaid jacket.

I saw a glimpse of him just before he disappeared behind a stack of tires lined up against an old car shop.

I was in a near jog.

I could hear footsteps in the gravel of the lot across the street. More glass breaking, metal shattering to the ground.

Why is this man following me? Oh, God, I don't want anything bad to happen. My breath was short and fast as a million and one thoughts trampled through my head. What if I never have the chance to apologize? What if I never have the chance to confess to everyone? What if the situation with my brother escalates and I'm not able to explain what happened, how it happened, and how I was trying to fix it?

These thoughts kept my feet moving, my mind sharp as one primal instinct kicked in: survival. I had to get somewhere safe and seek redemption.

A storage unit was to the left of me. Its tall brown and brick façade stood like a sentry, a fortress, a buffer for protection. There were a couple of cars in its lot. A pickup truck was parked by the plain entrance. The door to the building was propped open by a large, plastic bin. Noting that the footsteps crunching in the gravel across the street sounded faster, closer, I finally broke into a run and bolted for the propped open door. I crossed the threshold and kicked the plastic bin out of the way. The metal door slammed shut and I heard a loud click as it locked.

Only someone with a key or proper access would be able to get in.

That small fact gave me no comfort as my eyes adjusted to my dim surroundings. A long hallway. Doors on either side. An elevator. A 'Closed' sign on what appeared to be the main office.

Okay, so where was I supposed to go? Clearly this wasn't a smart idea.

The elevator.

I just wanted to get away from the front door for the time being. I got on the elevator, took it up to the top floor, floor three. When it landed, I pushed the button to the ground level. If that man got in the building, I didn't want him to know what floor I was on. There was a digital screen that dinged floor numbers above the elevator doors.

"Hello?" I yelled out as I stood on the third floor, remembering that cars were parked in the lot.

What if they were abandoned cars? What if nobody was here?

I pushed those thoughts away as I began running down the hallway, trying doors to see if any would open.

Nope, this was not fun or funny.

A loud, scraping noise echoed through the building.

Could have been someone moving furniture. Or opening a storage unit.

Or breaking into the building.

Hey, I wasn't taking a single chance on this one. I kept jogging through the hallway, turning corners, trying doors up and down the corridors.

I found one unlocked.

I rolled the door up as quietly as I could and exhaled a little at the brightly lit, messy unit filled with overflowing boxes. Dishes, small household appliances, coat hangers.

If necessary – and my gut told me it was a real possibility – I could use something in there as weapon.

I slid the door back down as quietly as I could behind me. I maneuvered around the boxes, and hid behind an old water heater leaning against a corner of the unit.

Finally.

A loose feeling of safety.

The room was a little suffocating and clammy with the door closed, but at least I had light. I reached in my pants pocket for my cell phone.

No signal.

So much for trying to dial 9-1-1.

"God, what am I supposed to do right now?" I searched deep inside, looked up to the heavens, seeing only the cement ceiling. "I've really messed up here. I am so sorry. Please, God, let me at least have a chance to say I'm sorry to everyone I've lied to, to everyone I've hurt.

Then an idea.

I didn't have a signal, but there was plenty else I could do with a cell phone. If something were to happen to me, if and once my cell phone was found, I'd be redeemed.

I pulled up my video recorder, turned the lens to face me.

Whoa, I look really bad! I frowned at the image of the scared, broken, desperate, guilty girl in the camera. Sweat poured from every pore in my face, partially from the clammy quarters, largely because of my current state of panic.

"Hello, I'm Berry. Berry Martini Jenkins." My voice bounced off the walls. I lowered it. "A few weeks ago, I began the most incredibly stupid and painful journey of my life. It has cost me nearly everything, financially, emotionally, physically, and, well, spiritually. I know God is not pleased with my actions, especially the way I've lied to my family, my friends, my coworkers and church members – people who have loved and supported me in their own ways. What did I do? What did I do." I licked, bit, twisted my lips. Swallowing hard, I looked down, and then looked back at the camera.

"I created a man who doesn't exist. Malikai Carter. He's not real. He's a total figment of my imagination. I made a profile for him on a dating website and carefully crafted an online presence. I pretended to be dating this fake man. Yes, I created a picture and then used someone else's man to continue the lie. I made up a website for his job that was completely imaginary. There is no Adilson Enterprises.

"I never thought anyone would get involved. I pretended that this fake man, Malikai, had a charity abroad for which he was trying to raise money. I did this not to get people's money, but to make him seem like a genuinely nice guy. I traveled across the country on a ski trip that didn't happen, and I've racked up more debt in the past three weeks than I have in the past three years.

"Even worse, I've put my mother out of money and I've betrayed the wallets of my church family and my co-workers. And now my brother." I shook my head, wiped a trickle of tears off the tip of my nose. "My brother had no idea that this wasn't real. I am so sorry." I shut my eyes as more tears fell and prayed a silent prayer that my brother would be safe.

"Why'd I do it? Why'd I do it." I sighed as I opened my eyes, looked back into the camera. "I don't know. I guess… I guess I did it to feel like enough. I think I've never felt like enough. And, even more than that, I felt like everyone else in my life didn't see me as...enough. The way I look, my hair," I reached up and patted down a soft wad of coils, "my job, the goals I haven't reached.

"I guess I felt unlovable, unworthy of love, and this was my terrible attempt to prove to the world that...that I was… worthy. I know. Terrible. Pathetic. And, now, I haven't proven any of those things. If anything, I've shown just how low I am. Everyone thought I'd found the man of my dreams when, in reality, I was just courting the fantasy man of my schemes. I'm sorry." I wiped my eyes, stared intently into the camera.

"So, this is me. No disguises, no pretending, just me. You

can rightfully hate me. You can have grace, and forgive and love me. I know I'm not worthy of love right now, but that's why I ask for grace."

The idea of grace, God's grace, took on new meaning for me right then. Maybe that's why grace was referred to in the Bible as a gift. Something not earned, but given.

I sure enough hadn't earned the right to be forgiven.

"Again. I'm sorry, and I will ensure that every dime spent on behalf of this crazy lie will get back to the right pockets. Well, that's if I survive today."

That man in the plaid jacket.

I became aware of where I was again, and why.

I just wanted to get to my mother, see about my brother. Watch Celeste walk down the aisle and meet Raina's baby.

What if this really is my end? I shut off the video.

As the room fell quiet again, I became aware of footsteps, slow plods that echoed through the halls. *Oh God, had I recorded myself for nothing?* If – no, when – something happens to me, will anyone even find my cell phone?

An idea.

I pulled up my *Facebook* account, uploaded my recording. Signal bars faded in and out. I had to believe that the upload would work.

I was #BerryWrong. Now, trying to be #BerryRight #ImSorry

That was the message I typed before hitting 'Post.' I tagged my mother, my brother, NaTosha, my church's page, my co-workers. And the police department.

"Please, God, let this upload," I whispered and then shut my eyes as the footsteps drew near.

The metal door rolled open.

I was still hiding in a rear corner, crouched behind the old water heater. Several boxes filled the space between where I hid and the open door.

I looked at the man who entered.

Older black guy. Long gray dreadlocks pulled back into a thick ponytail. Blue jeans. T-shirt.

This wasn't the same man who'd been following me.

He had boxes in his arms. This was his storage unit, I surmised. That pick-up truck by the front entrance was probably his.

And it looked like he had a holster on his belt.

Look, I wasn't going to spook the man with the probable gun on his hip by jumping out of his belongings in his storage space. Something told me that yelling, talking, shoot, even whispering, would be enough to get bullets flying my way. I held my breath as he unloaded several boxes. I was amazed at how much he'd been able to carry in one trip, though it explained why his footsteps had been slow and heavy. I waited for him to put down the last box and then exhaled as he walked away, leaving the door open.

I waited to hear the ding of the elevator and then I eased out of my hiding space.

This is crazy. Completely absurd. I didn't know what to do, what I was doing.

I grabbed my phone, stepped lightly around the boxes and darted out the opening. And then I froze.

"Hello, Berry."

The man in the brown plaid jacket stood just outside the entrance.

I took two steps back, reached for a box near the open storage unit, and threw it at him, all in one move. A collection of metal tools splattered onto the floor. I took off. There was no waiting for the elevator. I bounded down the steps.

I'd never felt my legs move so fast, my lungs fill so full of air. As I ran down the stairwell, I heard steps just overhead. Nothing to do but keep running.

Out the front door.

The pony-tailed man was pulling more boxes off his pick-up truck.

"Help me," I whimpered. "Someone's chasing me."

The man gave me a once over and then reached for whatever was on his belt. "Wait here." He headed back into the building.

I wasn't waiting for anything. Trees lined the area behind the storage unit. I headed toward them, praying there wasn't a fence on the other side of the forestry to box me in. I could make out what looked like the back of Davis' garage. *Yeah, that's his place.* A boatload of cops surrounded it from all sides. It was a scary thought, but a strangely comforting one. If the police were still on guard, nothing disastrous could have happened inside. The situation was still ongoing.

I needed help. I needed this nightmare to be over.

So, of course there was a fence.

I got to the other side of the trees and a tall privacy fence separated me from my brother's place.

I was indeed trapped.

I had nowhere else to run, no place to hide. I dropped to my knees, but I couldn't even pray.

"Berry Jenkins, you might as well come on out." A voice, strong and certain, sounded only steps away.

I squeezed my eyes shut then opened them again. I looked down at my phone. My post had uploaded. Amongst the critics and condemners, there were already over 300 likes.

Hope.

The man in the brown plaid jacket stood in front of me. I was already on my knees. I dropped my head to the ground and prepared for the end. *This is it.*

I looked up to see what the end would be.

He was holding up a badge.

"Ms. Jenkins, I'm Agent Summerville with the Federal Bureau of Investigations. We were contacted by some very influential people who wanted to get to the bottom of Adilson Enterprises as these people were about to make significant investments and there were too many questions about the company's legitimacy. All my research and investigating led back to you. Your brother is okay. The SWAT team just managed to get his captor, but you, on the other hand, have a lot of explaining to do."

Now, I had no idea what the full consequences would be for my actions and lies. At the moment, I didn't care. I felt complete freedom. No more stories to tell. No more money to lose or people to hurt. No one or nothing else to fear. I took one step forward and collapsed onto the agent. He frowned, but I wrapped myself around him nonetheless.

"Thank you," I whispered as he pretty much pushed me off him. I checked my phone one last time as he led me to a car to take me somewhere for questioning. A new comment and a friend request had popped up on my screen.

#BerryRight. Honesty looks good on you. -Bmore Jogger.

Part 5:
Hope

Chapter 29

"So, Berry, we can put the glass display cases over here, the fixtures on this side, and the models will walk down the middle. Did you want Huxley to come down the catwalk wearing one of your designs, too? Maybe one of the headbands? I can go get him. It would be cute and different. I know it may be difficult, but I had this idea of using catnip and his favorite food to bribe him onto the stage and then–"

"–Celeste, stop," I interrupted. "No. My cat will not be part of the show.

"Oh, Berry," she squealed and gave me a hug. "This is going to be the best fashion line debut ever. See, booking this hall worked out. We thought it was going to be for your wedding, but look what's happening instead." She squeezed me again and skirted off to the display cases to help fill them with the hair bows, scarves and other accessories I'd designed.

"Yeah, this is happening instead," I mumbled to myself as a smile finally formed on my lips and tears of pure joy filled my eyes. The past few months leading up to this event had been intense, but the night was finally here. The venue was fierce, the decorations fitting, and the ambiance was fabulous, darling. "Thanks, Lord. I owe you."

So, you're probably wondering what's going on. Let me get you up to speed.

I lost everything.

After my string of lies broke, every area of my life came crashing down like loose beads. I lost my job, for one. Not a good thing when you owe a lot of people a lot of money.

The company didn't appreciate having an employee whose dishonesty had gone viral, and Carolyn, Gina, and Naomi made sure HR knew every detail of my illegitimate late days and absences to seal my fate.

Celeste was the only one of my former coworkers who still talked to me.

I couldn't blame any of them for being angry. Aside from just the wrongness of me leading them on, the hall they'd reserved with a non-refundable deposit had put them each out a thousand bucks.

Yup, a thousand each.

Who fronts that kind of money for a coworker?

I planned to pay back every cent, and didn't even mind too much that they'd found ways to benefit from my downfall. Shoot, Gina managed to get a little side hustle as a paid blogger detailing the apparent torture it had been to work with me.

Oh, well.

I could only hope they attributed my sins to only me, and didn't fault all brown-skinned people for my lunacy. However, I couldn't control their perceptions, regardless of how uncomfortable that made me feel. Worrying about changing others' perceptions was a lesson in futility at best, and a several thousand dollar expense at worse. I had to work on fixing my *self*-perceptions.

"All right, Berry, the hors-d'oeuvre tables are all set up and ready, including the crab beignets and stuffed mushrooms you wanted. Thanks for letting me put out my business cards."

"It's the least I could do, Davis."

He nodded and walked away, but not before I saw the remnants of pain in his eyes.

We never talked about the day my lies literally held him hostage. The media firestorm that followed though was enough to light a spark inside of him. Anxious to get out of the shadow of my shortcomings, he figured out how to make a name for himself that went beyond the club where he deejayed. Well, used to deejay.

He'd made catering his full-time gig – I mean, business plan, new equipment, website, and all. Though I was sure it pained him to provide service at my event tonight, we both knew it was a door-opening opportunity. Celeste had been right about this place in D.C. Davis getting on the approved list of caterers for the venue was sure to open doors to the glitziest wedding receptions and events this side of the Potomac River.

He'd bought a condo in Silver Spring. Far enough to be away from the rest of us, but close enough for us to still see his growing success.

My mother was pleased.

I was proud.

We'd both had to start over from scratch. He'd lost all credibility with his former circle and I'd lost my ability to be hireable.

Turns out potential employers aren't that kind to Internet villains. And forget about me getting references from my former job.

Long story short, Davis and I both had no choice but to turn our passions into work plans. Him, cooking. Me – I was finally using my fashion degree.

Tonight, the grand roll-out of my hair and fashion accessories line was a make-or-break moment for both of us.

This had to work.

Like I said, I owed too much to too many.

"Berry!" My mother's raspy voice nearly knocked me over along with her sudden grab of my shoulder from behind. "Some little toothpick in the back just told me that she's supposed to be first on the stage? I thought we agreed that I was opening the first set. I got my hair especially done to wear that show-opening, rhinestone-studded haircloth. You know the one from your Botswana-inspired collection?"

So, yes, part of my business plan included making amends for faking a charity. A portion of my profits would be donated to a foundation in the Motherland. A group of respected businesswomen in Botswana had contacted me at the height of my Internet fame and connected me to efforts they already supported.

It was the least I could do.

"Uh, Berry? Did you just hear what I said?" My mother's arms were crossed. "Skinny-minny in the back thinks this show is about her. I told her this is about my baby doing the darn thing and that as the proud momma, I get to be featured first."

These days, my mother had been alternating between regally-styled flat twists and twist outs, and high quality flowing weaves and silky blow-outs. For the show, her hair was all natural, a crown of crinkly curls with her silver strands gleaming in the well-placed spotlights hanging around the room.

"Yes, mom, of course you're the headliner."

"Humph." She still looked a little miffed as she walked away. I was just glad she was speaking to me again. I used to jokingly think that it would be great to have a little break from my mother's mouth. But the two months that went by when she didn't speak nary a word to me following my worldwide confession were, admittedly, tortuous.

Not until I sent my mother an invitation for tonight's grand debut and fashion show did she start returning my calls.

Well, okay, after I said she could be in it, she began returning my calls.

Right or wrong, that's my mother. What can I say?

We are all in need of grace.

I wish I could tell you I learned that lesson from the members of my church. Not so much. Actually, take that back. Pastor Beamon showed me a lot of grace. With the exception of a few members who asked for their donations back, the majority agreed to have their generous contributions begin the long-awaited building fund. Pastor Beamon embraced me every time he saw me.

Well, I guess that's grace on some type of level.

God can take major mess ups and transform them into miracles.

Yes, I still go to that church from time to time, though my mother doesn't. People rarely talk to me when I do show up for service. That's okay. I'm not mad. Like I told my mother, not showing up is the ultimate bow to haters. Besides, I'm not going there for any of them. Going to that church where everyone knows how low I can be surprisingly gives me a sense of freedom. I don't have to pretend. Love me or hate me, I've learned that I can be just as much a faker as the ones I condemned.

That's why we all need grace.

To cover our short-comings and forgive our failures.

If I hang on to guilt and shame, how will I ever be able to feel the warmth of love?

I publicly apologized and am working to rectify my wrongs.

Who can judge me?

I plan on joining a new church one day. For now, I'm working on growing closer to the One who still finds me lovable despite my unloveliness.

"Okay, half an hour until show time. You need to change now, Berry." Raina waddled by, papers in one hand, walkie-talkie in another.

Yeah, she still talked to me.

"Berry," she commanded as she passed by me a second

time, "Go. Change. Now."

"Yes, lieutenant." I smiled and followed where her finger pointed. The hall's bridal suite. My clothes for the evening were in there.

I stepped into the room alone and admired the ornate gold-framed mirrors that covered each wall. I ran my fingers over the mahogany dressing table. I admired the silk and satin curtains and sniffed the fresh flowers my mom had delivered to the room. I held up the soft violet chiffon dress I was about to put on.

I know what you're probably thinking. Where is the happily-ever-after? The mystery man who will finally show up at the end of my story and whisk me away to 'I do?'

That may come.

But I told you from the get-go that this wasn't that type of story.

I don't have that right now.

What I do have is the woman staring at me in the mirror. A golden-bronzed beauty with hair that expresses a different mood each day. A dreamer with gifts and talents that are paving a way to success (and hopefully debt-freedom). A believer who has a God, family, and friends who still love her just because.

I'm an imperfect person who has hope for the future and appreciation for the moment.

This woman right here will not let the perception of others control her, or her own self-perception destroy her.

I still have more lessons to learn and more fall-out to clean up, but, staring in the mirror, all I see is a reflection of grace and glory.

My phone beeps. A notification. *Do I really have time to check it before I go out to begin the show?* Music is already playing. The models are poised and ready to head down the catwalk with my mother at the lead wearing what looks like a jeweled crown over her luscious curls.

The notification is a message on *Facebook.*

Congrats and good luck on your new fashion line. Do you have any plans later? –Bmore Jogger.

Plans? No. I'm done with planning and scheming and plotting and angling. I'm embracing the moment and celebrating whatever God gifts me.

We'll see, I type back.

The door to the bridal suite opens. A single aisle leads to the stage in the front of the room. Surrounding the stage are the people who've decided to support me, waiting for the festivities to officially begin.

Second chance.

New beginning.

New understanding of the word 'love.'

I smile and exhale, now ready to walk down the aisle.

DISCUSSION QUESTIONS

1. Berry has a sudden intense desire to be in a relationship although she's spent most of her adult life not worrying about finding love. Why the change?

2. What are Berry's biggest issues, if any, that feed into the nightmare lie she creates?

3. Describe Berry's relationships with her mother, brother, co-workers, and church friends. Are they positive or negative relationships? Explain.

4. Berry shares strong feelings about her church. Are her reactions justified? Why or why not? What experiences have shaped your own view of church? What role, if any, does church attendance have in your relationship with God?

5. In what ways, if any, does race and culture impact the story? How can these sensitive topics best be addressed, especially among people of all colors and cultures who profess Christ?

6. Which character would you want to spend a Saturday afternoon with and what would you do? What questions would you ask him or her?

7. What are your thoughts about Berry's ending? Is it a happily ever after? Why or why not?

CPSIA information can be obtained
at www.ICGtesting.com
Printed in the USA
LVOW12s1607231217
560657LV00001B/149/P

9 780692 980163